THE LIBRARY OF TIME

BOOK 3

NIKKI BROADWELL

ALSO BY NIKKI BROADWELL

Wolfmoon series:

Moonstone-Book 1

Willow-Book 2

Raven-Book 3

Faery-Book 4

Loki's Bargain: (formerly Gypsy series)

The Tower-Book 1

The Page of Pentacles-Book 2

The Ten of Swords-Book 3

Coyote series:

Just Another Desert Sunset

Coyote Sunrise

Dreamcatcher

Summer McCloud paranormal murder series:

Murder in Plain Sight

Saffron and Seaweed

Black and White and Red all over

Finlay's Folly

The Night of the Jaguar

The Case of Missing Books

Fehin and Airy series:

The Bridge

Time Gap

PROLOGUE

Annie gazed around the familiar room. Aside from the neglect and the dust it looked the same as it had been before Sam left for the 1300's. This Edge was not where she'd been when a bomb caused her to flee and where she'd joined up with a bunch of fighting women and where Jack had nearly become more than just a friend. This was the familiar Edge where she'd met Sam and Cecily and worked in The Library of Time, and where she'd fallen in love with the man who ran it.

The day the door appeared in that other Edge, and took her to Atenua had changed her in ways she was still discovering. The planet Atenua was connected to the Dog Star, Sirius, and was where Sam's father lived. The Library of Time was sentient, and despite the fact that she'd been in another Edge altogether, had apparently known where she would be safe to give birth. She hadn't even called up a door. It had appeared out of nowhere, and since she was about to die, she stepped inside. What had happened over those many months was life-changing. Being back here felt like a miracle, as though she'd come full circle and ended up in her true home with the father of her newborn. Her heart was full as she gazed at Sam holding their baby.

"Have you been working?" she asked.

Sam turned from where he was gazing down at the cooing baby in his arms. "Without you? I've been pining, Annie, unable to do much of anything since I returned. I spent months trying to figure out where you went. I didn't see any sign of you. And no one could answer my questions."

"And Cecily?"

"She gave up on me—said I needed to come out of my funk before she could work here. That was six months ago."

"What about your magic…" she asked tentatively, afraid of his answer.

"It's spotty. When I tried to conjure a door to lead me to you, the library refused. But when I begged, it did manage to get me back here from the 1300's. I feel like I'm still earning its trust." He held the baby against him with one hand as he raked his fingers through his dirty hair. "I thought you were dead." His gaze went into the distance, a bleak expression appearing on his face. "I've been contemplating suicide," he muttered.

"Oh Sam," she whispered. She put her arms around him, the baby snuggled between them. Sam was crying now, sobs making his shoulders shake.

"I was such a fool," he muttered. "I have no excuse for how I behaved."

"It's over now—we're together. We have a baby."

Sam pulled back to look down at the baby girl in his arms. "What's her name?"

Annie smiled. "I couldn't name her without you."

Sam smiled despite the tears in his eyes.

When Wolf joined them, Sam reached down to pat his wide head. "Wolf was with you all this time? I kept wondering what happened to him."

"He was my touchstone. Without him I might have given up all hope of seeing you again."

Sam smiled a ragged smile, shaking as he reached for her hand. "You have no idea the agony I've been going through. I was sure I'd lost you."

"I hated you after what you did. But after the baby was born all those thoughts disappeared. I knew something had come over you to make you act like that."

Sam shook his head. "I don't deserve you, Annie. I behaved like an ass. I can barely believe the things I did."

Annie leaned in and kissed him gently. "I forgive you."

Sam pulled her close, his need to bridge the deep chasm between them evident. Her mouth opened under his, all her pent up feelings rising to the surface as tears coursed down her cheeks.

MANY HOURS WENT BY AS THEY TALKED, ALL THE EVENTS OF THE past that led to this moment brought up and explored. Annie sat close beside him as she fed their child, his look of love as he gazed at the baby girl, warming her heart.

When it came to talking about the last days in the 1300's with his mother, he let out a ragged sigh. "I found her in a ditch, Annie. She'd just given birth and was bleeding. I took her to the Inn, but when I left to get food she disappeared." He looked at her, his eyes wide. "One minute she was there and then she was just plain gone."

"Your father came and took her to Atenua."

When he asked, Annie described the planet as best she could, remembering all the strange happenings over the time she was there.

"Is that where you've been all this time?"

"Earth basically blew up. Nuclear bomb. So many people died."

"You were in the wrong timeline."

"I guess I was, but I didn't know it at the time." When she

told him about Gaia, the goddess, he sat with his mouth open, his wide-eyed stare making her laugh.

"She inhabited your body?"

Annie nodded, and launched into all the rest of it, including the library that existed in Seris. "Your father, Apollo, helped me so much."

"Was I there?"

Annie laughed. "Yes. You were eight years old, and your mother was expecting again. Don't ask me to explain how you found her with a newborn and you were already eight—I have no idea." She laughed. "I have a suspicion you have a sister by now."

"My mother and Apollo had another baby?"

Annie nodded. "I left before she was born."

"I want to meet my father," he finally said. "But I'm not willing to do anything about it now. I just want to bask in us," he murmured, reaching for her.

When his lips brushed hers, Annie began to cry again, but it didn't stop her from deepening the kiss. Her heart fluttered against the cage of her chest as they clung to each other, the baby sleeping peacefully between them. Words of love were whispered and whispered again.

Much later, after eating the dinner that Sam prepared, they climbed the stairs to the familiar room she knew. It was dark outside, and her heart felt full as she looked out the window at the star-filled sky and the waxing moon. She placed the sleeping baby in a basket that had held a bunch of papers and climbed onto the bed next to the man she loved. When he removed his shirt she saw the scarab hanging around his neck. She reached for it and gazed at him. "You got it back."

Sam nodded. "I found it out by the stump."

Annie thought about that for a minute or two, trying to figure out how it had happened, but her mind was now on other things as Sam's fingers brushed against her skin as he undid the buttons of her blouse.

She felt like she was in a dream, a wonderful dream that she could barely believe. But as his fingers moved across her body and his lips touched hers she knew it was all true. Sam was here, solid and real, his love for her palpable. Their baby rested asleep in her basket as they connected, the words he whispered in her ear bringing her with him into the world they created together.

What they did together that night was beyond her wildest dreams, exquisite, magical, and the most perfect reunion she could ever have imagined.

If only she had known then what the future held.

CHAPTER 1

EDGE 2325

Wind blew past the living room picture window, rattling its frame, but all Annie could see was a beautiful mountain scene with the sun shining, big billowy clouds and conifers moving in a light breeze. Sam had his magic back, at least partially, his need to make up a fake view irritating her. When she replaced the fake scene with what really lay outside the window, the mountains disappeared, revealing a charcoal sky, branches, leaves and trash hurtling by at an alarming rate.

Nearly a year had gone by since she and Sam reconnected. And when they finally found each other she had a baby that he'd never met. After recounting what had happened on Atenua, they decided to name her Gaia. The Earth goddess had been instrumental in Annie's life and needed to be remembered. The past months had been heaven as they filled in the gaps of the time they'd been apart and found their way back to each other, basking in the miracle of their child.

But Sam was restless and it was worrying. She could see his frown from where she sat at her desk, his default setting for the last few days. Wolf gave a bark, seemingly warning her that Sam was about to explode.

She ignored him as she gathered her Tarot cards together, ready to lay out the reading for herself. What did the dreams she'd been having mean?

"Why did you just do that?" he barked, pointing at the view.

Annie turned, trying not to react to his tone. "I wanted to see the weather. Am I not allowed?"

A fake smile appeared on his face as he tried to hide his irritation. "Sorry—still surprised by what you can do."

Surprised that she could overturn his magic, was what he meant. He was a proud man who now felt that he had to compete with her. Certain aspects of his former abilities had not returned, and one of them was the wards that he'd placed around the town of Edge. Without them raiders came in whenever they felt like it, stealing and creating chaos until they were chased out. So far no one had been killed.

She sighed and laid the cards out on the desk. Her globe, or what Sam called her crystal ball, caught her eye, another symbol that had appeared in her latest dream.

Three cards to represent past, present and future—from left to right she gazed down at the the *Magician*, the *King of Cups* reversed, and the *World*. She let out a gasp.

"What are you doing?" Sam asked, moving close to look down at her desk.

She placed her hand over the spread. "Just working with the cards."

Sam made a face and headed toward the door.

Annie didn't hear whatever he muttered as he left, her focus on the layout. The magician was about her—the gifts she now had. Or at least that was her interpretation. It could also represent Sam, but she didn't think so since her question to the Tarot was about her dreams. The king of cups represented Sam—the way he was now and how it affected her. Reversed it meant that he was in a state of inner chaos, his ego at the fore. The card that represented the future was the world. It represented change, travel and completion.

Her recent dreams had taken her back to the late 1800's to the time of the Golden Dawn and where Elizabeth had come from. Elizabeth was her doppelgänger and had arrived at their doorstep when Annie was only a worker at the library. Jack had been around during that time, had charmed her and then both of them had disappeared. Did Elizabeth manage to take them into the past? There had been no explanation for how she'd arrived in Edge in 2323 or why she and Annie looked so much alike.

Two years had gone by since then. Sam and Annie were now together and had a child. They'd gone to hell and back to reach this point. Glancing down at the world card confused her— she had no desire to go anywhere. But from what she knew of this card, it seemed that it was to be some kind of completion for her.

She remembered her discussion with Sam's father, Apollo, about her parentage and background. He'd intimated that she was more powerful than she realized. She remembered very little of her childhood, as though it was shrouded in an impenetrable mist. Her parents were dead and she had no siblings, so there was no one to ask.

When Annie heard Gaia waking from her nap she rose and went to feed her, inner turmoil making her feel slightly ill. She had to talk with Sam, but Sam in this mood was not easy to approach.

She watched Sam through the window as he gathered wood, his hair tangling in the wind. He raked it back, his frown deepening. Annie was suddenly worried. She knew the signs. She'd been here before. Sam was spring-loaded.

EDGE WAS AS IT HAD BEEN, THE TOWNSPEOPLE DOING WHAT THEY had always done, barter system in place and Sam in charge of the boats that brought in supplies from across the ocean. What had changed was the absence of Cecily, who after listening to Annie about Sam's unwillingness to return from the 1300's, wasn't sure she trusted him. When Annie tried to reassure her, she tilted her head, saying, "I'll give it a year and see how things go."

Annie missed her and hoped Cecily would show up at the door asking for her old job back. The year marker was pretty much upon them now. She heard the door open, a gust of wind bringing in leaves as Sam appeared. He slammed the door behind him and gazed at her, his eyes narrowed.

"I'm ready," he muttered.

"What did you say?"

"I'm ready to go."

"Go...where?"

"To Atenua, of course, to meet Apollo. Gaia is old enough to travel now. We've had our honeymoon and I want to meet my father and discover who I am."

Annie shook her head in amazement. "Yesterday you were talking about how much you love our quiet life. We've barely gotten into the rhythm of our work again. What happened?"

Sam looked down. "I'm bored," he admitted, "and I'm still lacking what I used to have."

"Magic, you mean."

"Yes, my magic. I've tried various ways of testing it, but the library is still on your side."

"There are no sides, Sam," she murmured. Annie thought about the little she'd revealed to him about her own abilities, half of which she didn't even know herself. Where they'd suddenly come from was a mystery. She wondered if it was a residue from the goddess who had inhabited her body for so many months. All sh knew was that Sam didn't like it, his narrowed eyes when she demonstrated her visualization techniques, testament to his annoyance. So far the library had not given Sam back his power over the doors.

Apollo's take on why this was happening was something she had not yet had the courage to mention. Apollo felt that the library had taken away his privileges because he used them for himself, thereby abusing what the library had bestowed on him. Sam needed to prove himself to regain the library's trust, and so far his pride was preventing it.

Annie placed the baby on the floor, watching as she used the couch cushions to pull herself up to standing. She would be walking soon.

Sam came over and lifted the baby up in the air, making her laugh. Annie watched the two of them, gladdened by how close they were. Gaia was adorable in her new/old clothes Annie had bartered for, her blonde hair curling around her rosy face. The T-shirt and red corduroy overalls were a bit big, but would last a while.

Annie smiled at the two of them—so alike in features and hair color. "I'm not sure I'm ready to go anywhere right now."

Sam put the baby on the floor and glanced at her. "Why not?"

Annie made a face. "I don't want to disrupt our life; I have a pile of work on my desk. And I'm afraid of what might happen. Apollo and Constance were glad to get rid of me, and..."

"But I'll be there. What are you afraid of?"

"I don't know, really. It just seems that whenever we travel though time and space something bad happens. And what about the younger you who lives on Atenua? That could be a problem, right?"

"Two of me? If you remember, I've done that before with the version of me I met in the past—the one I rescued from the Institute. What matters is meeting my father and connecting with him."

What he really meant was his father could help him become who he *had* been—a magical being with unrestrained power. Annie let out a heavy sigh and pulled the baby into her lap. She was still breast-feeding even though she knew it was time to stop. When she pulled up her shirt the baby latched on. She leaned back and relaxed into the pleasurable sensations.

Sam watched her, his gaze unfocused. "I love this," he murmured, settling next to her.

"It's time for her to have more solid food, but I love the connection with her."

Sam smiled. "I wish I had been there through the entire process. When do you think we can make another one?"

Annie laughed. "Not yet, please. She's ready to walk, which means a lot more energy to keep her under control." She glanced at him next to her. "And I'm still fighting the extra weight."

"You were as thin as a rail when you got back here from Atenua. At least now you have some meat on your bones. I like how you look."

Annie laughed. "That's obvious," she said, thinking about the nights they spent in each other's arms.

Sam waggled his eyebrows. "Why aren't you pregnant yet?"

"Because I'm still breast-feeding."

"In that case you're right— it's time to stop."

Annie had to admit that the thought had crossed her mind. She'd missed him being involved the first time around. "If you're serious about Atenua, I would rather wait until we get back. I've already gone through an entire pregnancy on the planet of no nighttime."

Sam glanced out the window for a minute before he changed the scene with a flick of his hand. The quiet mountain scene reappeared. "Yeah, well I haven't," he muttered.

When the baby decided that her father was more interesting than Annie's breast, she placed Gaia in his arms and went to her desk. It was littered with projects, and her limited time to work on them was frustrating her. Another baby right now would be disastrous.

THE GODDESS GAIA'S VOICE WHISPERED IN HER EAR AS SHE SLEPT, Annie's dreams taking her back to Atenua.

You must speak to him, Annie. Do not let him bully you. I know you love him but he has to understand and respect you.

"I'm not worried. I understand him," Annie mumbled, waking herself up. She sat bolt upright, her gaze going to the empty bed beside her. All of the horrible things that had happened between them in the past raced through her mind, a sick feeling rolling though her. When she jumped up she noticed that Gaia was not in her cradle. "Sam!" she shouted, panicked.

A second later Sam pounded up the stairs and burst in on her. "What's wrong?"

Annie glanced sheepishly at the baby in his arms, the makeshift bib he'd made out of a kerchief, and the oatmeal on her chin. "I...I had a bad dream," she muttered, trying to slow her fast-beating heart.

"You scared the shit out of me," he said, placing the baby on the floor and settling next to her. He took her in his arms and kissed her. "Better now?"

Annie sucked in a deep breath and let it out slowly. "Demons from the past," she muttered.

Sam frowned. "Demons—you mean my behavior in the 1300's."

Annie nodded, trying to smile. "Gaia was in my dream—the goddess, not our baby. She thinks that you're bullying me."

Sam looked at the baby who was now standing next to the bed. "I can be a bully," he admitted. "Maybe this dream is because of what we spoke about the other day. I'm trying to push you into going to Atenua before you're ready."

"And the other thing," she mumbled.

"Another baby?" He scoffed. "I was mostly teasing. Another baby will happen when we're ready, not before."

Annie glanced at him. "The first one wasn't planned. It's not like I have birth control." That was sort of a lie—she knew exactly what herbs to take to prevent pregnancy, not that they always worked. John's wort, goldenseal, gingko and pennyroyal were all possibilities that could decrease fertility. As far as chemical pills, they hadn't been around for a long time. A better solution was just to count days and not have sex when she was fertile. But that system required discipline and paying attention. And it was always when she wanted him the most.

"You worry too much," he said, getting up from the bed. He picked up Gaia and headed for the stairs. "Can I finish feeding her now?"

Annie watched him go, her thoughts scattering. Something was bothering her, but other than the talk she needed to have with Sam, she couldn't quite get at what it was.

CHAPTER 2

Gaia let out a scream, waking Annie and Sam at the same time. Sam got there first and lifted her out of the crib he'd recently fashioned for her. He brought her over to the bed and handed her to Annie. "She must be hungry," he muttered, settling into bed next to her.

It was barely dawn and Annie had not slept well. She and Sam had argued late into the night, and after that she had lain awake for several hours. She pulled her T-shirt up and settled the baby, her eyes closing. But instead of being able to rest, her mind went back to the angry words they'd thrown at each other.

"You do not respect me!" she remembered yelling at one point and Sam's retort of, "I feel the same way about you."

They'd resolved nothing, only setting up a wall between them.

Once the baby was fed and changed, Annie headed down the stairs with Gaia in her arms. Sam was already outside stacking wood, his back to the picture window. She could tell just by the slope of his shoulders that the tension from the night before was still present. When he turned, the scowl on his face proved it. Her stomach did a small flip, the breakfast she had planned disappearing from her mind. She and Sam had to finish what they started. Otherwise the tension would continue and ruin the day.

Taking the baby with her she left the library and headed to where Sam stood staring out at the ocean. The day was chilly and there were whitecaps. He was wearing his warm wool pea coat, his hair mussed. He looked handsome with his windblown hair and the red in his cheeks. "Sam," she murmured, placing the baby on the ground next to the stump. Gaia clung to the wood and stood there gurgling in pleasure, before she began to work her way around what they used for a table.

Sam turned. "What is it?"

Annie frowned. "What do you think? We have some talking to do."

"Do we? I thought we came to the end of it last night. We don't agree and I'd rather not go over it all again."

Annie moved next to him and put her hand on his arm. "We need to figure this out, Sam. I hate this."

Sam narrowed his eyes. "Do you? Because to me it seems you want all the control. I'm just here to service your needs."

Annie let out a gasp of surprise. "Why would you think that?"

Sam made a sound in the back of his throat. "You liked me fine when we were screwing every night. Now that I've raised the possibility of going to Atenua, you've withdrawn your affection."

Annie thought about the past few nights of arguing. How could they make love with the tension between them? "Not true! What I said was I wasn't ready until we came to some conclusions—or at least stopped being angry with each other. You're jealous of me and I don't like it—you're acting like a spoiled brat."

Sam's skin turned blotchy and red, his eyes darkening. "I don't have magic, Annie! How do you think that feels?"

"You *do* have magic, just not all of it. And you don't like it that I can do things too. Please admit this, Sam. I hate it when we're at each others throats like this."

Sam turned away and let out a heavy sigh. "You're right. I'm annoyed. If I was my normal self it wouldn't bother me, but..."

"You're used to being in charge," Annie interrupted. "And the doors...the library..."

"Don't remind me."

"Why can't we be partners in this? Do you always have to be the one in charge? This is exactly what happened in the 1300's. Your ego."

"My ego?" he bellowed. "What about yours? You come back from another planet and proceed to lord it over me with what that goddess imbued you with. And meanwhile I'm struggling to maintain any sense of who I am."

Annie shook her head, her attention going to the stump. "Where's Gaia?"

Sam whipped around, scanning the area. "She's over there," he muttered, hurrying toward the hill where the baby was now crawling.

Annie rushed after him. By the time she reached him he had the baby in his arms, crooning to her as she giggled. He glanced at Annie. "She's really something, isn't she?"

Annie smiled. "Yes, she is."

It was later that afternoon that Annie and Sam ended up in the bedroom. Annie was flustered and unable to keep her hands off him, and he obviously felt the same. They stripped off their clothes and fell into bed together.

It was an hour or so later, when Annie lay snuggled in Sam's arms that he said, "Why do we do this—why do we argue like this?"

Annie snuggled closer, the feel of his warmth healing whatever had hardened her heart. "Maybe we're too much alike? We need to be able to talk these things through. I have some abilities now and you need to accept it. And I have to accept your frustration about not being all-powerful."

Sam kissed the top of her head, his arm coming round her to pull her closer. "I love you, Annie. I love who you are. It's my view of myself that's the problem."

Annie nodded. "I get that. And I understand why you want to meet your father—you think he can help you. But that can't be the only reason to go."

Sam pulled back to look at her. "You think that's my only reason? Am I so shallow and self-absorbed?"

Annie grinned and raised her eyebrows. "All I'm saying is that you can't count on Apollo to give you back what you've lost. He has his own set of problems."

"You told me that he's trying to bring the factions together there. Maybe I can help."

"That's true, but…" Annie stopped speaking as his hand slid along her thigh, the conversation drifting away as her body responded. A second later his mouth had found hers and she forgot everything they were talking about.

It was Gaia who woke them up later. She was wet, hungry and annoyed at being stuck in her crib for so long. Annie extricated herself from Sam's arms and pulled on her shirt and jeans.

When she tried to feed the baby, Gaia would have none of it, turning away from the nipple and letting out a screech.

"Seems she's weaning herself," Sam muttered from beside her.

"Seems like it." Annie took Gaia her and headed for the stairs. This meant she could no longer count on breastfeeding as her birth control. Sam was not one to think about such things, and she could get caught up in the moment quickly when it came to his charms. She didn't have her menses back, but once she did, she would have to count the days. Another baby was just not in the cards, especially with a possible trip to Atenua in their future. Sam was determined to go and she was sick of arguing about it.

~

IT TOOK A FULL WEEK AND A HALF BEFORE THEY BEGAN TO ARGUE again. Sam was as restless as she could remember, heading into town at all hours and walking along the beach alone with his head down. Annie continued her work, trying not to let him distract her. It happened gradually, the tension building. And then he just exploded, coming at her verbally when she was working.

"I have to get the fuck out of here!" he shouted at her. "I need to meet my father, Annie. You must understand how I feel!"

Annie turned from her desk, gazing at his red face and the bulging veins in his temples. "You want me to get you a door--is that it? Or do you want me to leave my work and come with you?"

"Why do you insist on working? It makes no difference anymore."

"Why do you say that? I thought you cared about preservation."

"After everything I've been through? What matters now is connecting with my father and having a project that means something."

"Like fighting."

Sam pressed his lips together, his fingers sliding through his long hair. "If that's what's needed, yes."

Annie let out a long sigh, her gaze going to Gaia on the rug. She'd given her some wooden blocks she'd discovered in the land fill, cleaning them carefully before allowing her to play with them. Everything went into her mouth now. "That stint you did in the 1300's did a number on you, Sam. You can't seem to be happy with anything now."

Sam frowned. "Not true—I'm bored is all, and you aren't helping."

"Because I'm content with our quiet life and our child? I don't want to go back there yet. You have no idea what it's like."

"Exactly. I want you along, but...I'll go alone if that's what it takes."

"Separated again? I've had nightmares about this. I see myself slogging though snow trying to find you."

Sam let out a huff of annoyance. "I want my powers back, woman!" he bellowed. "I'm sick of asking for your help."

Annie stood, her hands shaking as she took in his wide-legged stance, the veins bulging in his forehead. "Just go, Sam. I'm sick of fighting about it." She headed toward the back wall that led into the stacks.

He caught up to her and grabbed her arm. "Wait a fucking minute. We need to discuss this properly."

Annie pulled away from him and crossed her arms in front of her chest. "I'll send you to Seris where your father lives. You can take Wolf. He'll lead you to your father."

"Gods damn it, Annie! I can't take Wolf! You need him here to guard you! Those fuckers from across the hill could rape and kill you if I'm not around."

Annie glared at him. "So what do you suggest? You're not happy here with me. If I conjure a door for you how do you propose to find your father?"

Instead of answering he stormed outside and slammed the door. It was freezing and he hadn't bothered to wear a coat. Annie watched him head down the hill, his hair blowing back as a gust of wind went by. By the look of the sky, it would either sleet or snow later on in the day.

Annie thought about her recent dreams, the feeling that everything was about to hit the fan. This was the same way she'd felt before he left for the 1300's. But how could she convince him to stay? He wasn't happy with his life. It hurt to realize that she and Gaia weren't enough for him. The only way out of this mess was for him to do what he wanted to do, but if her dreams were right, there was a shit storm in his future. Why wouldn't he listen to her? But that was obvious—when she told him about her visions it only made him more adamant about going. It pissed him off.

She went into the kitchen to fix a meal for Gaia. Maybe when he got back from his walk they could talk sensibly about things.

CHAPTER 3

Sam's attitude did not improve. It was like the weather outside—volatile and unpredictable, his sudden outbursts scaring Annie and Gaia as he lost his temper. She tried to talk to him but he was having none of it, his general annoyance preventing any serious conversations between them.

"I can conjure a door, Sam," she told him quietly a few nights later. They were in the bedroom and she was trying not to wake Gaia. "I can make it very specific. Perhaps if you went to Ares and Gaia it might be better for you. They could help."

Sam glanced at her after removing his shirt. His muscles bulged from the work he'd been doing to ease his stress—chopping wood for the winter and stacking it. The pile was enormous. "I'd rather go straight to Apollo. I don't know this god, or Gaia, for that matter."

"Just a suggestion. I'm tired of your moods and your lack of interest in what we do best together."

Sam sneered. "You mean sex?"

"Among other things, yes. I think you should go before I kick you out."

Sam's face reddened. "Kick me out of my own home?"

Annie stared him down. "Your irritation is taking a toll on

your daughter and on me. I have a right to be here now. The library..."

"I know!" he shouted. "The fucking library is yours!"

When the baby woke and began to cry, Annie pointed toward the door. "You can sleep downstairs on the couch. You leave tomorrow."

Sam gave her a dark look and stormed out. She heard him pounding down the stairs and the sound of the front door opening and slamming shut. She wondered where would go at this time of night--it was dark and snowing. Had she just pushed him into another woman's arms? There were many in town who would be happy to have him. She picked up the baby and rocked her back to sleep, tears welling. She couldn't believe what was happening between them. *Déjà vu* all over again.

ANNIE WAS IN THE KITCHEN PREPARING OATMEAL THE NEXT morning when Sam appeared. "I'm ready to go," he muttered. He looked like he hadn't slept, his clothes wrinkled, hair mussed and dark circles under his eyes.

"Can you wait until after Gaia has breakfast?"

He didn't answer as he took the steps two at a time to their bedroom. She heard him pulling out drawers, the sound of something scraping before he let out a string of curse words.

She lifted the baby into the high chair Sam had fashioned for her, placing a bowl of porridge down in front of her. Instead of eating, Gaia picked it up and threw it, the porridge flying every-where. Annie stopped herself from screaming at the baby, knowing that Gaia was feeling every bit of tension that Annie and Sam were feeling. Instead, she burst into tears.

When Sam pounded down the stairs he found Annie curled up on the couch with Gaia in her arms. "What's going on?"

Annie wiped her eyes and looked up at him. "What do you think?"

"I won't be gone long."

"Heard that one before. Where were you last night?"

Sam's gaze slid away. "I have friends here."

"Women friends?"

"Gods damn it, Annie! First you can't wait to get rid of me and then you're worried about me sleeping around?"

Annie glared at him. "I don't want you to go anywhere, Sam. But if you feel you have to go, what can I do to stop you? I hate all of this—the arguing, the tension…I love you. I'm worried."

Sam placed his pack on the floor and sat next to her. "I love you too. I'm sorry I'm like this, but I…I can't stand being who I am right now. I want my old self back."

"What if you can't get it back? What if Apollo doesn't have the ability to help? What then?"

Sam let out a sigh and rubbed a hand across his stubbly face. "I don't have an answer to that."

Annie looked into the distance for a moment, trying to collect her thoughts. "We love each other, but if you can't be the man you were before, we can't be together—is that your answer?" She took hold of his arm. "Want to hear what Apollo told me about you?"

Sam frowned. "He hasn't even met me."

"I told him about the doors, how you lost your ability to control them. He said it was because you abused the privilege, Sam—that you used them for yourself."

"And you don't?"

"Mostly I've used them to help you in some way, and to leave Earth when it became uninhabitable."

Sam sat staring at the floor for several moments before he looked up. "Why didn't you tell me this?"

"I didn't think it would be useful and I didn't want to hurt you."

"But now it's okay to hurt me?"

"I wanted you to understand who Apollo is. If he thinks you aren't deserving, he won't help you."

"Maybe he can help me become a better man," he muttered.

"I thought I could do that. I'm really sorry that it's come to this."

"You thought you...?" He glared at her. "You put yourself above me, Annie. It's why I have to go."

"I don't put myself above you. I've been trying to help. You just can't get past your ego."

"So now it all comes out, just before I leave."

Tears welled and she tried to swallow the lump in her throat. "I love you and I want the best for you. This ego thing wasn't a problem before..."

"Before I went to the 1300's—yeah, I know that's what you think. Maybe this is just me. We weren't together that long before I went into the past. We didn't know each other very well."

Annie rose from the couch. "I'll conjure a door as best I can, but don't expect me to be waiting for you when you get back."

"Is that a threat?"

"It's the truth, Sam. I can't go through this again. I love you with all my heart, but seeing you unhappy makes me sad. I want you to want me, to want Gaia, to want what we have."

Sam rose and reached for her. "I do want you, Annie. I'm hoping that meeting Apollo will help me find myself. I'm no good for you the way I am."

Annie let him hold her, tears falling on his sweater as she sobbed. When he kissed her the tears came faster. A moment later she pulled away and hurried toward the door into the stacks.

CHAPTER 4

EDGE 2325

Annie stared at the place where the door had been three seconds before. A sheen remained, glittering dust motes swirling in the vacuum created. The last view of Sam had been his sad gaze on her as he raised his hand in farewell. She could barely see him through the haze of tears.

Gaia crawled along the floor of the stacks, pulling out books as she went. When Annie went to get her she had risen to standing, one hand resting on a shelf as she took two hesitant steps forward. Annie felt an overwhelming sadness as she watched her. Sam had just missed his baby's first steps. When she picked up the two books lying on the floor she was surprised to see the titles. One was called *The Golden Dawn,* and the other was *Using Dreams to Discover the Future.* The third was a book about life in the 1800's. She glanced at the baby looking up at her. How odd. She scooped up Gaia, held onto the books with her other hand, and headed for the other room.

The house seemed cold and lonely without Sam. She couldn't believe he was gone. If this turned out like the 1300's she didn't know what she would do. At least she wasn't pregnant this time. But how she would survive his absence was another matter. *Keep busy,* she told herself, moving toward her work table. When she left Gaia on the rug with her blocks and took the books to her desk, she noticed a note in Sam's handwriting.

Dearest Annie,

If this is the last time I see you please remember how much I love you and our baby. I am sorry I've turned into this person. I don't understand it, but I do know that in order to heal I have to do something drastic. Going to Atenua seemed like the best choice. I don't expect miracles from Apollo, but I do want to meet him. From what you've told me he is an extraordinary man. I am hoping that somewhere deep inside I take after him.
I already miss you. Please wait for me.

Sam

After Annie read the note she crumpled onto the floor sobbing.

∽

IT TOOK ANNIE A LONG WHILE TO REGAIN HER EQUILIBRIUM. SHE was shattered by the note and devastated that he was gone. Her mind cast back to the moments before he left. She'd placed her thoughts squarely on the green door that led into the compound, visualizing it clearly with the snake carvings and the shadows she remembered. When the library provided the door it was tenuous at first, making her wonder if this was a bad idea. Perhaps something terrible was going on there. What if Apollo was in jail or had been killed? What if the compound no longer existed?

As the door settled she'd become more confident, sending her thoughts toward Atenua and Sam's arrival where he was supposed to go. Just before he stepped through he'd pulled her to him and kissed her, a pirate's kiss, wild and deep, one strong arm holding her tight against him. When he released her she gasped, which made him laugh. "Remember that until I get back," he'd whispered in her ear, his breath causing shivers.

Annie felt sick with wanting as she thought of him. She should have gone with him. It was too late now.

The rest of the day was made up of a few minutes of work followed by tears and then repeated. In between she fed the baby and changed her, playing with her for a few minutes before placing her down for a nap. While Gaia slept she opened *Using Dreams to Discover the Future*. She'd been dreaming a lot recently and the imagery was clear in her mind. Cold, desolate landscapes and a feeling of being lost. Was this about her or Sam? It was hard to know.

> If you are one of those people who are a little bit off, a tad different than others, then you are the right one to be reading this book. Having mystical powers can be daunting, and this book is dedicated to helping you through it, step by step. Do you already know who you are and what you can accomplish, or are you still finding out about it? Do you dream often? Dreams are the key to the soul's purpose. And if you pay attention, your dreams can predict the future.
>
> First of all you need to ask your dreams to show you what you want to see. Symbols are key. Do you know your own symbols? We all have our unique set. Try and remember yours before you attempt to track your dreams. Otherwise you will become lost in imagery that you don't understand.

Annie closed the book and stared into space. She knew there was more to what she could do, but with Sam and his resentment she'd decided to ignore it. With him gone she could explore who she was. But even the thought of that gave her a twinge of guilt. Sam thought she placed herself above him. It wasn't true. He had to be in charge—it was who he was. If only they could be equals. She let out a sigh. He was very far away now, possibly meeting his father. How long would he be gone?

She thought about her dream symbols. She nearly always knew what her dreams meant. Tonight she would ask her dreams to connect her with Sam—to know what he was doing and thinking. They'd always been able to do this...except when he was in the 1300's. Was it merely the distance of that time period, or was it that he'd been taken over by what was happening? Annie thought he'd been taken over—it was why he was so restless now. Whatever had hold of him back then had not let him go. Apollo would know what to do.

Wolf nosed her, as though he knew what she was thinking. They had a bond now. Wolf was Sam's dog, but now he belonged to Annie, just like the library. Tears welled. No wonder Sam was so upset. She'd taken over his life.

CHAPTER 5

ATENUA

eavy snow covered everything. The wall Annie had told him about was nearly obscured by drifts. When he finally found the door through the layers of snow and banged on it, no one came. He was freezing, his ears uncovered and his coat not warm enough. After trying several times to rouse someone, he tromped through the drifts around the wall to the place Annie had mentioned where the bricks had disintegrated. Perhaps Apollo and his mother couldn't hear his knocking. With the wind whistling the way it was, he couldn't imagine they could hear much.

His boots were wet through by the time he reached the spot he was looking for. He stepped into drifts that came up to his thighs, having a hard time extricating himself before he was able to climb the wall. He headed to the mound of white that had to be the house. Snow came up so high it obliterated any hint of windows or doors. Somehow he found his way to the portico and then struggled through drifts to find the door. He used his bare hands to swipe at the snow, finally discovering the front door. He banged on it and shouted for some time, finally giving up. *One last try*, he thought, reaching for the knob. The door swung open and he went with it.

Sam landed on his hands and knees inside. He rose, his ears attuned to voices or any sign of habitation. Snow blew in, ice crystals hitting him in the face as he struggled against the wind to get the door closed. Inside there was nothing but silence. He moved down the hall opening doors, the icy temperatures causing him to shiver. No one could live in this house now. There was obviously no heating system, or if there was, it was off. The temperature had to be below zero.

As he progressed through the house he had the feeling that no one had been in it for quite a while. Thick dust covered the furniture and despite the chill air, there was a musty smell. He was exhausted, his eyes at half mast. It felt like night with the windows mostly covered over with snow. He found a bed and some blankets and curled up, falling asleep almost immediately.

SAM WOKE SHIVERING. WHY HADN'T ANNIE WARNED HIM ABOUT the snow and cold? He would have packed warmer clothes. The sky was the same gray color it had been when he fell asleep—it was still snowing. If anything, it had grown colder inside the house. He rose from the bed and pulled a blanket around his shoulders as he explored to find something to eat. In the kitchen he could find nothing but a few pieces of leather-like jerky. He ate it, using his incisors to rip it apart. His strange dreams came back to him—snakes and caverns so dark he couldn't see his hand in front of his face. He pondered his next move. Where would Apollo and Constance go? Was this some annual migration or had something happened to them? Annie had told him about the dark side of the planet. This wasn't it. But why was it so cold? From her descriptions the sun shown every day—unrelenting light. The sun was out, but it hung behind clouds so thick that its light barely reached the planet's surface. *And forget about any warmth,* he thought, pulling the blanket tighter around his shoulders.

It was a while before he decided to brave the elements. There was a town down there, if he accurately remembered what Annie had told him. Maybe someone was around and he could ask what had happened to Apollo. He searched the cupboards and closets, finally discovering a warm jacket with a hood which he put on over his other clothing. He left the house and worked his way up the path he'd made coming in, heading for the wall.

He was down the hill when he spotted several huddled figures. He hurried toward them, hoping to find answers, but instead they were frozen solid, their eyes wide open. For a second he was unable to move, the horror of it and the reminder of his time in the 1300's taking him over. He shook uncontrollably as he moved through the drifts toward the buildings in the distance. He worked his way by more bodies lying still under a layer of snow, others sitting up and leaning against trees.

His mind was shot, his thoughts wild. This was a place of nightmares. Had this storm arrived out of the blue? Was everyone dead?

THE HARBOR WAS FROZEN SOLID, BOATS STUCK IN PLACE AND rigging like cobwebs of ice. No one was on them—Sam checked.

He couldn't feel his feet, and his hands were blue despite shoving them in his pockets. He would die here if he didn't find a way to get warm. He was starving and had no food. What had he been thinking when he left Edge?

Where in hell would Apollo be if he wasn't in the compound, and why hadn't Annie explained this damn weather? Sam let out a huff and scanned into the distance. A bright light flashed in the sky above him, blinding him with its intensity. He crouched down as it hurtled toward the planet. An explosion deafened him, the smoke billowing toward him from where the thing had landed. He couldn't hear and he could barely see.

Hours went by. Smoke covered the landscape, making him cough. His eyes burned. He was freezing, his thinking mind slipping. He was so sleepy, but he knew if he succumbed he would die.

CHAPTER 6

"Looks like a meteor hit Atenua," Ares said, squinting.

Gaia stared at the dark clouds rising. "Is that what it is? Who is in Seris, Ares? I feel someone's presence."

Ares turned to her. "It's Apollo's son."

"Is Annie with him?"

"No."

"He knows nothing about this time of year on Atenua. There is no one in Seris now."

"Perhaps we should help him?"

Gaia let out a an annoyed sigh. "From what Annie has said about the man, I am loathe to meet him."

"We are gods, Gaia. It is up to us to help mankind, especially now."

"Why 'especially now'? Things are better on Earth and those who live here are familiar with the weather patterns. They've gone underground."

Ares frowned. "And how will he find them? He could die out there."

"And Annie would blame me," Gaia muttered.

"That is correct."

"But it's snowing down there!" she complained, gazing at the flowers blooming and feeling the sun on her bare arms.

Ares scoffed. "You do not feel the cold. And neither do I. We have an obligation."

~

"HE'S HERE," ARES SAID, HURRYING TOWARD TWO ENORMOUS boulders.

"Is he dead?"

"Not quite, but almost." Ares took hold of Sam's shoulders and blew his breath onto his face, thawing the ice crystals and warming him. "We need to take him to the castle," he muttered to Gaia, who was staring at the man.

When she nodded the two of them took hold of Sam and flew upwards into the heavy dark clouds that had now covered over Seris and everything within sight.

By the time they got him back to the castle his cheeks had a bit of color. His eyes were still closed, but life had been restored.

~

SAM WOKE IN AN ENORMOUS BED IN A ROOM DECORATED WITH PALE tapestries and columns of marble. "Am I in heaven?" he muttered, looking around.

"Not heaven," a female voice said. A beautiful fair-haired woman came into view dressed in a gown fit for a queen. "I am Gaia, formerly from Earth."

Sam stared at her in confusion. His last memory was huddling between two boulders trying to protect himself from something that fell out of the sky. "Where am I?"

"This is Ares' castle. We found you near death and brought you here."

"And my father and mother? Are they here?"

She laughed. "Most everyone on the planet has gone underground for the cold time. They should be safe."

"Annie didn't mention anything about this," Sam grumbled.

"Annie knew nothing of this," Gaia answered. "She was here during the warm season and no one informed her about what happens when the planet is at its farthest point away from the sun."

"Atenua has an elliptical orbit," a tall well-built man said, arriving next to Gaia. "One side is always dark and the other always light, but both become very cold when the orbit reaches its outermost point. I am Ares, by the way."

Sam stared at the larger than life red-haired god. "Where do all the people go?"

"Some have tunnels under their houses, others travel to the dark side of the planet where the creatures live deep underground. It is there that Apollo and Constance have gone with their two children. The meteor you experienced was unexpected."

Sam raised his eyebrows. "Little Sam and...?"

"Thea, your sister."

"The goddess of light," Sam muttered. "Sounds about right considering Atenua. But what happens now with this meteor? Has it destroyed Seris? There were many dead in Seris, but that was before the thing hit."

"Hard to say until the weather down there clears. I hope it has not done major damage. In many ways it is a lovely city. As for the dead, there are many homeless—they have nowhere to go when the weather changes. I have to say that the cold this year seems more extreme than others."

"How do I find Apollo and Constance?"

Ares and Gaia exchanged a glance. "I suppose we will have to take you. That is unless you wish to remain here until the weather warms."

Sam glanced out the door at the beautiful gardens, birdsong reaching his ears. A warm fragrant breeze touched his cheek, the scent of flowers reaching his nostrils. He took in a deep breath. "If Annie were here I would say yes, but without her I need to find my father. He has the answers I seek."

"What are the questions?" Gaia asked him.

Sam glanced at her and away. "I would rather not say."

"Annie has confided in me, Sam. I know what happened between you. It was from here on Atenua that she found her way back to you and tried to convince you to leave the 1300's."

Sam hung his head, embarrassment flooding his senses. He didn't know what to say.

"Annie loves you deeply. She refused to give up on you."

"I know that. It's why I need to talk with my father."

Gaia cocked her head as she watched him. "Apollo cannot help. It is up to you. Right now Annie is pining for you and worrying about what has happened here."

"She has the power to do what she wants," he muttered.

"You do not trust her? She has done nothing to deserve that. I hope you can come to your senses and realize what you..."

Ares grabbed her arm and dragged her away before she could go on. Sam could hear him whispering in her ear as though his hearing had become more acute. "He is in no shape to hear your opinions," Ares told her. "He is confused and searching. He nearly died. Do not make things worse for him."

Was being here on Atenua reviving his magic? He wished it was so, but he also had the sense that this was not what he should be concentrating on. This preoccupation with magic had caused his problems. "I need to find Apollo," he said, looking at Ares.

Ares nodded. "I will take you there if you feel up to it."

Sam swung his legs over the edge of the bed. "I certainly feel better than I did. What did you do?"

"Aside from breathing life back into you? Nothing but a bit of magic to give you back your strength."

A bit of magic. Just the word *magic* annoyed him these days. Sam found his clothes at the end of the bed and quickly pulled them on. He felt stronger than he had, his resolve growing as he dressed. Soon he would have the answers he needed and he could head back home to Annie.

Gaia stood with her arms folded as Ares led Sam toward the edge of the mountain. Steep dark rock jutted out in layers leading downward. "Gaia became very close with Annie when they shared a body. She is protective and can be a bit off-putting at times. Try to understand."

"I do understand. I was an ass and still am. It's why I'm here."

Ares laughed. "At least you can admit it. Do not listen to Gaia—Apollo will help you, Sam. Your father is a good man."

CHAPTER 7

EDGE

When Annie concentrated on Sam all she saw was white. Snow? Was it possible? If so, no one had mentioned that kind of weather while she was there. Perhaps some unexpected storms had come through. She sent a prayer out to Gaia, hoping that the goddess would help. He should have been back by now.

The last month had been hard for her as people began to turn up at her door. When they asked to borrow the books the library housed, she allowed it, understanding their thirst for knowledge. Edge was attracting inventors, creatives who were making things, both mechanical and organic. They came and dug deep in the landfills to discover parts they could use, but they needed instructions. The library was becoming what its name implied, and she was now the custodian.

As the days went by and more people arrived, she devised a system so that they could borrow the books. She made cards and filled them out with dates and times for their return.

Another group came for her. It was as though she had an advertisement on her door, reading PSYCHIC. She wasn't psychic, at least not in the way they hoped. When she asked what made them decide to knock on her door she was met with blank stares, as though she'd always been there for them to consult. She dealt with them by inviting them inside, making tea and pulling out her tarot deck. She set up her place to read the cards at Cecily's old work space, using her crystal ball, aka, globe, as a hint of her authority. At least it gave her something to do.

The more she read the cards the more she realized that her intuition seemed to have increased ten-fold. Visions came unbidden, visions that contained the people sitting in front of her and the answers they sought.

It was odd, and felt as though Sam's leaving had ushered in some strange new energy, winds that brought messages from beyond Edge. The weather had been harsh, ushering in freezing rain and sending any remaining leaves flying. Even with the bad weather people sought her out, turning Annie's and Gaia's solitary life to one of strangers roaming in and out with books in their hands, and others sitting on the couch reading. Gaia loved it, her eyes bright as she sidled up to everyone, babbling in a language only she understood. Wolf, on the other hand, hid under the table, watching warily.

The world was waking up. And what Annie saw in the cards corroborated this. Things were changing fast. Only time would tell if this was a good thing.

MORNING CAME TOO SOON, THE NIGHT BEFORE FRAUGHT WITH disturbing dreams of snow and cold. Gaia had managed to climb out of her crib and was playing on the floor at the foot of the bed. Annie panicked, her gaze on the open door and the steps that led down. Gaia could have tumbled down the stairs. She hastily rose and grabbed the baby, carrying her down to make coffee and breakfast.

As she worked on the oatmeal she went over the dream imagery from the night before—*symbols* was what the book called it, but for her it was as though a tableau had been laid out revealing things as they really were. She had seen Sam wearing a strange coat with a hood and a woman dressed in an elaborate gown leading him somewhere as snow accumulated around them. Who was the woman? Her immediate jealousy was followed with rationality. It had to be Gaia—she was the only one who wouldn't feel the cold. Gaia was taking him to the castle in the clouds. But what had happened to cause this development?

Her supply of coffee beans was getting low. Her hand grinder was now empty. Later today she would have to go to town for more—if they even had them. Supplies had run low since Sam had been gone, the ships coming less often. She had a strange premonition that money would be coming back soon. If that was the case she would have to charge for her readings; many of those who needed help did not have any. She sighed and lifted Gaia out of her high chair. Her mind went to Sam who was missing out on the baby's development—every phase was important. Where was he?

ANNIE WAS DOING A READING WHEN THE VISION TOOK HER OVER. A headache followed, so severe she thought she might be sick. It only lasted a moment, maybe two, the imagery pulsing around her. Something had happened on Atenua, something that lit up the planet and caused great damage.

"What does that card mean?" the woman asked, pointing at the three of cups.

Annie had to force her thoughts back to the reading. "For you I would say it's about coming together with others for a common goal. You've been wanting to form this group, Eliza. It looks to me as though now is the time."

"Oh, thank you," Eliza gushed. "I wish I had something to give you, Annie. You've saved my life." Eliza rose and headed toward the door. "Can I send Ben over tomorrow? He's the one who doesn't want me to form the group."

Annie thought about the taciturn man who raised the sheep and goats. "Only if he wants to, Eliza. You cannot force him."

Her eyes narrowed. "He's being a beast and I'm tired of it."

"Be that as it may, I won't do a reading for someone who doesn't want to be here."

When Eliza left, Annie went into the kitchen to make tea. She was exhausted and worried, her mind on Sam. When she heard a knock she hurried to the door. "I'm closed..." she began before noticing who it was. Jack stood on her stoop. "What are you doing here?"

He held out the talisman—the green scarab created on Atenua. "This belongs to Sam," he said.

"I thought he gave it to you."

"My mother finally told me the truth. Sam and I aren't brothers. I have no right to this."

Annie stared at him in surprise. She hadn't seen him in this Edge since before Sam went to the 1300's. So much had happened since then. When Gaia gave a cry and toddled toward the door, Jack's eyes went wide. "Who is this?"

"Sam's and my baby. Her name is Gaia."

Jack leaned down to say hello and a second later he lifted her into the air, making her laugh. "I'm surprised you and Sam were together long enough to make a baby," he muttered.

"We were together in the 1300's Jack. We were close until..."

"Until he lost his mind," Jack mumbled.

Annie watched him interact with Gaia, surprised by the feelings that rose up in her. It had to be because of the other reality, the one in which she and Jack had almost...but Jack had been different in that reality—kinder and loving toward her. And she'd been so lonely. She pulled her attention back to the man standing in her doorway. "Thanks for bringing it back."

He placed the baby on the ground and peered past her into the living room. "Is Sam here? I'd like to talk to him."

Annie shook her head. "I'll tell him you came by."

"Okay," he said hesitantly, glancing at her. His eyebrows rose as though he could read her mind.

"I'm busy right now," she said quickly, moving to close the door.

He put his hand out to hold the door open. "Sam's gone, isn't he?" Where did he go this time?"

Annie blinked back tears. "I have to go," she murmured, managing to push the door closed. She watched him through the window, his hands in his pockets as he turned in a circle, seemingly unsure what to do. A moment later he headed off with his head down.

Annie slipped the talisman around her neck, feeling a buzz in her chest when it touched her skin. Everything lit up for a second, as though the green stone had ignited her senses. But it was Sam's talisman, not hers.

She paced for a few minutes, her fingers holding the talisman, which was becoming hot in her hands. Jack's appearance had stirred something up that she'd tried to ignore. She'd loved him once and then again in the other reality, before the bombs sent the planet into a tailspin and she walked through a door into Atenua. She'd come perilously close to sleeping with him. And here she was again—Sam gone, lonely, confused and vulnerable.

CHAPTER 8

ATENUA

S am stood in driving snow staring at the smudge of darkness in the distance.

"I could take you all the way if you prefer," Ares said. "The weather is certainly not conducive for a hike."

"No. I have some thinking to do and I need the time."

"Try and stay warm, Sam. I provided you with a heavy cloak, but you must hurry. The weather will get worse until the planet moves closer to the sun again."

"Thank you, Ares. I never thought I would meet a god I liked."

Ares laughed. "I am only a minor god—perhaps I am not as arrogant as others."

Sam smiled. "You are less arrogant than I've been. I need to think about that."

Ares smiled. "I wish you all the best."

Sam moved off, barely noticing when the god disappeared into the snow-filled clouds. His mind was on his father now and what his future held. If Seris was destroyed, what then? When he stared into the distance it felt like he was heading into hell, a wall of darkness in front of him.

He hadn't told Annie the true reason he needed to speak with his father. She thought he had lived too long to remember his past, but it wasn't that. There were huge chunks gone from his memory, empty spaces that he couldn't fill with anything but blankness. It was one of the reasons he'd stayed in the 1300's for so long. He'd hoped that being there would have jogged something loose, but it never did.

At first he'd thought that his stint in the Institute had done it, but looking back on several periods of time, that theory didn't cut it. Everything was confusing now, as though his entire life was a series of strange encounters with big blank periods in between and no continuity.

Annie was the only thing he could hold onto. Since he'd been with her his lapses had disappeared. She was his grounding, and yet he'd he'd left her alone with their child in order to find a father who might or might not be able to help him. It wasn't about magic at all, it was about his sanity. He couldn't take Annie down with him—it wasn't fair. He was half a man and she deserved more.

THE WIND CAME UP AS HE STRUGGLED THROUGH DRIFTS AS HIGH AS his thighs. Ice crystals were in his lashes, his nose numb. The darkness was closer now, but he still had a long way to go. He was tired, so tired, his lids lowering as he began to move more slowly. He had to rest, even for a few minutes. His belly growled with hunger. But there was no food on this ill-conceived trek he'd put himself on. Why hadn't he allowed Ares to take him to the caves? He was an arrogant fool, full of himself with the idea that he could overcome the weather. There was no overcoming this weather. He could easily end up dead. He hunkered down under a tree and closed his eyes—*just for a few minutes*, he told himself.

Sam was a hawk circling in the sky looking for rodents. He dipped down and zeroed in on a dark shape, carrying it in his sharp talons while he found a perch where he could eat it. It was dead by the time he landed on a branch and he ripped the flesh off the bones, devouring it with the fur still intact. After it was gone, his hawk eyes searched the sky and the landscape of white before he put his head under his wing to rest.

He woke with a start, the dream still with him. There was blood on his hands. He smeared it off on the snow and looked around. A few feathers lay scattered about, as well as pieces of regurgitated fur. An owl or hawk must have spent some time right beside him eating some rodent it had found. He wished it had left some for him.

His belly didn't feel as empty as it had. Maybe he was so hungry that it didn't register anymore. Snow still fell from a leaden sky. His brain seemed off, and he was shaking with cold. That's when he realized that he was naked. His clothing lay scattered about as though he'd pulled them off quickly. He hurried to dress, watching his skin turn from red to blue. He couldn't think any further than the dark space in the distance. He pulled his hood up, tucked the cloak closer and went on.

CHAPTER 9

EDGE

Annie sat up in bed, her heart beating wildly. The talisman buzzed against her chest. Sam was lost in a snowstorm. She sent a message through the ether to Apollo. Maybe he could hear her; every time she tried to contact Sam it was like a wall had come down between them.

When she glanced at the crib, the baby was standing up holding the top rail, her eyes wide. Wolf was beside the crib. He gave one bark.

As she rose to retrieve Gaia, she heard someone banging on the door downstairs. She pulled on a robe, grabbed the baby and hurried down. Wolf ran past her barking, his hackles raised as he raced toward the front door.

By the time she got to the door whoever had been there was gone. Perhaps after hearing a large angry dog barking they'd decided to come back later. Wolf's bark was nothing to fool around with.

Annie was curious as to who it was. Most of those coming to the library were either here for her readings or wanting a book on a certain subject, mostly regarding building windmills or water wheels or something similarly useful for the community or for themselves. There was a resurgence of energy in creating at the moment, every young person she met either talking about something they'd thought of or describing a friend's project. The excitement was palpable, as though Earth was coming back to life after a long snooze. A woman she knew who studied the stars told her that it was an alignment that hadn't been seen for over one hundred years. "Women are rising up," she whispered, her eyes bright. "We are as much a part of this new world as men are—for once!" she added emphatically.

Annie thought about that. Women had not been under men's thumbs so much since the last war. They were becoming more creative in their pursuits, and men had more respect for them. After living in the 1300's where women did all the work and got none of the respect, she'd come to appreciate what she had here.

When she peered out the window it had begun to snow. The parallels seemed weird, as though there was a conduit running between the two planets. Her fingers went to the scarab, feeling it shiver. She had the sudden impulse to go through a door to Atenua—she should never have let Sam go alone. The baby gave a little shriek from where she'd placed her in her high chair. First things first— Gaia needed to be fed.

Annie had calmed by the time Gaia was fed and changed, the simple actions turning her attention to the present moment. Today was the day she usually visited the shops to replenish the supplies she needed. She left the baby in Wolf's care and hurried upstairs to dress.

Once she was dressed she grabbed Gaia and left the library. She put the baby on the ground and took hold of her hand, giving her the chance to practice walking. The sun had come out, but the gray clouds in the distance would return. There was definitely snow in the future. Fifteen minutes later, despite Gaia's protests to the contrary, she had to pick her up. "I have to get my shopping done," she whispered, trying to console her, not that it did much good.

By the time she returned, there was a line outside the library and Cecily was there screening people.

"Cecily!" Annie cried, hurrying to the pixie-like woman with the triangular face. She hadn't seen her since her return to the Edge she knew. It was a welcome sight.

Cecily greeted her with a kiss on both cheeks. "I came by and noticed all these people waiting at your door. Looks like you could use some help."

Annie widened her eyes to indicate the craziness going on before she whispered, "Thank you."

Cecily allowed one person in at a time, either to go into the stacks or to have a reading. Annie was at her desk, ready with her cards. The others who wanted books had to stop by Cecily on their way out so that she could write the name of the book down and tell them how long they had it for. It was all very orderly. Cecily's presence was a godsend and helped Annie concentrate on the people sitting in front of her expecting answers. She'd come to realize that what she was doing with the cards was coming from within her—the answers appearing like magic. But if she was worried or fretting, the answers did not arrive, frustrating her and the person who awaited her wisdom.

IT WAS DURING A LULL THAT ANNIE FINALLY GOT THE CHANCE TO talk with the woman who had worked with Sam for all those years. "Where have you been?" she asked her.

Cecily smiled and cocked her head to one side, which made her look even more like a sprite or a pixie. "I have a man in my life," she said shyly. "He lives about ten miles from here. I came back to see if Sam was doing any better. Last time I was here he was so depressed I was afraid for him."

Annie nodded. "He was a mess when I got back. But the baby cheered him up."

Cecily laughed, her gaze on Gaia. "A baby between you? Never expected that. He must have been thrilled."

Annie nodded. "It certainly helped. This is Gaia," she continued, putting the baby on the floor.

"And where is he now? It looks like you're single-handedly running things."

"He went to Atenua to find his father."

Cecily frowned. "Atenua—isn't that a planet in the Sirius system?"

She nodded. "I sent him through a door. But I think he may be in trouble."

"When isn't he?"

Annie laughed. "I know—it's like he seeks it out."

"Keeps him feeling alive," Cecily responded.

"You would know better than I," Annie said. "How long have you known him?"

Cecily stared into the distance. "More years than you might believe."

Annie decided not to pursue it—she didn't want to find out that they'd known each other for a century or more. She'd never been sure how old Cecily was—it seemed like the woman was as ageless as Sam. She looked up to see Jack coming through the open door, his gaze on her. "I need a reading," he muttered.

Cecily waved him through. "I'll watch Gaia," she offered, glancing at where the baby played on the floor.

Annie pointed Jack to the desk where two chairs had been set up. "Why are you here?" she hissed.

"I need to figure out my next move."

"Your next move—for what?"

Jack frowned and looked down at the deck. "I prefer to have you read the Tarot, Annie, not psychoanalyze me."

She let out an annoyed huff and handed him the cards. "Shuffle three times and then cut the deck into three piles from left to right. What do you need answered?"

He picked up the cards and shuffled. "I just told you—life."

"That isn't very specific."

"I'll take whatever I can get," he muttered, watching her lay out the cards. "Are you in charge of the cards, or is it me that controls the reading?"

Annie glanced at him. "It's you, Jack. I am an instrument of the Tarot—I read what the cards tell me."

"That means your opinions are in the reading."

"I try to keep my opinions out of it. The answers I get come from somewhere else. With you it might be harder, but I'll do my best." She turned over the first card—*Temperance*. "This first one is all about timing. This suggests that you must have patience, that everything happens in its own time."

He let out a heavy sigh. "And that one?" he asked, staring at the *Moon* card she had just turned over.

"Confusion and illusion, possibly deception."

He looked up at her, his dark eyes boring into hers and making her uncomfortable.

"Were you here earlier this morning?" she asked to break the tension.

He looked away for a moment, finally turning back to her. "I was, but no one seemed to be home."

"It was early. I heard you knock, but I didn't get to the door in time. Seems you're anxious to figure something out."

He nodded. "I am."

"But you don't want to reveal what it is? Maybe if you shared a bit more I could help."

"I can't share with you, Annie. We know each other—we've had a relationship. The less you know the better."

Annie pulled another card and laid it face up. "I thought a short reading might work since you seem so impatient." She glanced down at the *Ten of Swords*. She was reluctant to tell him the meaning.

"Well?" he asked, frowning at the disturbing image.

"This card is about endings. And loss and pain."

He let out a humorless laugh. "I'd say so, considering the swords sticking out of his back."

"What does it signify for you?"

He shook his head. "I thought this would help, but it's making things worse," he said, standing.

"This isn't the way I work. I first listen to your issue and then I read the cards that come up. Without any information it's very difficult to know what the layout is trying to tell you."

"I can't tell you about this—you wouldn't approve. It's my business anyway. What do I owe you?"

"Nothing," she said, rising from the chair.

"Come on, Annie. I know you do this for money. With Sam away you're on your own."

"So it's true? Money is coming back? Where's it being made? I don't get any news about the rest of the country."

"Thats because you never leave Edge."

"Where would I go if I left? I have everything I need here."

Jack smirked. "The cities are coming back to life—industry is turning its wheels again. There are banks now."

"Banks—I'd forgotten all about them. I like the barter system."

"You would. You live in a dreamworld." Jack pulled out a few bills and put them down on the desk.

Annie's gaze went to him. "I didn't help you, Jack. Therefore you don't owe me anything."

"How do you know you didn't help me?"

Annie handed him back his money and rose to walk him to the door.

When he headed off, Wolf followed him. "Wolf!" Annie called out. Wolf stopped, but Jack didn't turn around, his hands deep in his pockets as he walked away. Annie felt a pang of something akin to caring. That man…he was such an enigma. What in hell was he up to now? The ten of swords did not bode well. Probably involved in several schemes to make money—he had always been a wheeler-dealer. And he was about to experience a betrayal—and be stabbed in the back. But maybe whatever this was would change him…it could happen.

"What did *he* want?" Cecily asked.

"A reading."

Cecily's eyes narrowed. "Jack wanted a reading?" She scoffed. "I don't trust him."

Annie thought about this Jack and the one she'd met in the Edge that had no magic. They were like night and day. But bringing the talisman back was a good thing. She had to admit that she felt a certain kinship with him. Was he her friend? He'd sought her out for a reading which meant he trusted her. But he wouldn't tell her his plans. Her intuition told her that he was doing something that would change his life in one way or another.

She nodded to the next person in line, gesturing toward the desk.

CHAPTER 10

Dreams plagued Annie all night long, visions of strange places and times, and Jack, who wanted something from her. She woke in a panic. Sam. A few days had turned into weeks.

When she came down to the kitchen with Gaia, Cecily was already fielding people. After placing the baby in her high chair and handing her a piece of bread to gnaw on, she hurried toward Cecily. "I have to speak with you," she whispered.

Cecily told those waiting to be patient and turned to Annie with a frown. "What is it?"

"It's Sam. I expected him back weeks ago."

Cecily made a face. "And what can I do about that?"

Annie hesitated, glancing at her daughter who was still in the high chair. "I can't take Gaia with me if I go to Atenua."

Cecily's eyes widened in alarm. "You...want to go to Atenua and leave her with me?"

"Something's off, Cecily. Jack being here and his reading... something isn't right."

"And you know this, how?"

"I had a vision."

Cecily shook her head. "You and your visions." She let out a sigh. "How long?"

"All I have to do is find Sam and bring him home—I figure no more than a day or two."

"And what about what he's doing there? Didn't he go for a reason?"

"To meet his father, yes. But...I don't feel safe here without him." She glanced at the crowd outside the door. They were milling around impatiently. "With this new development I need him."

Cecily nodded. "I get that—it's not a job for one person, or even two, not with people going into the stacks and taking books. I have a sense that Sam will not like what we're doing."

Annie let out a humorless laugh. "I totally agree—he's going to be pissed at how many books are checked out."

"Doubt he would allow it at all," Cecily muttered.

"I'll leave tomorrow. Too late for today and I haven't packed yet. Tell the ones who want readings to come back next week. As to the others, deal with them as you have been."

Cecily sighed, glancing at the baby. "I can't believe I'm agreeing to this."

Annie smiled. "You'll do fine. And Wolf is here."

"Wolf? How can he help?"

"He watches over her, Cecily. He's like a babysitter."

"Okay—go. But please do not be gone long."

Annie gave her a hug. "In the morning please keep people out of the stacks for a while, okay?"

Cecily nodded, a resigned look on her face.

ANNIE SPENT THE REST OF THE DAY PREOCCUPIED ABOUT HER upcoming trip. She could barely concentrate on the cards or the people sitting at the desk expecting answers to their questions.

When she gazed at the baby, a chill went down her spine. What if something happened and she couldn't get back? Or even worse, something happened here while she was gone.

CHAPTER 11

Annie wasn't surprised when Jack re-appeared at her door early the next morning. Her dreams had intimated that he was on his way back to the library. "Are you looking for another reading?" she asked, opening the door.

He shook his head, his narrowed gaze moving by her into the interior. "I need a door," he muttered.

Her worst fears were confirmed. "A door? What are you talking about?"

"You know very well what I'm talking about," he said, grabbing her by the arm.

When she tried to twist away he grabbed both her arms and pinned her against him. "I want a door," he hissed in her ear. "Now."

"Gaia's in her high chair. I can't just leave her there."

"It won't take long," he muttered, pulling her with him toward the stacks.

"I thought you could travel without doors," she muttered, looking up at him. His eyes looked very green and over-bright. Was he on drugs? "And besides, the library won't allow it."

"Why the hell not? You have control of them."

"Yes, but you don't." Annie pulled away and rubbed her

wrists. "I can't just send anyone through, Jack. The library only allows it if it approves."

He scoffed. "So now it's sentient? That's rich. For some reason my normal methods aren't working. Why do you care if I use the doors?"

"I'm the custodian."

"Yeah, so? I'm only going back in time—I'm not trying to ruin your life or anything. In fact I have a surprise for you if you come with me."

Annie glanced out the window, hoping to see Cecily, but she wasn't there. "Where do you want to go?"

"London, late 1800's—you know where and when."

Annie took a step back. "For what?"

"I have friends there, and for that matter, so do you."

"The library won't allow it."

"Bullshit. You can't tell me it has ethics."

Annie realized that he was not going to give up. All she could do was prove it to him. "Okay. Come with me," she said, heading into the stacks.

He followed on her heels, his breathing loud in her ears.

Once they were in the corridor she stopped. "So, Golden Dawn time? September, 1893?"

Jack smiled and nodded. "Very good, Annie. Your memory is working well."

"I need a door to take Jack into the past," she murmured, expecting nothing to happen. To her surprise a door immediately appeared.

Jack laughed. "I told you so."

He glanced at her before he pulled the handle down, but instead of stepping through, he grabbed her and pulled her with him. "You're my ticket back, Annie."

Annie tried to pull away, but it was too late. The door closed behind them. A moment later she was standing on cobblestones and the door was gone. Panic rolled through her. Gaia was sitting in the kitchen in her high chair. "Gaia!" she cried out.

"Cecily will be there any second. Get a grip."

Annie narrowed her eyes, recognizing where she was. "If you can move through the ether, why did you bring me along?"

"Because for some reason I can't now."

"Maybe you've stepped over the line, Jack—taken your magic one step too far." The building where the Golden Dawn had conducted their business stood in the waning light, shafts of the lowering sun brightening the stone. It was late afternoon and there was wispy fog lifting from the river, streaks of color painting the western sky. Annie tried to breathe.

"Beautiful, isn't it," Jack whispered in her ear.

Annie grabbed Jack's sleeve. "I have to get back!"

Jack shrugged. "She'll live until Cecily gets there."

Annie tried to calm herself as she looked around. The Golden Dawn building was an ornate affair with columns and marble and wide mullioned windows and set apart from others like an embassy or a special monument. It was one of the few places in this timeline where women were on an equal footing with men. The light was different here. Lack of pollution, she suspected. She wondered about Edge and all the new creativity and the inventions. What was happening in the future reminded her of this time period when everything was possible. It was after the industrial revolution but before pollution became problematic. A second later she was in panic mode again, imagining Gaia screaming and crying. "Jack, please—where is the library in this time period?"

"Weren't you planning to leave for Atenua this morning?"

"How do you know that?"

Jack grinned. "I know a lot of stuff. Cecily is there by now. I can feel her."

Annie frowned at him. "You can feel her?"

Jack nodded. "I'm a wizard—I told you that. She came early because of the trip you planned this morning. And Wolf was at the door when she arrived."

Annie stared at Jack, trying to figure out what had just

happened. A wizard? She'd heard him say it, but what did that even mean? "If you're a wizard why did you need me?"

"I told you—something isn't working. Not sure why."

"It's because you're misusing it. Are you sure about Cecily?"

He nodded. "Stop worrying. Your baby is fine. And I have another little surprise for you."

For some reason she believed Jack about Cecily. She felt it too —Gaia was safe. "What surprise?"

Jack smiled. "You have a twin sister in this timeline. You don't know about it because you were sent to the future when you were a baby to keep you from being hung as a witch."

Annie's mind was still on home, his words shocking her into a reaction. "A baby? Who would hang a baby?"

Jack laughed. "Twins are considered an ill omen. The people here are superstitious about it. Your parents sent you away to hide the twin thing from their friends. Your mother and father were witches, Annie."

Annie was trying to process what he'd said when a cart came out of nowhere and nearly ran them down. "Pay attention," he hissed, glancing at the darkening sky and the chaos on the street.

Annie was in complete shock as Jack took hold of her arm and steered her off the street.

CHAPTER 12

THE DARK SIDE OF THE PLANET

S am shivered violently, fighting to open his eyes.

"Keep him still," a female voice said.

"I'm trying, but he's a big man."

"Pour this down his throat—it will calm him."

Sam choked and coughed, but his eyes refused to open. In the next few minutes he felt himself drifting, his thoughts drifting along with him. He was floating in warm water, held up by some unseen force. When hands moved across his body an erection rose in response. He felt like an animal, reacting to stimuli but unable to go any further. He let out a groan.

"He seems…"

"Better? Yes, I think so. Now we will leave him to rest."

The presence he'd sensed retreated. Women—it was women who touched him, women who were helping him. He imagined them, beautiful, with long hair like Annie's, their hands soft where they touched him. In the silence he let go of all thought, falling into a deep sleep.

SAM OPENED HIS EYES TO SEE WHAT LOOKED LIKE AN ALLIGATOR standing next to where he lay under blankets. Next to the alligator was an upright snake. He had to be dreaming. This couldn't be what he'd felt earlier.

"You are not dreaming," a voice said. He turned to see a man come into the room, his indigo eyes reminding him of his own.

"What is happening?"

The man smiled, running a hand through his thick graying hair. He waved at the two creatures. "Manasa and Salir have been tending to you. I am Apollo. I suspect that you are my son."

Sam felt shock in the deepest part of him. His heart began to race. "You're my father," he muttered inanely.

Apollo glanced at the two creatures standing next to the bed and said something under his breath. Sam watched as the alligator turned and walked toward the door, the serpent following.

"They have been tending…who are they?"

"As I said, the snake is Manasa, the other is Salir. You nearly died," he added.

"I remember being in snow."

"That is correct. Do you remember anything else?"

"I was in Seris, but the city was abandoned."

"And you thought to travel to the dark side of the planet. Why?"

"I…don't really know," he said, thinking back. He looked up. "It was Ares and Gaia. They took me to their castle. Ares brought me back to life. They explained about the dark side of the planet. I seem to be a burden to everyone here."

"Ares brought you here to the tunnels. What happened then?"

"I asked him to leave me once the tunnels were in sight. I wanted to make the trek myself. I had some thinking to do."

"Stubborn *and* foolish," Apollo murmured.

"But here I am," he said defensively.

"Annie let me know you were here. I sent my people to find you."

"Annie? She communicates with you through the ether?"

"Yes."

Sam was angry for a split second, jealousy rising as he wondered why he hadn't heard from her. "Your people—I don't remember anyone."

"That's because you were not yourself, Sam. Not only were you near death, you were also in another form."

"What do you mean?"

"You don't know?"

Sam stared at him. "Know what?"

"You were in hawk form. We only found you because you fell out of the tree where you were perched. By that time you were unconscious."

"Bird...? What are you talking about?"

Apollo made a face. "You seem to have blocked out half your life."

Sam tried to make sense of what he was saying, but found that he was drifting off to sleep again. He could not keep his eyes open no matter how hard he tried.

"HE DOESN'T REMEMBER," SAM HEARD SOMEONE SAY. HE STIRRED and woke fully, his eyes opening on Apollo and his mother staring at him.

"What don't I remember?"

Apollo let out a sigh and turned to Constance who said, "Nothing, darling. We are so glad you're here and feeling better."

Sam pushed himself up to sitting, looking around at the earthen walls and intricately woven tapestries in deep blues and reds hanging on them. There was a smell of dirt and mustiness that tickled his throat.

"As you know this is the dark side of the planet and we are in the tunnels that weave through the mountain above us. There has been an explosion and we have not been back to check the damage in Seris. You were there?"

"I was, but no one was there aside from several people who had frozen to death."

Apollo frowned. "The ones who live outside," he muttered. "I tried to persuade them to come along, but they refused—we have not had this much snow in eons."

Sam swung his feet to the floor, feeling awkward lying in bed. "I should get up—where are my clothes?"

"You didn't have any on when we found you," Apollo answered.

Sam frowned, trying to remember taking his clothes off. "Why would I be naked in a snow storm?"

"I have clothes you can wear," Apollo said, ignoring his question. He pointed to a pile of garments on a chair by the opening that led into the other room. "We will leave so that you can get dressed." He took Constance by the hand and they left the room.

Sam felt fuzzy-headed and confused. Everything about this trip seemed off. He stood shakily, placing one hand on the wall to steady himself before making his way slowly toward the chair. He had not intended to come upon his father this way, nor had he known that Annie was in contact with Apollo. Why hadn't she contacted him?

The clothes fit him well, and were warm and soft, made of wool. Once he was dressed he left the room, heading toward the voices in the distance. In another room that appeared to be the kitchen, he found his mother sitting in a chair breast-feeding a child. The baby was sandy-haired and chubby—maybe close to a year old. His sister, as he remembered from what Annie had told him. Gaia was not much older. "What's her name?"

"Theia."

Sam recognized the name from Greek mythology. Theia was the goddess of divine light. Yes, Ares had mentioned her. "Makes sense considering the constant light on Atenua. Wasn't she the child of Gaia and Uranus?"

Apollo chuckled. "I would rather think of her as a goddess of sight and vision. She gave sight to mankind and..."

Before Apollo could go on, both men's attention were taken to Constance as she rose abruptly from the couch, the rustle of her heavy skirts loud in the closed in room. "How are you feeling?" she asked Sam as she buttoned her sweater and put the sleeping baby in a handwoven basket. A moment later she went to the kitchen and poured tea from the earthenware pot. She handed Sam a cup of tea and a plate of bread and cheese.

Sam sat at the table where she pointed. "I...I'm a bit shaky, but better."

"We did not know you were on your way. If we had we would have told you to wait until the planet is again closer to the sun," she said, looking him over. She placed her hand on his head and bent to kiss his cheek."I have not seen you since that fateful day when I gave birth...to you..." She widened her eyes and gave a little laugh.

Sam smiled, remembering his shock when she disappeared from the Inn. "I was worried about you—you disappeared into thin air."

Constance glanced at Apollo. "Yes. My dearest Apollo brought me here and healed me. Your birth was not as easy as the more recent one," she murmured.

"Considering that I found you bleeding in a ditch, I would say not," Sam agreed. "I had no idea what happened to you."

"How could you, my darling boy? You had no knowledge of Apollo. I did try to tell you but you were too worried about me to hear what I said."

"Your mother was in grave danger when she called out to me," Apollo added, "the first time she'd done so since the time I spent with her on Earth. Your birth was a surprise to both of us."

Sam glanced from one to the other, the love they shared palpable. "I'm glad of it—since I'm the result. It's good to be alive," he muttered, feeling as though his mind wasn't working as it should.

Apollo smiled. "This time of year on Atenua can be deadly. I wish I had known your intent. I'm just glad you have survived so far."

Sam looked at Apollo sitting across from him. He'd nearly forgotten his reasons for coming. "I wasn't thinking straight. Annie was not in favor—she told me about the orbit, but I chose to ignore her. But she never mentioned weather like this."

Apollo looked down, his fingers combing though his long hair. "We make this pilgrimage nearly every year, but this one was more difficult with a new baby in tow."

Sam glanced at the doorway leading into the rest of the apartment. "Where is my...my..."

"Your other self? He'll be along shortly." Apollo fixed him with his gaze. "Why *did* you come now?"

Sam ran nervous fingers through his tangled hair, aware of how similar his gesture was to that of his father's. "I...I've been restless and needing to meet you, for one thing. I've also wondered about my magic and what has happened to me."

Apollo's eyebrows rose as he glanced at Constance. "It seems you have forgotten who you are."

CHAPTER 13

EDGE

"Explain, Jack—I don't time for this."

Jack laughed. "Always the impatient one."

"I am not impatient. I'm only..."

"I know," he said, taking hold of her elbow, "you just want to be in control," he muttered, guiding her toward the cluster of brick buildings in the distance.

"I am here under duress. I would appreciate some understanding on your part."

"I understand—believe me. Aside from becoming a mother and gaining magic, you haven't changed since we were together."

She turned to look at him. "Are those two things connected?"

"I don't think so—but you need to ask your sister." He hurried her across the road filled with newly imagined cars and the horses and buggies they would soon replace. There was a certain amount of chaos without stop signs or lights or lanes, as the traffic moved willy nilly in all directions avoiding each other by inches. When she stepped in manure and let out a cry, he chuckled. "Watch where you put your feet."

"Thanks for the warning. You're saying that Elizabeth and I are twins."

He raised his eyebrows. "Thought you probably realized that by now. How could you have missed it when you two met? You're identical."

Annie stopped in the middle of the street. "I thought it was a fluke of the universe. Doesn't everyone have a doppelgänger?"

Watch out!" he yelled, pulling the two of them to safety as another horse-drawn cart rolled by.

Annie caught her breath, her gaze roaming the lively street where gas lamps were currently being lit. It was dusk and the gas light was soft, not garish. It felt oddly familiar—the men on ladders turning the valve and lighting them with tapers. Before she could think about it further Jack tugged her toward an inset door in a line of brick townhouses.

"Elizabeth's house," he told her, lifting the knocker in the shape of a lion's head.

Annie glanced at the small garden filled with rose bushes. Some were still in bloom and others had turned a beautiful ochre color. "Does she know I'm coming?"

Jack's gaze slid away. "Not exactly."

When the door opened, her doppelgänger stared at her out of wide eyes before turning to Jack. Her eyes narrowed. "How dare you come here," she hissed.

"My sweet Elizabeth. I thought you would be happy to see me. Look who I've brought along."

Elizabeth frowned. "Happy to see you after what you did? I will never forgive you."

Annie's glance went from one to the other. Jack was up to one of his tricks.

Elizabeth turned to Annie. "Last time we saw each other things were not very cordial. Would you like to come in?"

Annie nodded, glancing at Jack.

"Shall I go away and let you two ladies catch up?" Jack asked.

"That would be my choice," Elizabeth said. She grabbed Annie's hand to pull her inside before slamming the door in

68

Jack's face. "That man is insufferable," she muttered, leading the way into a parlor that faced the street. Lace curtains moved in the light breeze from the open window, the sweet aroma of late fall roses coming with it.

"What happened between you? Last I heard you were…"

"Do you not remember what he did, Annie? He asked me to marry him and then forsook me for that horrible woman who ran the seances."

"Izzy," Annie murmured.

"Yes, Izzy." She glanced at Annie."Why did he bring you here?"

"He told me that you and I are twins and that our parents sent me into the future when I was a baby."

Elizabeth turned pale, her eyes widening even further. "He *told* you? He was forbidden to speak of it. I should never have opened up to that man."

"Is it true?"

Elizabeth looked away. "Make yourself comfortable while I prepare tea."

"But are we sisters?" Annie called out as Elizabeth turned to walk out of the room.

Elizabeth stopped. "Yes, we are sisters," she answered.

Annie sat heavily on the pink damask couch. Her memories of Elizabeth in the future were mixed up with the new romance she was experiencing with Sam. They'd shared their first kiss while Elizabeth was there. When Jack and Elizabeth disappeared, no one was quite sure where they'd gone. It was Cecily who discovered a newspaper article in an old history book that detailed the scandal that occurred in the past because of Jack. Elizabeth was well-known, part of the Golden Dawn Hermetic Society, and their upcoming marriage, or lack thereof, had made the papers. What in the world was he up to now?

~

Hours went by—hours in which Annie learned about her parentage. Her mother and father were both witches trying to disguise their identity. And when her mother gave birth to twins, they felt they had to do something to prevent the fallout.

"Twins born to a witch is an ill omen," Elizabeth told her, "At least to the superstitious ones that would have come after our family."

"Are they alive?"

"Sadly no. They would have loved seeing you as an adult. According to correspondence I have under lock and key, they were heartbroken. And as twins are so close in so many ways, I grew up feeling like part of me was missing. I didn't find out about you until after my trip to the future. That trip was a mistake, by the way. I have no idea how I got there." She glanced away for a second, her hand going to a locket around her neck.

"I had some strange experiences as a child too—I actually made up a twin sister who I talked to," Annie said.

"Was her name Elizabeth?"

Annie smiled and took a sip of her tea. "No," she murmured, sliding her cup carefully onto the saucer. "I called her Emeline—Emmy for short."

"That was our mother's name," Elizabeth said.

Annie blinked and stared. "How odd."

"Not so, Annie. You were aware before they sent you off. You must have heard the name." Elizabeth went to a desk and opened a drawer, pulling out several daguerreotypes. She handed one to Annie.

Annie gazed at the stern features of a handsome man wearing a frock coat standing behind a dark-haired woman wearing a severe black dress that came up to her neck. Her eyes looked like Annie's, but the expression in them was worried, fearful even. In her lap were two identical babies dressed in lacy caps over light curls and wearing long frilly dresses.

"You haven't said much about the magical part of us. Apollo, Sam's father, seemed to think my parents must have been powerful. What magic did they use, or did they die before you got a chance to know?"

"They gambled and won, Annie. They sent the magical one away and kept the dull one, me. As far as their magic—they kept it hidden. This incarnation is not one in which they could exhibit it. They were part of high society here and worried about their reputations. You are married now, or are you with Jack?"

"Not married and definitely not with Jack. I'm with Sam, the man you met in the future. We have a baby. He's on another planet and in trouble—or at least it felt that way before I left 2325."

"You have premonitions?"

"Yes...I can see things happening in other places."

"Jack took advantage of you in your vulnerable state."

"I suppose he did. I've known him a long time—I met him when I was sixteen. I had no idea he was a wizard until today, although I have to say I wondered."

Elizabeth picked up her cup and sipped before she lifted her eyes to Annie's. "When I met you in the future I was not aware that we were sisters. If I had been, I would have told you. It did not occur to me until months after that experience. And of course I confided in Jack. He knew right away, Annie. He told me that you had special abilities. But he promised not to say anything."

"It was so odd seeing myself reflected in you. And Sam nearly lost his mind."

Elizabeth laughed. "I do remember his face reddening a few times, especially after you removed my arsenic dress."

Annie thought of the bright green dress Elizabeth had been wearing when she arrived—the dye was very popular back then before they discovered how poisonous it was. It was also used in wallpaper.

"My parents went to their graves hoping that magic would somehow appear within me, but it never happened," Elizabeth continued, looking down at the floor. "They hoped that magic would be more accepted in the future. The hangings have stopped, but the stigma has not."

"Jack led me to believe that you have it too. He said it appears at this age we are now. Between 25 and 28." Annie let out a scoff. "He's probably plotting how he can use the two of us in some nefarious deed."

Elizabeth raised her brows, "If he's correct, I still have time," she muttered. "But you...tell me what you can do?"

"I can read minds—not always, but often. I can conjure things, like fire, just by visualizing. The library is now mine to command, which irritates Sam no end."

Elizabeth's eyes widened. "Sam has lost his magic? As I remember he was...not sure of the word...he had an aura of power about him. Rather intimidating, as I remember. Jack was so jealous. He raved about it whenever he had my ear."

Annie smiled. "I won't bore you with the details of what went on during that time—I will say that Jack was quite the ass, but honestly, Sam was too. We thought for a long time that Jack and Sam were half-brothers."

Elizabeth glanced out the lacy curtains at the dark sky before rising to close the window. "Will you stay the night? I have an extra room."

When Annie pictured Gaia she was laughing and playing with Wolf. As far as Sam, she had a strong sense that he was now with Apollo. "I would love to."

CHAPTER 14

1893 LONDON

Dawn light filtered in through the lace curtains, the brightness landing on Annie's eyelids where she lay cozy under a down quilt. She'd been dreaming about a beautiful hawk, its wide wings spread as it lifted into a snowy sky. She yawned and sat up, remembering where she was.

A gray silk dress had been placed at the end of her bed, one more in keeping with the 1800's than her jeans and heavy sweater. A full skirt was gathered at the waist with a tight bodice and a lacy square neckline. Next to it was a corset. Annie sighed and rose from bed and dressed, her body rebelling against the corset as she fastened it as best she could. The dress, of course, fit her perfectly—it belonged to her twin. She tried to take in a deep breath and was stopped by the article of clothing tight around her rib cage. "Crap," she muttered. Without it this dress would not fit her.

She felt claustrophobic as she left the room, afraid she might suddenly have a fit and rip everything off her body. Either that or faint. As she remembered from her reading, fainting happened often among the women of this time. She tried not to think about it as she headed toward the kitchen and the dining room where Elizabeth was already drinking tea and munching on a bun.

Elizabeth looked up and smiled. "Good morning! How did you sleep?"

Annie thought for a moment. "I slept well, although I had many dreams." She took the cup Elizabeth held out and sat at the table covered with a lace tablecloth, trying to breathe shallowly. The wall sconces were still lit, the flickering light sending shadows up the flowered wallpaper. "Are you still connected with the Golden Dawn?"

"Oh yes—it is the only activity that keeps me sane these days. I keep hoping that I can learn magic, even if I do not have it naturally. We've been learning about the Sirius system which is associated with the goddess Isis. When the star rises it coincides with the flooding of the Nile. The alchemy of all of this is complicated, but simply put, the ancient Egyptians had a system of decans or decades, and each one was ruled by a different group of stars. Alchemy is known as an Egyptian science." Elizabeth let out a sigh. "It is beyond my abilities, I'm afraid. Too complicated for my feeble mind to comprehend. I must admit I have not advanced since we have been studying all of this."

"That is interesting in that Sam is now in the Sirius system on a planet called Atenua. That's quite the coincidence, don't you think?"

Elizabeth's eyes widened. "My goodness. Yes, I would say so. Perhaps we will need to take at trip to the Golden Dawn today. I can ask about all of this—perhaps someone might have answers to questions you might have."

"I would like that." Annie glanced at her sister, noting her hair done up in a chignon of sorts. Elizabeth did not employ either the meek style of dress of this time period or the elaborate and unbecoming hairstyles. Her clothing spoke of a woman who knew her own mind. "Are you wearing a corset?" she asked, glancing at Elizabeth's loose silk dress in an asian motif so unlike the one she wore.

Elizabeth laughed. "No. It is one of the best aspects of being involved with the Golden Dawn."

Annie glanced down at her tight dress. "Why do *I* have to?"

"It was all I had to lend, Annie. My other two comfortable dresses need to be cleaned. I am sorry."

"I can barely breathe," she muttered. Annie glanced out the window. The sun had disappeared behind clouds and it had begun to rain, the patter of it against the wavy glass reminding her of home and her baby. "It's raining," she said, glancing at her sister.

Elizabeth shrugged. "The weather is changeable this time of year." She glanced at where Annie tugged at the bodice of the dress. "I have a seamstress I employ who can alter it if you like."

Annie sighed. "I won't be here long enough for that. But I thought before I leave that I could try and help you. Your magic might lie dormant, especially if you don't know what you're looking for. Perhaps we can coax it out."

"That can be included in our trip. I have not spoken to anyone there about my heritage. But now that you are here, perhaps you would be willing to bring it up?" She glanced at Annie with a critical look. "If we are to go out in public we must do something with your hair."

A few moments later Annie stood in front of the large mirror in Elizabeth's bedroom. She allowed herself to be turned and twisted, her hair brushed and braided and put into a strange configuration consisting of a chignon high up on her head and loops of hair hanging around her face.

"You have soft hair and I do not have the proper tools to do this properly," Elizabeth muttered, her mouth full of hairpins.

When Annie looked into the mirror she was shocked. "I don't know how you did this, but what a lot of work for the few short hours I'll be here!"

Her sister smiled. "If I did not, people would gossip. I have a reputation to keep up."

Annie laughed, flipping her head and making the curls fly. "And yet look at you! Totally free in dress and manner."

"The women know who I am. I only get by because of my affiliation with the Golden Dawn."

"They must be jealous."

Elizabeth shook her head. "Not at all," she murmured. "They tolerate me and do not aspire to be involved. Now, about my magic…"

They donned their wraps and umbrellas and left the house a moment later, heading toward the river in the distance. Light fog played across the surface of the water, wispy and light as the rain drifted through it. The sun was an afterthought behind the heavy clouds.

Once at the wrought iron railing along the bank, Annie turned to her sister. "I want you to think of something you would like to happen. It could be as a simple as a pigeon coming down next to you, or a fish jumping from the river. You must concentrate on it and let every other thought go."

Elizabeth frowned, looking down. In the next second she had an expression of concentration on her face, her lips pressed together. Several moments later she let out a sigh. "Nothing," she muttered dejectedly.

Annie sighed and grabbed her sister's hand. "Let's go to the Golden Dawn—perhaps they will have answers for you."

They walked together to the ornate building that housed the Hermetic Order.

As soon as they entered, they were met by two men and a woman, who frowned at Annie. "Elizabeth? Why are there two of you?"

Elizabeth laughed. "This is my sister, Annie, from the future. She has traveled back in time to meet me."

"And I have a few questions," Annie added, smiling.

The two men raised an eyebrow, but no-one seemed surprised by the time travel revelation. "I am Curtis Monroe," one of them said, holding out his hand.

"Annie Morgan at your service," Annie said gripping his hand.

By this time the other man had walked away—not interested in what was going on, but the woman still stood there, eyeing them both with a certain amount of suspicion. "If we are to speak I suggest we do so privately," she said, glancing at Curtis.

Curtis nodded and gestured for them to follow him.

As they walked down the hall the woman said, "I'm Eva Haight, by the way. Sorry for being so impolite."

Curtis led them into a small room containing a beautiful roll-top desk and several cushioned chairs covered in a paisley fabric. A Tiffany lamp adorned the desk and he switched it on. Electricity was not in full use yet, but the more wealthy establishments had it. "Please make yourselves comfortable. We have a few minutes until the next lecture begins. Elizabeth? Will you attend today?"

Elizabeth shook her head. "I plan to spend as much time with my sister as possible," she murmured, her cheeks reddening slightly.

"I am only here for a short while," Annie explained, gazing at her sister. She turned to Curtis, pointing to the lamp. "That's a Tiffany lamp, is it not?"

His eyebrows shot up. "How could you know that? He is a friend of mine and was kind enough to make this lamp for our offices. Will he become famous?"

Annie smiled. "Yes, very famous. You are a lucky man."

He smiled and placed his hands in his lap. "Now, what can I do for you?"

Annie gazed at Elizabeth who began haltingly. "My sister has some special abilities that I do not. I have wondered and hoped, since my parents were..." she glanced at Annie. "They were witches, I suppose you would say."

"We do not refer to those who have alchemy as witches, Elizabeth. We know who your parents were. It is why you are here."

"You...I mean..." Elizabeth's voice drifted off, her hand moving nervously to the neck of her dress. "You are aware of..."

"We are aware that you have potential, my dear."

"But I have not shown any indication of...magic."

Curtis laughed. "Or the ability to learn our complicated systems."

Elizabeth blushed furiously, her gaze going to Annie, a pleading expression on her face.

"My sister is wondering if there might be a test of some sort, or perhaps a way to bring out her...abilities."

Curtis turned his pale eyes on her. "And what is it that you are capable of, Miss Morgan?"

"Please call me Annie," she murmured. "I have an affinity with fire," she continued, demonstrating with her fingers.

His eyes widened as he watched her. "We are more interested in the esoteric, Miss Morgan. This sort of parlor trick is not what we are after at all. It serves no purpose in our world."

Elizabeth rose to her feet. "I am sorry that you feel this way," she said haughtily. "Come, Annie. We have more important things to do with our time."

Annie glanced from Curtis to Eva, who had not spoken a word. Eva gave a slight nod as Annie and Elizabeth exited the room. Once they were in the reception room Eva joined them.

"Curtis is one of our most conservative members," she whispered. She put her hand on Elizabeth's shoulder and steered them out the door and into the sunshine that had just appeared from behind clouds. "Curtis believes in the step by step approach. He does not have the luxury to do otherwise. You, on the other hand," she said, turning to Annie, "have real magic. It is what we all aspire to. I do not have the time to speak with you at length, but I would suggest that if you have this ability, your twin sister Elizabeth does as well." She glanced over her shoulder. "It is time for the lecture to begin." She gazed at Elizabeth. "Seek me out later. I may have an idea or two for you." She smiled and left them there as she hurried back inside.

Annie and Elizabeth stared at one another. "That's good news," Annie said into the silence.

Elizabeth nodded, but she didn't seem convinced. "Curtis is insufferable," she muttered. "I am so sorry you had to hear his diatribe."

Annie smiled. "At least he's polite." Annie glanced at the man hurrying toward them. "There's Jack."

"Time to go, Annie," he said, gasping as he caught his breath.

"What ? Why?"

"Cecily is worrying. I just saw it."

"You did not!" Elizabeth said, frowning at him. "Why are you bothering us again?"

Annie glanced at both of them, her heart skipping a beat. She believed him."I have to go, Elizabeth. Talk with Eva and keep practicing."

"When will I see you again?"

Annie shook her head. "I will make sure it happens soon. You need to meet your niece." She embraced her sister before turning to Jack who was waiting. "Goodbye, Elizabeth. I am sure the next time we meet you will have uncovered the mystery of who you are."

Elizabeth tried to smile, but her eyes filled with tears. "I have enjoyed this very much."

Annie felt the heaviness behind her eyes. She did not want to cry. "I have too. I wish I could stay longer."

Jack grabbed her hand. "Come on, Annie..."

Annie waved as he dragged her away. As soon as Elizabeth was out of sight she began to cry.

"Where's the library?" Jack asked.

Annie wiped her eyes with the sleeve of her cloak, realizing she was still wearing her 1800's attire. "I thought you were taking us there."

"Is there one here?"

Annie stopped and pulled her hand out of his. "Why did you suddenly appear? I was enjoying getting to know my sister."

"I wasn't kidding about Gaia and Cecily. I did see them. There are other ways back and forth."

Annie frowned. "Didn't you tell me you'd lost your ability to do it?"

"Yes, but even without the actual building you are able conjure a door. You've done it before. Your sister can move through time without a door. Did you know that?"

"What? How do you know?"

"How do you think she arrived in 2323, Annie?"

Annie stared into space. "She doesn't think she has magic," she muttered to herself. She glanced at him. "I should go back and tell her, but I have to get home." She headed into an alley between two buildings, concentrating on where she wanted to go. It was only a moment before a door hung in the air in front of her. She let out a sigh of relief.

Jack was saying something, but Annie wasn't listening as she pulled the handle down. "Are you coming?" she asked, glancing at him. She stepped inside, but before Jack could follow, the door closed behind her. "Crap," she murmured, frowning. She was sure he intended to come along.

"Welcome," a voice said, making her jump. When Annie looked around the dim interior she saw a faint image of a dark-haired man. Usually she walked straight through, but now it seemed there was an internal room and another door to open.

"Who are you?"

"I am the library in human form. I thought it was time."

"Time? Time to make yourself known?"

He nodded and raised his eyebrows. "Perhaps Sam would not enjoy my presence, but I had a feeling that you would appreciate this version."

"I do, but I'm in a hurry to get back. Will you open the door for me or do I open it?"

He grasped the handle, his dark eyes meeting hers. "I am fully cognizant of what is waiting for you on the other side." The door swung open.

Annie didn't have time to think about this new iteration of the library or his veiled warning as she stepped out—she was too concerned with Cecily and Gaia. Cecily was not a person who got ruffled easily, so if her premonitions were correct, something bad had happened.

She didn't hear the door close behind her, or the slight hum as it disappeared.

CHAPTER 15

EDGE 2325

Annie arrived in the stacks and rushed into the front of the library. No one was there.

"Cecily?" she called out.

A second later Cecily ran through the open front door looking panic-stricken. "I can't find her—she's gone."

"Gaia is gone? How? Where?"

"She was here in the morning and playing with her blocks like she usually does. I was working at my desk. It was around fifteen minutes later that I looked over and she wasn't there. A bunny was hopping around the room—have no idea where that came from. I haven't seen her since and there is no way she could have left the library. I would have noticed."

"Where's Wolf?"

"Last I saw him he was playing with the rabbit."

"Playing? A rabbit is prey to him. Where are they?"

"I saw him go upstairs a while ago."

Running to the stairs she took them two at a time. When she reached the bedroom Gaia was sleeping on the bed and Wolf was lying next to her. "She's here!" Annie yelled.

Cecily arrived a moment later out of breath. "What the hell?

How did she get up here? I've been watching those stairs like a hawk to make sure she doesn't try to climb them."

Glancing at the sleeping baby and back to Cecily, she asked, "Where's the rabbit?"

Cecily shook her head, her eyes going wide. "Did Wolf eat it?"

"If he did, he did a good job of cleaning up the blood." She swept her hand around the pristine room.

Cecily frowned, glancing at the dog and then the baby. "What is going on?"

"I have an idea, but it's so far-fetched I hesitate to say it out loud."

Annie closed the bedroom door and led the way downstairs, leaving the sleeping baby and Wolf upstairs.

"Well?" Cecily asked when they reached the living room.

Annie stared out the window, her thoughts all over the place. She finally turned to Cecily. "I think Gaia's a shape-shifter."

Cecily let out a laugh. "Come on—is Sam a shifter? You certainly aren't. Where would it come from?"

"Sam...he doesn't remember large swaths of his life. Maybe this is why."

Cecily didn't speak for a moment, her eyes narrowing. "I've known Sam for too many years to count." She stared unseeing at the wall. "This is weird, but he's disappeared on me several times over the years. Long time ago—before he met you, that is."

"Disappeared—in what way?"

"Like he was there one night and in the morning, gone."

"Were you lovers?"

Cecily grimaced. "Nothing like that. We shared a house is all."

"And did you see another animal in his place?"

"A bird got in once, flew around the room until I shooed it out."

"Got in...maybe it was Sam." Annie and Cecily moved as one

and sat heavily on the couch. "If he is, he doesn't know it," Annie murmured. "He has major lapses in his memory."

Cecily nodded. "If he knew he'd be bragging about it and doing it all the time."

Annie had to laugh—this was so Sam. "I'm sure of it," she agreed, giggling. "And lording it over me."

Cecily laughed and the two of them were giddy for a few minutes until the baby let out a wail. Annie rose and hurried up the steps to get her.

Once she returned with Gaia, Cecily was back at her desk, her head in a book.

"What are you doing?"

"Trying to make sense of this."

Annie looked over her shoulder at the pages that detailed shape-shifting. "My gods," she muttered, staring at the grotesque pictures. Glancing at the baby in her arms she felt a shiver. "Hope it's only a rabbit," she muttered.

"And maybe a bird," Cecily added.

THEY WERE BOTH AT THEIR DESKS WHEN ANNIE TOLD CECILY WHERE she'd been—that instead of going to find Sam, she'd been whisked away to the late 1800's. And that Jack was involved.

"What about Sam?" she asked, after Annie filled her in about her twin and everything else that had happened.

"I think he's ok. I sent a message to Apollo and...I don't know...it just feels that they found each other."

"Maybe they're both birds," Cecily muttered, "Flying around Atenua."

Annie let out a laugh. "Maybe. All I know is I don't feel anxious about him anymore."

"So you'll stay here until he gets back?" Cecily asked hopefully. "I think several of my hairs turned gray while you were gone."

"I'll try, Cecily. I have enough work to keep me busy...but..."

"But what?"

"I keep thinking about my sister. She doesn't know she has magic."

"Maybe Jack will fill her in. Where is he, by the way?"

"He stayed there. But Elizabeth hates him after he jilted her."

"He can't get back without a door, right?"

Annie stared out the window, thinking. "Honestly, I'm not sure what he can do. He told me he's a wizard, whatever that means. Does that book have anything in it about wizards?"

"Isn't that just male for witches?" Cecily leaned back in her chair. "You know Annie, you having your mind on something besides Sam seems healthy to me. He takes up too much of your head space."

"Did I tell you that the library came to me in human form?"

Cecily straightened. "What?"

Annie nodded. "When I conjured a door there was a man inside—like a weird time-traveling doorman." Annie stared into space. "He was handsome," she muttered, remembering.

Cecily laughed. "Competition for Sam."

Annie glanced at her. "He isn't real—he's a manifestation."

"Really?"

Annie was quiet after that, thinking. Was this man, who didn't have a name, real or just a shadow who lived inside the space between here and where she went? She was ready to go through a door just to see him again. Would he be corporeal this time?

When Annie looked up, Cecily was looking at her with her head cocked to one side. "Could work as a way to keep Sam around," she said teasingly.

"I would never try and make him jealous."

Cecily shrugged one shoulder and bent her head back to the book on shape-shifting. "There's a section on wizards. It says shape-shifting, elemental manipulation and spells."

"Elemental manipulation means he might have control of air,

fire, water and earth—he could be way more powerful than me or Sam." She thought back to her time with him and how he aways managed to not get caught stealing. And his mother—Serena was a powerful witch.

ANNIE TRIED TO SORT THROUGH WHAT WAS ON HER DESK, BUT HER thoughts were on Jack and her sister and the strange man she'd found behind the door. It felt to her as though another world had opened up, one in which she had a twin and another man in her life, as well as a shape-shifting daughter. Not to mention an entirely new idea about who Jack really was. She was excited in a way she hadn't been for a long time, but also nervous. How long was Sam planning to be gone? Was he a shapeshifter too? Or would she have to test the door and go and find him?

She rose from her desk and went to play with Gaia. The baby was on the floor in her usual spot and looked up at her innocently. "Will you change into a rabbit?" Annie whispered. But the baby only stared down at her blocks before picking one up and trying to stuff it into her mouth.

CHAPTER 16

ATENUA

S am was getting to know his baby sister. It made him miss Gaia all the more. Theia burbled and laughed when he lifted her into the air, just as Gaia did.

Constance was friendly and seemed to enjoy having him around, but Apollo remained remote. The days were passing by and he still hadn't found out how to get his magic back. Aside from intimating that there was something Sam needed to remember, Apollo had been evasive and standoffish.

Sam had not been outside since he was brought here over a week before. He was just returning to feeling more himself, the meals Constance and her cook prepared giving him his strength back. He was anxious to leave the claustrophobic tunnels. His few days had turned into weeks and the way things were going it seemed it might be a lot longer; he could not leave here until he connected with Apollo.

He woke as he always did, in darkness, his body going rigid as he realized that this was another day that he would not see the sky. He left his cell-like room and headed toward the area lit up with candles. At least there was light and life, as young Sam yelled and ran around, knocking things off tables and letting out whoops of laughter. Theia was still too young to be much of a problem. Younger than Gaia, she was walking, but not yet running as he was sure Gaia would be doing by the time he returned home. A wave of sadness broke over him as he watched her. He was missing out on important milestones.

"Today you will meet and learn about those who saved you," Apollo told him as he handed him a cup of tea. "And soon we will go back to Seris and find out how much damage was done."

No good morning or anything to loosen the ongoing tension between them, Sam thought to himself. "Do we know for sure there was damage?" Sam asked. "I saw it hit but I'm pretty sure it wasn't in the middle of the city."

Apollo shook his head, his dark blue eyes on Constance who was now sitting on the couch spooning pabulum into the baby's mouth. "I am hoping it is not as bad as I imagine."

"Maybe your nemesis was wiped out," Sam said, thinking about the dreaded minister who Apollo had told him about.

Apollo chuckled. "Wouldn't that be wonderful. But no, he has tunnels to protect him."

"Here?"

Apollo shook his head. "His are in Seris, under the tower where he lives."

"Why don't *you* have tunnels in Seris?"

Apollo glanced at him and rubbed a hand over his face. "I have many friends here, those who I want to support. This trip to the dark side is a pilgrimage we try to make every year."

Sam felt chastised, as though his question was impertinent. He realized that he often felt this way around his father. Was it his sensitivity, or was Apollo perpetually annoyed with him?

After a breakfast of cooked grains, he followed Apollo out of their apartment and into the tunnels that led off in all directions. After a long time of walking in darkness Sam asked, "Where are we going?"

"To the community room. It is the day they conduct their business. Best time to meet everyone."

Again, Sam wondered why Apollo was so short with him.

How was he supposed to know what went on? "I get the feeling that you either don't like me, or I irritate you," he mumbled.

Apollo held the lantern out, peering at him in the darkness. "Perhaps I have formed an unfair opinion, Sam. Annie shared a lot of what went on in the 1300's. I am sorry if I do not have an open mind."

"Annie and I are fine now. We got through all of that. I am not that person."

"And you have come here, why? I have a strong sense that you want something from me."

Sam was taken aback by his frankness. "I wanted to meet you," he began, "to connect."

Apollo's eyes glittered in the low light. "There is no more to it? You do not expect me to return your magic to you?"

Sam's chest tightened. "I did—I do. Or at least I hoped you could help me find it again. I thought you would be happy to meet me."

Apollo turned and headed off, his voice drifting in the darkness. "I would be happy if you were open to my wisdom. But it seems that you have come here with the express purpose of getting what you want."

Sam felt a sudden anger, words spilling out before he could stop them. "That isn't true! I nearly died, and I..."

Apollo stopped again and held the lantern up. "And you expect sympathy? I am not sympathetic to those who do not attempt to know themselves. I have mentioned that you have blocked out your memories. You have not questioned me about this. Shall I give you what you want without the wisdom necessary to understand yourself? You are arrogant, Sam."

Sam didn't answer as he followed the older man down one tunnel and up another. It felt like hours before he could see a line of light ahead. What he wanted to do was leave this place and never return. As they neared the door he angrily wiped tears from his eyes.

When Apollo swung the door open, the scene inside was

such a shock that Sam backed away. Apollo motioned him inside with a look that brooked no refusal. Sam walked through the door, eyeing the strange creatures.

"So, this is your son grown up," the buffalo-headed creature bellowed from his place on the dais.

Apollo glanced at Sam. "A version of him."

What in hell did Apollo mean by that? "I'm Sam," he muttered, holding out his hand.

The buffalo creature did not shake his hand as he looked toward the snakes and the creatures that resembled alligators. "Those who helped rescue this fool, please step forward."

Sam bristled. "Ares left me too far from the tunnels. I was freezing out there."

Apollo gazed at the buffalo creature, obviously addressing him. "He does not realize," Apollo whispered.

Realize what? Sam wondered. *That I'm an idiot?*

A snake came forward, eyes trained on Sam. She moved her head from side to side, but Sam didn't hear any words.

"She is greeting you," Apollo said. "She is Manasa, the wisest of the beings on this planet. We hold her in the highest esteem."

Sam bowed, unable to think what else to do. "Thank you," he said, wondering if his hearing had gone as well as any sense of himself. He felt naked here, without defenses. He'd seen this creature once before, felt her touching his body, but they had not been formally introduced. His face heated, remembering.

He stood quietly while Apollo conversed in a foreign language, gesturing to Sam as he made some point or other. The buffalo- headed creature laughed at one point, staring at Sam like he was an object of foolishness.

As the conversation continued, Sam's anger and frustration rose to the boiling point. He finally couldn't stand it a second more and rushed from the room, hurtling down a corridor in the dark. And to add insult to injury, he was crying.

It was a minute or so later that a feeling of otherness came over him. His breathing changed and his eyesight improved. He could see in the dark. He felt the presence of small creatures behind the walls of mud. His feet no longer touched the ground and he heard a sound like air rushing by. When he reached the end of the tunnel and moved outside, he soared upward, feeling free of something he couldn't name.

A sound came out of his mouth, rough and discordant. His thinking mind was gone.

CHAPTER 17

1893 LONDON

"Please, Elizabeth. Annie made me promise to give you this message."

Elizabeth stood in her doorway, staring at the man she hated the most in the world. She folded her arms over her chest. "What is it?"

"You have magic," Jack said.

She shook her head. "I do not. We tested it."

"You do—you can move through time."

"I cannot move through time."

"Don't you remember arriving at the library in the year 2323?"

Her eyes narrowed. "I wish I had never met you."

Jack tried to force his way in, but Elizabeth shoved the door against his foot. "Listen to me," Jack continued. "You have the ability to move through time without any device such as the library. Even your sister can't do that."

"And now you want me to prove it to help you go to the future?"

Jack stared into her familiar and perfect face. He'd been with both twins, made love to both of them at different times in his life. He wouldn't mind bedding her right now, but he doubted there was any chance of that. "Wouldn't you like to see your sister again, meet your niece? We could leave right now."

"Today is a Golden Dawn work day."

"So what? there will be more of those." He inched closer. "I am not the same man that went off with Izzy, you know. I've mended my ways. We could get back together."

Elizabeth made a face, her nose crinkling in the process. "If I decide to try this out, it will not be with the likes of you," she hissed, slamming the door.

Jack laughed. Being stuck here was not such an imposition, he thought, visualizing Izzy.

As Jack wandered the streets searching for Izzy's apartment, he realized that he might be staying for a while. He was in the beginnings of a money-making scheme. Lying was second nature, and with what he knew of the future he could come up with any number of business models. He focused on Izzy as he let go of his frustrations. He had an urge to take her to bed. Would she be amenable? They had not parted on very good terms.

He found her in her apartment getting ready to go out. When she opened the door the shock on her face was almost laughable. "Surprised to see me?"

"What are you doing here? You left me alone in that horrible town and never returned."

"I couldn't get back, Izzy," he lied. "You know how I feel about you."

"Do I?"

Jack moved closer and took her face in his hands. He kissed her gently and ran his thumb along her cheek. "I would never hurt you," he murmured, nuzzling her neck.

"Oh for goodness sakes, come in. You know I am unable to resist you."

Once he was inside he removed her hat and kissed her properly, and it wasn't long before they headed up the stairs together. When he undressed her he marveled at her creamy skin, the ample breasts he hadn't seen for a long time. He was so involved in what he was doing that he didn't notice the indistinct figure in the shadows watching.

Before Jack had completed what he came for, the man had slipped out the door.

~

JACK SPENT THE NIGHT WITH IZZY, HIS LUST SATIATED BY THE TIME they parted at the door.

Izzy pulled her silk robe around her body. "When will I see you again?"

Jack paused, wondering what to say. He had no idea what the day would bring. There was no shortage of ways to scam people out of their money in this timeline. It was how he survived. He felt his pocket where he'd stashed the bills Izzy had given him. His sad story had plucked at her heartstrings. "I will try to stop by tomorrow. Today I have business to attend to. Thanks for the loan."

Izzy made a face. "Loan? Have you ever paid me back?" She smiled and reached up to kiss him.

He kissed her back before heading out the door and into the rain. He had a plan in mind. The cobbles were shining and wet, images moving in the puddles as he walked away with his head down and his hands in his pockets.

~

JACK WAS UNDER AN OVERHANG BETWEEN TWO BRICK BUILDINGS smoking a cigarette when a door appeared. He stared at it in wonder. Had it picked up on his thoughts about the future? *Take cookies as cookies is passin'*, he thought to himself, an adage he'd heard more than once. He didn't think any further about it as he pulled the handle down and stepped inside.

When he stepped out again he was met with a blinding snowstorm, tiny crystals of ice hitting his cheeks and nose. Because of Izzy's insistence, he was in full 1890's regalia, crisp linen shirt and puff tie, vest and dark woolen frock coat, his charcoal trousers clean and pressed. His shoes were leather and not suited for snow. Where was he? There was no sign of a house or a street as he scanned the terrain. When he turned back, thinking this might not be quite the hospitable place he'd envisioned, the door was gone.

CHAPTER 18

When Sam woke up he was lying on his back under a tree. He was naked, his clothes scattered around him. He quickly dressed, wondering why in hell he'd removed his clothing again. What dreams were making him do this? The snow had stopped for the moment and there was slightly more light here—must be the area that lay between the two sides of the planet—the section of twilight.

A dark figure in the distance caught his eye, moving toward him. Was the man wearing a top hat? He had to be dreaming. The last thing he recalled was being pissed off at how Apollo was treating him. After that there was nothing...he must have blacked out. How did he end up here?

As the man drew closer Sam recognized who it was. He rose to his feet. Things could not get any weirder, he thought to himself, staring at Jack. "What in hell are you doing here!" he called out.

Jack tipped his hat in greeting as he made his way slowly toward him, fighting through the heavy drifts. "Came through a door," he said.

"A door? How are you in charge?"

Jack held out his hands and shrugged. "I'm not—the door

just appeared for no reason. I thought maybe Annie sent it. I walked through and here I am. Is she here?"

Sam pinched the inside of his arm, letting out a yelp. This wasn't a dream. "Annie isn't here. You didn't ask for a door?"

Jack grimaced and let out a sigh. "I've never had control of them. Elizabeth was my means into the past the first time, and now I hitch rides—either with Annie or others who have this ability."

"Others? Who else controls the doors?"

"There are other ways to travel through time, Sam."

Sam ignored this statement as he looked over Jack's archaic clothing. "You were obviously in the past somewhere—where were you?"

Jack leaned down to brush the snow off a boulder and sat. He crossed one leg over the other and rested back on his hands as though he was sitting in a garden in the height of summer. "I was in 1893. Annie was with me until I got left behind."

Sam's eyes narrowed in annoyance. This man had a way of pushing his buttons. "Annie? Why?"

Jack smiled. "To meet her twin sister, Elizabeth."

Sam stared at him. "What are you talking about, Jack? You've really gone around the bend this time. I left Annie in 2325 with our baby."

"And she and I went back in time."

"Why would she go with you?"

Jack raised an eyebrow. "I wanted to introduce her to her sister."

When Sam's anger rose, he tamped it down. "What sister?"

Jack smiled. "Elizabeth. Surely you remember her—you were certainly smitten, as I remember. After Annie conjured a door to go back to Edge, another door appeared. And here I am. Not sure what the library's playing at."

Sam gazed at Jack's bare neck under the collar and the tie. There was no leather thong to be seen. "Where's my amulet?"

"Gave it to Annie—it doesn't belong to me—I know that now."

Sam let out a heavy sigh and lowered to sit on an adjacent boulder. "So, Annie has my amulet as well as control over the doors," he muttered darkly, "and she went into the past with you."

Jack laughed. "Poor Sam—literally left out in the cold. Speaking of that, why are you here?" he asked, scanning the area of drifts and snow-laden conifers.

Sam shook his head. "Damned if I know. This trip isn't going as planned." He glanced at Jack. "But back to Annie—where is she now?"

"She's home in Edge, or at least that's where she planned to go."

Sam felt dizzy for a second, his thoughts tangling in confusion."And you...what the hell is going on? What is this about Annie's twin?"

"Yeah, well, I checked her DNA, took a few hairs while she was asleep. They are definitely twins. And Elizabeth admitted the rest."

Sam put his head in his hands, a headache brewing. "Why didn't she say?"

"Apparently their parents sent Annie into the future when she was a baby—afraid that she'd be taken and killed because of the superstition regarding witches and twins."

Sam could barely hear what Jack was saying—it was too far-fetched. He couldn't think about this right now—he had to get back to the tunnels. The quicker he got things settled with his father the sooner he could go home. "I came here..."

"To find your magic—Annie told me. Any luck?"

"No. My father thinks I'm an idiot. He hasn't said one kind word to me since..." Sam had a strange sense of something odd that he couldn't bring into focus.

"Since what?"

Sam sighed. "Since I arrived. I should probably just go home

—there's a library here and Apollo can help me—that is if Seris isn't destroyed," he muttered mostly to himself.

"I'm confused. What is Seris?" Jack looked around. "Where are we?"

Sam had the sudden feeling that every muscle in his body was about to cramp. He was exhausted in ways he'd never felt before. "This is Atenua, a planet in the Sirius system. Didn't Annie tell you?"

Jack jumped and nearly fell off the boulder. "Another planet? I thought Atenua was a town in the mountains somewhere. Why did the library bring me here?"

"How would I know? Does seem odd, I'll give you that."

"Sometimes I feel like we're brothers. Just not by blood," Jack muttered.

"Brothers? You are a liar and a cheat, Jack. Annie tried to convince me, but I couldn't see it. Now I do."

Jack chuckled and shrugged. "I get by in my own way—I never do anything truly bad. I haven't killed anyone."

"Except me," Sam muttered.

"That was an accident."

Sam rose and looked around, spotting the darker smudge in the distance. "I need to find Apollo."

"Even though he's treating you badly?"

"I probably deserve it."

"What should I do?"

Sam looked at him in his outfit. "Come along—it will be good for a few laughs."

It was sometime later when Sam came to the end of his tether. Jack was pissing him off, his patience running thin. The man kept needling him. He was about to lash out when he felt the same sensation he'd felt in the tunnels. Suddenly he was free, looking down on the tiny figure of Jack below him.

∾

SAM'S HEAD WAS SPLITTING WITH A PAIN SO BAD HE WANTED TO scream. He was outside the tunnel that led to Apollo's underground dwelling. He had no idea how he'd gotten there—he was blacking out and seemingly covering ground while he was in a fugue state. He let out a heavy sigh, wondering where Jack was. Had he left him behind somewhere or was the man wearing a top hat and frock coat actually just part of a dream? Sam wanted to go home. He missed Annie and Gaia. This entire trip seemed like a strange nightmare leading nowhere.

He shivered, realizing he was naked again, but this time he had no clothing to put on. What was happening? As his body registered the freezing wind he began to shake, his teeth chattering. He took off at a run—if he'd didn't find shelter he'd be dead in fifteen minutes.

When he reached the door that led into the underground apartment, it was standing open. *Strange,* he thought, listening for voices. He hurried inside but no one was there. "What in hell now?" he wondered aloud. A trip through the rooms revealed a hasty departure, with drawers left open and several items on the floor. Sam looked around, rage sending his scream of "FUCK!" into the stale air. He searched and found some warm trousers and a sweater, which he quickly pulled on. A coat was hanging in another closet and he put that on as well. Boots were next, the ones he found not really his size, but he tugged them on anyway.

Hurrying outside, he wondered how many days it would take to reach Seris. He had no food and the cupboards had been bare inside the apartment. Apollo hated him—that was obvious. Why was he even here? "I want to go home," he muttered. "I want Annie."

He was in despair as he trudged off, heading in the direction of Seris, or so he hoped. He thought of calling out to Ares, but he couldn't ask the god for help again. If he died out here it was his own damn fault.

CHAPTER 19

The sky was an azure blue and the recent rains gone, at least for now. Clouds were visible over the ocean and there was a slight haze that indicated a change sometime later. Annie was outside under the birch trees, her ears attuned for Gaia's waking cry.

She'd been watching the birds over the ocean, feeling nothing but the bliss of the warmer temperatures and the taste of the licorice tea from the mug she held in her hand, when a vision came to her, sharp and immediate.

A feeling of despair hit her like a punch. She doubled over in pain. Sam. Sam was in despair. But how could that be? He'd been fine before she went to the 1800's—what could have happened? He was reaching out to her. But how could she leave again? The baby...and the rabbit situation. Should she take Gaia with her?

Cecily had not yet arrived, and Annie was just getting back into her projects. The Tarot readings would surely start up again once people knew she was home. She let out a worried sigh and hurried inside, her gaze going to the sleeping baby in the basket. She needed Sam to build another crib or enclosure for downstairs. It was time for Sam to come home, especially if he was in trouble. But why would he be okay and then not? Had he connected with Apollo? Surely the answer was yes.

Gaia had been fed and was taking her morning nap. She had at least an hour to contemplate a decision before Cecily arrived. But her mind was all over the place, trying to sort though all the strange happenings. Did she trust the library now that there was a man inside? And what about baby Gaia and her shifting? Sam was asking for her help. She had to go to him.

The baby woke a minute later and she hurried to change her and give her a snack. She was already planning what to wear to keep warm in Atenua.

WHEN CECILY ARRIVED ANNIE HAD GONE FROM WORRIED TO frantic. Something dark and terrible was happening on Atenua.

"I have to leave the baby with you," she said as soon as Cecily walked through the door."

"Well, good morning to you too," Cecily said, her eyes narrowing. "What's up now?"

"It's Sam."

"I thought he was with his father! Didn't you say…"

"He was okay—now he isn't. I can't imagine what could have happened, but I have to go."

Cecily stared at her. "I cannot deal with Gaia again. If something happens while you're gone…"

"Please, Cecily. I can't take her into a snowstorm in the wilderness. We now know what's happening with her. Just keep her confined. At least if there's a rabbit running around you'll know why."

Cecily let out a frustrated huff. "Go, but if you're not back in a couple of days I'm taking her to that social service place that just opened up in Edge—I'm not kidding."

"You wouldn't."

Cecily's stare hardened. "Watch me."

"I have no choice. You must understand."

"I know that Sam is a big baby and his calling out to you is probably because he's lonely."

"It doesn't feel like that to me."

Cecily waved her hands in the air. "Just go, but you owe me big time."

"Thanks," Annie murmured, reaching to give her a hug.

Cecily backed away and crossed her arms in front of her. "I'm not happy about this."

Annie gazed at her for a second before she turned and ran up the stairs to pack. She pulled on long underwear, heavy jeans and her boots, sliding her fur lined hooded wool cape over the sweater she'd tugged on. It would have to do.

Rushing downstairs she glanced out the window where Cecily was sitting in a chair, the baby and Wolf on the dirt in front of her. Annie waved, but Cecily didn't wave back. A second later she was pushing the door open into the stacks. Once she was inside she reached out with her mind to locate Sam. "I need a door to take me to Sam," she whispered.

When the door appeared she hesitated for a moment—was the man inside? But she had to go—there was no doubt about it. When she pulled the handle down and the door swung open, the same man greeted her. And this time he seemed more solid. "Where do you wish to go, my lady?" he asked her, his voice deep and low.

"Who *are* you?"

"Who do you think I am?"

"Do you have a name?"

"You may call me anything that appeals to you."

"Okay, let's call you Steve. So, Steve, I need to find Sam. Can you manage that?"

"Why do you need to find Sam?"

Annie was losing patience. "How is that your business...the library is mine to control."

"Is that so? Well, the library, as you call it, has other ideas now. Neither you or Sam seem able to keep things under control."

Annie stared at his bland expression with rising anger. "So you've taken over?"

"That is correct."

"I don't have time for this—Sam is suffering on Atenua."

Steve frowned. "And you are positive of this."

"He called out to me—what else could it be?"

"You do not think he is exaggerating? Sam does have a tendency to…"

"Omygods! Take me to Sam!" she shouted.

There was a strange whooshing sound that she didn't remember from past trips, and then the door opened and she stepped out into a blizzard. "Wait for me here!" she shouted over the wind. But when she looked back the door was gone. "What the hell?" she yelled, staring at the shimmering spot where it had been. *That bastard.*

She scanned the rough, hilly area, looking for Sam, but there was no sign of him and no tracks to indicate if he'd he been there. Ice crystals hit her in the face, freezing her lips and nose. "That doorman sent me to the wrong place," she muttered as she trudged forward. "I can't believe this."

She had at least thought to bring along some jerky, which she munched on as she fought her way forward. The snow was heavy and the wind was brutal. She was stepping into drifts past her thighs, nearly impossible to work her way through. She stopped to reassess, wondering why she'd picked this particular direction. Was her intuition kicking in or was she wandering in circles? She was obviously nowhere near the dark side of the planet, the light nearly blinding her as it reflected off the crust of ice that lay atop the boulders and on the branches of the trees. "Where is my magic now that I need it," she muttered.

With the unchanging light it felt as though time was standing still. The world of white was never-ending. She couldn't make out where the dark side began because of the snow that continued to fall, blinding her to what lay just meters away.

At some point she decided to take a rest, hunkering down beneath a conifer and pulling her scarf tight. She closed her eyes and laid her head back against the wide trunk. A dream pulled her in. The amulet around her neck was the link between them, the way to find him. When she woke she was holding the amulet and it was glowing. This was new. The amulet pulsed and pulled at her, the glow growing brighter as she stood and began to walk. She followed a circuitous path as the amulet glowed bright or dimmed depending on which direction she took. It was like the child's game of hot and cold, except it was the amulet that led her.

She'd walked for what seemed like hours when the amulet suddenly went dark, like a light had been switched off. Annie panicked and began to run. When she tripped over a hidden rock it pitched her forward. Her head hit a rock and everything went black.

CHAPTER 20

nnie sat up. There was blood on the snow where she'd fallen, and when she felt the spot on her forehead her fingers came away red. Dizziness made her sway when she rose to her feet, her thinking fuzzy and slow. She'd asked the door, or rather *Steve*, to take her to Sam, but all she saw around her was snow and more snow coming down. The amulet had not brightened again, as though its battery had gone dead. When she held it in her hands there was no hum coming from it. Was Sam dead? She went rigid with fear.

A hollow spot ahead of her under a tree seemed to resemble a man's body and she fought her way through the thick drifts to examine it. Her boots were already wet through; her feet felt like cubes of ice.

A few feathers and a muffler that belonged to Sam lay nearly hidden under the new layer of white, but when she looked for footprints she didn't find any. Possibly too much snow had fallen since he left. Holding the amulet in her hand she turned in a circle. But the talisman remained just a stone with no change in brightness. Her bond with Sam had to be enough. Turning slowly in a circle, she headed in a direction she sensed he might have taken.

The snow had stopped for the moment, allowing her to scan further into the distance. The dark side of the planet came clearly into view, a wall of black. She had friends there— Manasa, the snake she'd traveled with, and also the upright sort of alligator creature who had led her to the meeting room. Considering the freezing temperatures and lack of places to shelter, it seemed the best decision to head to the tunnels. Maybe that's where Sam had gone. She hoped he wasn't freezing to death somewhere close by. She'd sent him to Seris and the compound where Apollo lived; why would he come out here?

SHE WAS DEALING WITH THE UNEVEN GROUND AND TRYING TO navigate without falling again when a hawk came out of nowhere. It's harsh call startled her so much that she lost her balance and nearly fell. It flew right at her, and if she hadn't raised her hands to shoo it away, it would have attacked. "Go away!" she shrieked, holding her hands over her head. She moved through the deep drifts as fast as she could, trying to put distance between herself and the enormous bird, but it flew above her, staying close.

When she came to a small copse of evergreens she huddled under them, startled to see the bird land in the branches right above her. She was so weak after her head injury and then her rush through the thick snow, that bird or no bird, she had to rest.

When she opened her eyes again the hawk was right next to her, so close she could touch the feathers. She jumped up and promptly slipped and fell into a bank of snow. She yelled at it but it refused to move, only watching her out of one yellow-orange eye. "What do you want!" she shouted. The bird cocked its head as though listening and sidled toward her. "No!" she screamed, brushing the snow off her clothing as she righted herself from her fall. "I don't have any food," she told the bird as she searched through her pockets. When she found a piece of jerky she threw it at the bird.

It pecked at it, continuing to stare at her. When it let out a series of strange peeps she wondered if it was young—maybe it wasn't fully ready to be on its own. "Did you get lost?" she asked, trying not to look at the claws and the sharp beak.

The bird shook its head as though answering and then fluffed out its feathers. "Wish I had those feathers," she murmured. "I'd be a lot warmer. I think it's only a days walk to the tunnels, but with the snow it might take longer. I'm hungry and didn't bring anything along. Stupid me—didn't know I'd end up outside in a snow storm talking to a bird."

The bird spread its wings and took off, soaring away into the snowy landscape. Annie let out a sigh of relief as she gathered her hooded cape tightly over her head and around her shoulders and began to walk towards the smudge of darkness in the distance. Her cold fingers clutched the amulet around her neck, hoping for some glimmer from it, but the stone was as cold as ice.

ANNIE WAS PAYING CLOSE ATTENTION TO WHERE SHE WAS PUTTING her feet when she heard someone call her name. When she turned she was shocked to see Jack trudging through the thick drifts to reach her. His outfit was from the 1800's and looked ridiculous, especially the black top hat that was covered in a thick layer of snow. His nose was red, his cheeks too, his hands inside the sleeves of his frock coat.

"What in the world are you doing here?"

Jack grinned a crooked grin. 'The library brought me—did you see Sam? He's a shifter, Annie. He turned into a hawk right in front of me."

"What are you talking about?" Annie stared at him. He was a consummate liar.

"Sam shifted and flew off. I'm not lying," he said, noticing the skeptical look on her face.

Annie frowned. "I did see a bird—it scared me. But it flew away. Why are you dressed like that? And why would the library bring you here?"

"You do remember that you left me in the past, right?"

"I didn't leave you there; the door closed before you came through."

Jack frowned. "Well, another one showed up while I was smoking a cigarette in an alley. I didn't ask for it or anything. I figured it would take me back to Edge, but instead it brought me here."

"Did you see Steve?"

"Who the hell is Steve?"

"He's the gatekeeper of sorts, the new doorman who represents the library. He's the one who bought you here." She gazed at him, trying to puzzle out Steve's motives.

Jack lifted both hands, an expression of confusion on his face. "I figured the library wanted to show me something, but I never expected this. Why would it send me here?"

"I don't know. I think the library has grown sick of Sam's and my bumbling ways. But if Steve doesn't come back to get us we'll both freeze to death."

"Bumbling ways or arrogant ways?" Jack asked her as he skirted around a boulder.

"I'm not arrogant!" Annie shouted. "What have I done to deserve punishment from the library?"

"Didn't you just use the world bumbling? Maybe the library expects more seriousness. Maybe it decided to take its power back. And tell me please why it would choose to bring me into this chaos of you and Sam?"

Annie let out a frustrated sigh. "No idea. Unless...unless it wants all of us to make up—but that's ridiculous. There's no way I will ever forgive you for the crap you've pulled. And now that I've gotten to know Elizabeth I feel even stronger about it."

Jack didn't say anything as he trudged forward with his head down. Annie almost laughed at his top hat covered with an inch of snow, the shoulders of his black frock coat whitened from the stuff. But it wasn't long before the cold slipped under her cape. Any humor about their situation floated away as she contemplated the future.

It was sometime later that Jack noticed her holding the amulet. "Is that thing helping?" he asked, watching her.

Annie looked down. "It was glowing, but now it's not doing much of anything. I think it's the conduit between me and Sam."

"Makes sense if he's a bird now—no wonder it's just lying around your neck like a cold fish."

"Did it ever light up for you?"

He scoffed. "If it did I didn't notice. I don't need an amulet, Annie."

"So, if you are a wizard as you said, why are you still here?"

"I'm curious to find out my role in this drama."

Annie had to laugh. Jack had always been like this, letting the fates take him just to see where they led. "I like that about you," she said before she realized the folly of encouraging him.

He raised an eyebrow. "So there is something you like about me. I'm glad to hear it."

"Don't let it go to your head," she muttered, moving carefully around a snow-covered boulder that stood in her way.

Jack grinned, looking her over appraisingly.

"And don't look at me like that," she hissed.

"But you look so fetching in your fur-lined hood, Annie, with your cheeks rosy and your eyes so bright."

Annie ignored him and hurried forward.

CHAPTER 21

S am was lost in a haze of unknowing, any sense of himself gone as he flew from one tree to another. There was something he wanted, something that was here, but his mind was on other things. He scanned the snow beneath him, the little mounds made by burrowing animals. When he saw a point of darkness against the white, he dove, wings tight against his body. He caught the small rodent in his strong talons and lifted back to his perch to eat it. He picked it apart and devoured it, satisfying a portion of what was bothering him. The rest refused to reveal itself, but it nagged at him like something stuck in his craw.

He lifted off the branch and let the winds carry him upward where he caught the thermals, drifting as he watched for unsuspecting creatures below. White flakes landed on his feathers and he shook them off. He felt a hunger that wasn't about food. He'd seen the human below, had tried to get her to follow him. But why would he do that? Who was she to him? His hawk mind shut down as he twisted to search the ground below. When he saw two small specks of color, he dove.

"THERE HE IS!" A VOICE SHOUTED.

He hovered in the air trying to puzzle out the strange feelings going through his body. It wasn't hunger, but it felt like hunger. He wanted to tear the big one up, to rip his flesh off his bones. The other one was smaller, a cloak covering her body, fur around her hood. He needed her.

"That's Sam!" the voice yelled.

The smaller one squinted her eyes and looked up at him. "Sam?" she called out, beckoning to him with her mittened hands. When he flew down and landed on her shoulder she let out a screech and fell into the snow.

"Annie, are you all right?"

The other one was there helping her and sending him away with a flick of his arm. He hovered above them, his muddled thoughts taking wing as he attempted to fly back to her. She was his mate.

"Shift, you fucker!" the big one yelled.

"Sam! Please shift! I'm here to help you. Is it really him, Jack? It doesn't seem possible."

"It's Sam. I saw him shift into this hawk. Why won't he shift back?"

"It can't be him—if it was, he would have shifted."

When he flew close she yelled at him and waved her arms in the air. He landed on a branch close to where she stood.

"We have to keep moving. If it is him, he can't shift back for some reason. It's too cold out here to stand around waiting."

He watched and waited, knowing he was supposed to do something. When the two headed off he followed at a distance. Something burned inside him, a feeling that made him screech, which he did a few times before settling into a rhythm in the sky above them.

~

"WE HAVE TO STOP, ANNIE. YOUR LIPS ARE BLUE AND I'M WET through. We're both going to die out here if we don't find shelter soon."

He landed in a tree just ahead of them, their words making no sense.

He watched them dig out a hollow in the snow and settle into it. "Take off your coat," the smaller one said. "Come close and I'll put the cape around both of us."

His sharp eye focused below to the one he was connected to and the other one who was now holding her against his body. They lay down together as close as they could get. "You're shaking," she murmured.

"Yeah, well I'm fucking freezing," he said.

He let out a screech and fell off the branch to land right next to them. For a second he was lost to himself and then he felt the strangest sensation come over him.

"Sam!"

A second later her arms were around him, her head tucked under his chin. He sighed and tried to breathe, his heart so slow he wondered if it was beating at all. He couldn't speak yet, his mind caught up in another form, one that hunted for food and mated in the spring.

"Sam?"

"Yes, my love?" he finally managed to rasp out.

"Ohmygods," she murmured, tears falling to freeze against his bare neck. "You're naked."

Sam looked down at his body. "I guess I am," he muttered.

DESPITE NOT ENOUGH CLOTHING TO GO AROUND, THEY ATTEMPTED to dress him. Annie took off her sweater and Sam pulled it on. It was too small and looked ridiculous, but at least it was wool. Jack took off his socks and slipped them onto Sam's feet and Annie took her cape off and placed it around his shoulders. His lower body and legs were still bare. Without the cape or sweater Annie shivered, her arms around her middle.

"This isn't going to work," Jack said, looking at her. "I think Sam needs to shift back into the hawk—with feathers he'll stay warm and can lead us to shelter."

"I agree," Annie said, glancing at Sam. "You can fly and find the tunnels."

"Apollo and Constance aren't there," Sam muttered hoarsely, his voice rough from disuse.

"Where are they?"

"Damned if I know. My guess is that they went to Seris. A meteor struck a few weeks back and they went to check their house." He glanced around at the drifts and the falling snow. "The tunnels are close. I can lead you there."

Annie grabbed his bare arm. "What if you get stuck in bird form again?"

Sam shook his head. "I won't with you here, but not sure I can shift into the bird again—it's only happened when I was angry and at my wits end."

Annie raised her eyebrows. "Like now? We're in dire straits, Sam. If we don't find shelter all three of us will die out here."

Sam thought about being a bird, picturing how he felt inside as he spotted rodents and dove to catch them. It was brutal needs that did it—the search for food. At first nothing happened, but then, as he imagined it and allowed the bird in, the change began. When it was over he perched gently on Annie's arm, his head close to hers.

When he nuzzled against her she stroked his feathers. "Time to fly, Sam. Just take us to the dark side where the tunnels are. If it's too far we'll make another plan."

He didn't understand her words but something inside him told him what he needed to do. He lifted off, his screech loud as he circled above them. It was barely a minute before he spotted the dark wall in the distance.

"He's on the way," Annie said, turning to Jack next to her.

He nodded, grabbed her hand and headed in the direction the bird was flying.

Annie wanted to pull away, but her hand was warmer held in Jack's hand, and he was helping her maintain her balance as they pushed though the drifts. She glanced at his top hat, the cravat tied perfectly around his neck. She giggled.

"What are you laughing at?"

"You," she murmured.

He smiled and tipped his hat, making her laugh. Were they just characters in some fantasy story like *Alice in Wonderland*? Everything felt dream-like and strange.

CHAPTER 22

The tunnels were finally in view. And none too soon, Annie thought to herself. Jacks' cheeks were bright red, his nose as well. He could barely speak from the chattering of his teeth. Sam was still in bird form, landing beside them and waddling toward the darkness ahead.

"Sam?" she murmured coming up beside him. She kneeled down and stroked his feathers. "Can you shift now?"

He put his beak against her hand before he pressed the top of his head there. She drew her fingers through his feathers. "Time to shift," she whispered.

It was a sudden transition, the bird suddenly not there and Sam's shivering naked figure taking its place. He had an erection.

Annie laughed nervously and hurried to throw her cape around his body. "Guess stroking your feathers does more than soothe you," she whispered in his ear.

Sam glanced down and laughed. "I've missed you, Annie."

Annie grabbed his hand, tugging him toward the mouth of the tunnel as Jack hurried behind them.

"Tell me what's been going on," she whispered, not wanting Jack to be involved in their conversation.

"Aside from being a bird and having Jack turn up out of nowhere?"

Annie giggled and pressed closer to him. Despite his near nakedness he exuded warmth. "What's with Apollo? Have you had a chance to connect?"

Sam huffed. "I've gotten nowhere with him. Ares and Gaia were so much nicer than he's been. Don't know what I did to deserve it, but he did admit that he has an attitude about me because of what you told him."

Annie felt a jolt, remembering the way she was feeling about Sam when she was here. "It was while you were gone, Sam. I was hurt and depressed. And pregnant."

Sam squeezed her hand. "I know that. I told him we'd worked through it, but he thinks I'm arrogant."

"Maybe I can smooth things over."

"What are you two yammering about?" Jack asked, moving closer.

"Apollo, my father," Sam answered.

"Seems like a formidable dude," Jack said.

"He is," Annie answered. "Sam doesn't know him yet, and..."

"He likes you better than Sam?" Jack finished, laughing.

The sight of Sam with only her cape on, his feet and legs bare made Annie laugh again. Despite the freezing cold this entire trip was making her giggle. Sam's erection and now his hair plastered to his head wearing only her cape which came to his knees, and Jack with his top hat and long formal frock coat... she had to stifle her laughter, it was taking her over. In a minute she would be hysterically laughing and Sam and Jack would think she'd gone round the bend.

Her giggles disappeared when Sam stopped in mid-stride.

"Why are you even here?" he asked Jack, an angry scowl on his face.

"Didn't we go through this already? The fucking library brought me. I have no idea why. Annie says that Steve thinks..."

"Who the fuck is Steve?"

Annie looked up at him. "Steve is the library now. He's a dark-haired guy who looks to be around forty. He runs the doors."

Sam's eyes widened. "What?"

"I know," Annie said in a calming tone. "It surprised me too. I guess the library decided that neither of us are capable of doing a good job."

"Seems better than having you two at each other's throats," Jack added, a smug smile on his face.

The tunnel loomed up in front of them and Annie tugged Sam inside before he and Jack got into a fistfight. She could feel the tension in his arm as she pulled him forward.

Sam glanced at the ground, his voice echoing off the walls around them. "I don't get this at all. The library has been mine for...I don't know how many years—since the institute, and that was over a century ago."

Behind them Jack whistled. "Holy shit, Sam. You're a really old dude. Too bad you act like a young fool half the time."

Annie frowned, trying to contain Sam who was about to lose it. "Stop it, Jack. Sam is vulnerable and freezing cold. If you want to have a pissing contest at least wait until you're on even ground."

The tunnels veered to the right and left. When Annie turned to the right, Sam grabbed her hand. "That's not the way," he whispered, steering her down another long unlit corridor.

Annie used her fingers to provide light, taking the lead. All she could think about was getting warm.

"I've never been to their apartments," she said to Sam who was close behind her. When she pressed against him he put his arm around her, pulling her close. "Gods woman. I am so happy to see you."

∽

THE DOOR TO THE APARTMENT HUNG OPEN AND THEY HURRIED inside. The only light was from Annie's fingers as she searched for tapers. She found a few in the kitchen and lit them, sticking them into holders she found on the tables. When she glanced at Sam he was frowning.

"You can turn into a bird," she reminded him, thinking that his frown was about the fire coming from her fingers.

"I don't care about that," he muttered. "I'm trying to figure out what we do from here. This place is as cold as outside."

Annie registered the cold as her breath formed a cloud in front of her. "How do they heat it?"

Sam shrugged. "I wasn't paying attention."

Annie searched for clues, checking the kitchen drawers and scanning for a wood stove.

"I found it!" Jack called out from another room. "Stack of wood and a stove to burn it in. All we need are your magic fingers, Annie."

Annie lit the paper and wood that Jack had stuffed into the stove. A pipe led upward, disappearing into the earthen roof above them. The warmth was immediate. "Now what?" Jack asked as they huddled around the stove.

"Now we find something to eat and then we sleep," Annie answered. "We'll feel better after a rest."

"And one more thing," Sam whispered in her ear. She shivered in anticipation.

Jack headed off, coming back a few minutes later with news of how many bedrooms and how cold they all were. "Not as bad as outside though, and there are a lot of warm quilts. What about food? Is there any?"

Annie had just returned from looking through the cupboards. "There's cheese and jerky and crackers and some bread," she said, handing him a plate.

Sam looked surprised. "I searched through those cupboards and couldn't find anything to eat."

Annie smiled at him. "There's an entire set you must have

missed.When we wake up we can find the ones who live here. They'll help."

"Manasa," Sam muttered.

"You've met her?"

He nodded but didn't say anything else.

It wasn't long before they went their separate ways. Annie and Sam found what they supposed was Apollo and Constance's room and Jack went down a hall to one of the kid's bedrooms. As soon as they were inside with the door closed, Sam shed her cloak and pulled her close. She could feel him hard against her. "How long have you…"

"The entire time since I shifted," he whispered in her ear. "It's painful now. I need you badly."

Much had been left unsaid, but Annie was as anxious as he was. He tugged her sweater off and bent to kiss her breasts. The cold made the nipples stand up and goosebumps came out on her skin, but with his mouth there she felt warmer than she had in hours. "Sam," she whispered, her fingers combing through his long unkempt hair. She ran her hands over his scars and muscles, remembering each one.

"I must reek," he muttered, lifting his head. "I haven't had a shower since I've been here."

"I don't care," Annie whispered, her fingers tracing his belly to the part of him that stood at attention. He unbuttoned her wool pants, loosening them until they fell around her feet. She stepped out of them and then they both removed her long underwear, throwing them into the growing pile on the floor.

She was completely naked now, his avid look and what he was doing with his fingers making her crazy.

When she let out a gasp he picked her up and carried her to the bed.

"You want me?"

"Yes," she hissed out between spasms. He was bringing her close and then backing off. He knew exactly what he was doing.

"As you wish," he murmured.

When he pressed inside her she gave a shrill cry, unable to keep quiet.

"Jack is having an earful," Sam muttered.

"Let him—it's probably all he's had for a while," Annie whispered back.

When she twisted one leg over his back he let out a heavy groan. "If we aren't careful I could give you a baby."

"Give away," she shivered. The bed springs squeaked under them, the headboard slamming against the wall in rhythm as they made up for the time apart. He waited for her, only asking one more time if it was okay. Annie was unable to answer, a nod all she could manage. She let out another cry when it happened, Sam holding her tight as she let go. His release followed, a sound coming from him that she had never heard before. His face was wet with tears.

When it was over Annie snuggled into his warmth. They fell asleep in each other's arms, the quilts pulled over them.

CHAPTER 23

SAM

"Are you two trying to torture me?" Jack asked when they met in the kitchen many hours later.

Sam glanced at Annie and they both burst out laughing. "No, Jack," Sam answered. "Sorry, but we couldn't seem to be quiet."

Jack frowned and turned to search through the cupboards. "Not much to eat."

Sam was dressed now, wearing more clothing that had been left behind by Apollo. A wool shirt and pants and a sweater that he was pretty sure Constance had knitted. He felt strong and confident after the time spent with Annie. She was his rock, his grounding. He needed her more than he'd ever realized. He moved next to Jack and opened another cupboard. "Here's the gruel they mix up. It's hardy and will do in a pinch," he muttered, pulling out a container with a lid.

"We need to cook it in water," Annie said, looking at it.

Sam pointed to a heavy earthenware jar. "Water there and we can heat it up on the wood stove."

AFTER THE MEAL THEY TALKED ABOUT WHAT TO DO. SAM TOOK THE lead, bringing up what they'd been avoiding—his new-found ability and how to get to Seris. "The bird can come in handy. I can scout out the trip." He glanced at Annie. "Or we can call on Ares and Gaia. They could get us there faster."

"Can you take us with you, Sam? Like they can?" Annie asked.

Sam smiled. "I don't think so. I'm not a god, I'm just a hawk."

Annie took his hand. "Did I tell you about Gaia?"

Sam frowned. "No, what about her?"

"She shifted into a rabbit while I was gone. Poor Cecily didn't know what was happening."

Sam's current thoughts turned into dust. "I'll be damned," he muttered. "Where did this ability come from? Apollo hasn't mentioned anything about it."

"Why would he? You didn't know…"

"He saw it happen, Annie. I was angry and took off down the tunnels the first time. He followed me…I think he might be an eagle."

"Why didn't he say?"

"He hates me," Sam muttered.

"Stop saying that. It isn't helpful and it's untrue. He doesn't know you."

Jack made a sound in the back of his throat. "This is turning into quite the interesting drama you two are caught up in."

Annie sighed and looked away for a second. "So much to sort through—so many changes."

"As long as we're together I'm fine with all of it," Sam said.

"And yet you took off and left Annie alone with your baby," Jack said, his narrowed gaze on Sam.

Annie glanced at him and then at Sam. "He came here for a reason, Jack. Things haven't gone according to plan."

"Don't make excuses for me. I was a fool to leave you. If nothing else this trip has shown me how much I have to lose."

His eyes welled and he wiped at them, turning away to hide the raw feelings from Jack.

"If you can't get your shit together I can take over the care of Annie and Gaia."

Sam's anger rose. He tamped it down. The man was bating him. "Annie and I are bonded, Jack. You had your chance with her and you blew it. Stop trying to start a fight. You won't win."

Annie slipped her arm through Sam's. "How about we concentrate on the problems at hand. Jack needs to get back, and you and I have to find Apollo and finish what you started. He has to see who you are. We can't leave until that happens."

Sam bent to kiss the top of her head. "We need to get a move on then. Gaia is with Cecily, I imagine. How long did you tell her you'd be gone?"

Anna felt a shock remembering their conversation. "She said if I wasn't back in a few days she would take her to the social services that just opened up!"

Sam looked down. "How long would you say it's been?"

"Two days," Annie mumbled.

"Okay—we have two more days to get things wrapped up here. We need Ares."

"Unless the time is different here and there." She looked up at him.

"Is it?" Sam asked.

"I can't remember anything about it! It didn't matter to me then."

"What about me?" Jack asked, frowning.

Sam turned to him. "You need to call up a door."

"And I do that, how?"

Annie frowned and shook her head. "You've done it before, Jack—you admitted you're a wizard."

Jack's face turned red. "Yeah, well, I...

"All you can do is it try. And if it doesn't work, we'll figure it out," Sam said. He felt himself again—taking charge. And it felt good. "Time to go," he announced, heading toward the door to the tunnels.

"And Ares and Gaia?" Annie asked.

"Let's get out of the tunnels before we try and summon them."

"Summon—that's kind of arrogant, isn't it?" Jack asked.

Sam laughed. "It seems the right word though—how else do you call a god?"

THE CONTINUING DARKNESS WAS OPPRESSIVE, THE OUTSIDE NEARLY as dark as the tunnels. Sam felt it keenly, and when he glanced at Annie he could tell she felt it too. No wonder she hadn't wanted to come here again. Unrelenting sun or shadow were equally bad. "I understand why you didn't want to come with me," he murmured in her ear. "This darkness is bad, but in all honesty I think constant sun might be worse."

"It is. I was going crazy with no night. I can't wait to get home." She squeezed his hand.

"What should we do about the gods?"

"I can contact Gaia through the ether. She's there for me."

Sam nodded. "Do it." He glanced at Jack who was staring into space with a pained look on his face. "What are you thinking?"

"I'm trying to call up a door, but so far no luck."

"How did it happen when you came here?"

"I was in the 1800's and the door just appeared."

Sam rubbed a hand across his stubbly face. "I wonder why. Seems odd to send you here."

"I agree. I thought at first that I was to be a part of your plan. Then I thought, no, the library wanted us to mend our differences. Now I don't know what to think."

"You have a life in the 1800's?"

"Yes, for now. I'm trying to make some money."

Sam shook his head slowly. "These schemes of yours will get you in the end. Honest work isn't so hard, is it?"

Jack laughed. "I've never done honest work, Sam. You should know that by now. I have no qualms about who I am."

The sky was turning darker by the minute and snow had begun to fall. Sam looked up and frowned. "What's this then?" he muttered.

"Another fucking storm," Jack hissed.

Annie moved closer to the two men. "Whatever this is, it isn't a storm," she whispered, her eyes narrowing.

The wind came up, and with it ice crystals pelted the three of them. Jack ran for the tunnels and Sam grabbed for Annie's hand, but before he could get a grip she was pulled away. "Annie!" he shouted over the wind, trying to follow. The screeching wind hit him full in the face, pushing him backward until he fled inside the tunnel. Jack was yelling something that he couldn't hear and then everything went as dark as pitch.

"The wind—it's like an animal," he heard Jack say.

"You mean alive. If it's alive it just took Annie away on purpose. And you and I are stuck here until it dissipates."

Jack pulled a lighter out of his pocket and flicked on the flame. Sam stared at the blue flame, Jack's square face lit up from underneath. "You had this the entire time?"

"Yeah—what of it?"

"You could have said," Sam grumbled. But a second later his mind was on Annie. His heart was beating fast and he was suddenly sucking in air, unable to take in a full breath. "What the fuck is going on?"

"You would know better than I—this is my first time on Atenua."

Sam turned to him. "Did you do this?"

Jack glanced at him, his eyes dark. "Annie will be fine," he muttered.

Sam's rage rose faster than the wind, his fist clenched and

heading toward Jack's jaw before he could think about it. Jack stumbled backward and hit the wall and slid down.

CHAPTER 24

ANNIE

Annie was in a place of utter darkness. There was no wind and no sound. She struggled to see, but it was as though she'd gone blind. It was like several places she'd been in the past—places she didn't want to think about, much less be in again. Was this the Furies? "Who's there?" she called out, her voice high-pitched and scared. There was no answer.

She remembered Sam's amulet and pulled it over her head, holding it in her cupped hands. It put out a very slight glow, allowing her to establish that she was inside a cave of sorts, the aroma of wet earth suddenly strong. Something white caught her eye and she headed toward it, stopping in shock once she could see what it was. A skeleton stared up at her out of an empty eye socket. She backed up and ran into something soft behind her. She let out a hollow scream when she saw what it was. She felt for a pulse but she already knew. Sam was dead.

Annie didn't know she was crying until she felt the tears on her face. Her fear had blocked out everything. What was this place and how had she arrived here? The last thing she remembered was being with Sam and Jack and then the wind had come up. A beastly wind that seemed almost sentient. It had separated her from Sam and brought her here. Was Sam really lying dead behind her? How could he be? She'd been with him not ten minutes before.

Jack appeared in her mind. Jack, the self-proclaimed wizard, who had arrived on Atenua through a door. She began to cry, trying to hold the tears back as her hiccuping sobs grew louder. It came to her suddenly. Elemental magic. Jack could manipulate the wind. She thought of Serena, Jack's mother and the time she spent with her and her son in the other timeline and reality. Jack had been young then, but he knew what he was doing. She remembered the spells he and his mother put on her—the ones that made her need for him insatiable. The foamy drink she drank every single morning. She was suddenly deeply afraid. If Jack had inherited half of what his mother could do, he was a powerful force for evil.

She turned to the body of Sam again, gazing down on his blank expression, the unseeing eyes. She knelt next to him and gently closed his eyes as she took in a breath. *This isn't real*, she said to herself, repeating it over and over again as she rose to her feet.

After stumbling along several tunnels in pitch black darkness, Annie found the way out. The trouble was that outside was freezing and heavy snow was falling. She was in the area of twilight between the light and dark side of the planet. She held the amulet tightly in her hand, waiting for it to light up. But it stayed stubbornly dark.

Annie was walking through drifts when she heard Jack in her head. *We are connected, you and I. I never forgot that year we spent together or when we were younger and spent our nights fucking and our days stealing. Remember that? I want that again. Sam is washed up. He's old and has no magic aside from the bird thing—and what good is that? I can do so much—you have no idea how strong I am. We could have a baby. You still love me—I can see it in your eyes when you look at me. I can fix things so that we can be together.*

Annie gagged and had to stop for a second, afraid she might

throw up. What was he thinking? Unbelievable. The man was utterly deranged—as crazy as a loon. That was not Sam back there—it couldn't be. Was Jack going to try and kill Sam? Apollo was the only one she could think of who would have the power to stop a wizard. She called out to him in her mind but no response came.

It was sometime later when the goddess appeared in her mind. She was exhausted from trudging through snow, grateful to stop for a moment. "Gaia?" she whispered. "I'm in trouble." A few minutes went by with no response and Annie worried that Gaia was no longer there for her. But then she heard her.

I can see that you are, Gaia replied in her head. *I am on my way.*

Annie waited in the cold, her mind on what she'd seen and the terror running though her. She closed her eyes and tried to calm her erratic heartbeat.

"Annie?"

Annie's eyes opened to see Gaia standing in front of her. The goddess was wearing a caftan of pale gold silk, her skin flawless and her eyes bright with knowing. The snow did not land on her.

"What has happened?" the goddess asked, gazing at her tear-streaked face.

"I was with Sam and Jack and then I was in some horrible place of death and skeletons. I found Sam's body—he was dead."

Gaia frowned, watching her. "How did you get there?"

"A wind came up—it felt alive. Next thing I knew I was in a cave." Her mind went back to that terrible moment. "It's Jack, it has to be. He did this. He was in my mind, telling me lie after lie. He wants me for himself." She let out a gasp. "Is Sam really dead?"

Gaia stared into the distance. "Sam is fine." She turned to Annie. "This Jack is the one you thought was Sam's brother?"

Annie nodded, letting out a ragged sigh. It wasn't Sam—it had to be some sort of hallucination.

Gaia gazed into the distance again, her eyes narrowing. "This entire scenario does not feel right. I have no sense that this Jack is responsible for what happened. I see both Jack and Sam frantic about what happened to you."

Annie frowned. "Who else could have done this? And why?"

"That is my question as well. In order to discover the answer you will need to quiet your mind."

"You can't just tell me?"

Gaia closed her eyes. "There is darkness around the source."

Annie closed her eyes and attempted to blank her mind, but every time she thought it was clear, Jack's voice would break in, going on about how much she meant to him and how happy they could be. "It isn't working," she finally muttered.

Gaia's eyes opened, her gaze narrowing. "I see a dark door that I cannot move through. The answers are there but I cannot reach them."

"A door...the library," Annie muttered. She stared at the goddess. "Could it be the library?"

Gaia nodded slowly as though the truth was coming to her from some far away place. "There is darkness emanating from this library you mention. This is the same library that brought you to Atenua, the door where I joined you?"

Annie nodded. "There is an entity inside now. A man—I call him Steve."

Gaia closed her eyes, her forehead creasing. A moment later she nodded and opened them. "This is the source."

"The man inside is doing this? Why?"

"I do not have the answer to that. I can only see as far as where it emanates. You will have to find another way home. This is a dangerous darkness."

Annie shook her head, her thoughts twisting as she tried to understand. "First the library chooses me to be the custodian and then it turns on both of us? I don't get it."

"The only part of this that can be known is the source. And

the source is this entity you mentioned. It might be acting outside the library or in concert with it. It is evil, Annie."

"Evil?" she squeaked.

"Yes. You must find Sam and Jack and arm yourselves psychically. It wants something."

"Can you help me find them? I have no idea where I am."

Gaia laughed. "You are very close. Less than a five minute walk, by my calculations."

"What? I was in a cave and it took forever to find my way out, and then I walked for a long time."

"The place where you were is supernatural. It doesn't truly exist. Jack and Sam are where the dark side of the planet begins. Go to them."

Annie squinted toward where she pointed. But when she turned to say something, the goddess was gone. "Thank you," she murmured, pressing her hands together in prayer position. She heard an answering murmur, as though the goddess was whispering to her from far away: "*Take good care.*"

Annie took in a deep breath and began to walk.

CHAPTER 25

I t was less than a minute before Annie came upon Sam and Jack. Sam's eyes widened in relief as he grabbed her and pulled her close. When she glanced at Jack, his forehead was creased with worry.

"Where in hell have you been?" Jack asked. "We were flipping out. Once that wind came up you were just gone without a trace."

"I ended up in a cave. I swear that wind was alive," she said, glancing up at Sam. "The place was filled with skeletons, and you were lying there dead." A second later she was crying.

"What in hell?" Jack said, his gaze going from Sam back to her. "Sam's fine—he's right here with us. Are you sure it was him?"

"I felt his cold body when I checked for a pulse. It was horrible." She wiped at her eyes with the back of her hand, trying to get hold of herself. "And you..." she said, looking at Jack. "You were telling me lies and saying that you and I..."

Jack stared at her before he interrupted. "I've been here with Sam the entire time."

"We've been trying to find you," Sam continued. "I even

turned into the hawk and scanned for miles. I saw no caves, Annie."

Was he saying he didn't believe her? "I called out to Gaia. She came and helped me." As the words came out of her mouth she wondered—was Gaia real or had she hallucinated her too? She glanced at Jack before turning back to Sam. "I thought it was Jack doing it," she muttered. "He was in my head."

"Seriously?" Jack asked. "Why would I?"

Annie turned to face him, her thoughts tangling as she tried to unravel the experience. "You told me that you and I should be together, that Sam was old and washed up—that you were way more powerful than he is."

Jack's eyes widened. "What? I would never try and take you away from Sam! He's like a brother to me."

Annie looked down. "Gaia assured me that it wasn't you, but now I'm wondering if I hallucinated her too." *You did not hallucinate me, Annie.* The words were clear in her mind. She shook her head. "All of this is too creepy. Gaia thinks it's the library doing it. She said she couldn't see past the door, and that whatever this is, is evil."

Sam put his arm around her, a sympathetic smile on his face. "The library isn't evil, Annie."

Annie pulled out of his embrace. "Are you doubting Gaia? She's a goddess and she can see things that we can't. Maybe the library isn't evil, but the guy inside might be. I did tell you about him, didn't I?"

Sam frowned. "Maybe it's Gaia who isn't real," he muttered.

"She just spoke to me again. I have to believe her, Sam. Someone is doing it. The man inside almost didn't bring me here. He argued about you and how you exaggerate things."

Sam laughed. "I do exaggerate sometimes. I go off inside my head and make mountains out of molehills. Maybe he's who he said he is—the human manifestation of the library."

"That may be true, but it's none of his business, is it? And why is there an entity running the doors? It was you and then it was me…and now it seems that neither of us are in charge. Gaia said we will have to find another way home—whatever is going on is dangerous."

Jack stared at her. "I didn't see him when the door appeared for me. But I do think it's odd that I ended up on Atenua. Why would the library bring me here? It sounds like a game he's playing."

Annie nodded. "A game of cat and mouse," she murmured to herself.

Sam stared into the distance, his eyes hooded and dark.

THEY DECIDED TO STAY AT APOLLO'S APARTMENTS UNTIL THEY COULD sort things out. They found some crackers in a drawer and some moldy cheese that they had missed. Sam grabbed a knife and cut off the mold, slicing it up and passing it around. Meanwhile Jack got the wood stove going, using his lighter to start it burning.

After eating, Sam borrowed his lighter and lit a bunch of candles before searching for a lantern.

Annie sat huddled on the couch, her arms around her middle. She felt separated from Sam, his hesitancy to believe her making her feel very alone. The thought of the weird wind was even worse. "I'm not going out there until we're tethered to one another," she muttered, shivering. Gaia had told her the truth. And despite his quirks, Jack was their friend.

Sam didn't say anything as he carried a lantern in from another room. He placed it on a table and sat in a chair across from the couch.

Jack was in the kitchen opening cabinets in search of rope. "I don't like this," Jack muttered. "Why did this 'whatever it is' make it sound like it was me doing it?" He pulled out a coiled rope and held it up.

"I don't know," Annie answered. "It seems like whatever it is, has it in for the three of us." She reached out for the rope and

Jack brought it over to her, sitting on the couch to help her untangle it.

"Let's back up a step," Sam muttered. "Jack has never had our best interests at heart. Maybe the library is trying to get us to pay attention."

Jack and Annie both stared at him. "Jack may be a lot of things, Sam, but he isn't trying to take me away from you."

"Yeah—I don't like what you're insinuating, man. With your lengthy absences I've had plenty of chances."

Sam let out a heavy sigh. "The library has always looked out for me. It's hard imagine it doing evil all of a sudden. Tell me the honest truth, Jack. What are you doing here?"

Jack shrugged and shook his head. "Hell if I know. I thought the door would deposit me in Edge. I shouldn't have walked inside, but I did." He glanced at Annie. "You believe me, don't you? I was there talking to Elizabeth giving her the message you asked me to relay. It wasn't long after that when the door appeared. I was smoking a cigarette between two buildings. I thought, why not?"

"Guess you won't be doing that again," Sam muttered.

"Damn straight," Jack said, running his fingers through his dirty hair. "I need a shower—is there one here?"

Sam rose from the chair. "There has to be some set-up in one of the rooms…there's a toilet so there's got to be a shower or a bath." He glanced at Jack. "Let's take a look, shall we?"

They left Annie in the living room and disappeared down the hall. Almost as soon as they were gone, she felt a chill, as though a cold wind had blown through the room. "Who's there?" she whispered. There was no answer, but she felt something brush by her. "Stop playing games," she muttered. She heard a laugh and then silence. She had risen to go find Sam and Jack when they returned.

"There's a shower in Apollo's office," Sam said, coming into the room ahead of Jack. "Not sure how hot the water is, but I guess we'll find out. It seems like it might be piped in from some underground hot springs."

"I'm going first," Jack announced, grinning. "I won the coin toss."

"The entity, or whatever it is, was here."

Sam glanced at her. "What happened?"

"Nothing, but I know it was here. I heard it laugh."

Sam made a face. "You're keyed up. You imagined it."

Annie frowned at him, her anger growing. "I did not imagine it, Sam. It's doing this to put a wedge between us—first the Jack thing and now it comes to me when you're out of the room."

"For what possible reason?"

"How do I know?"

"Maybe it wants Annie for itself."

Annie turned to see Jack's somber expression. "Maybe," she answered. "But why?"

"You're a beautiful woman, Annie. If this entity has made itself human, perhaps it wants to experience…well, you know."

Sam stepped forward, his face turning red. "That's enough, Jack."

"It's the truth, isn't it? I'm trying to think like the entity."

"I don't want to be alone again," Annie mumbled. When both men nodded, Annie could see the animosity on Sam's face as he glared at Jack. "This is exactly what it wants—us to be at each other's throats," Annie muttered into the strained silence.

"I'm going for a shower," Jack announced, heading out of the room.

When Annie looked at Sam he turned away. "I don't buy any of this," he muttered.

"You don't believe me."

Sam gazed at her. "I know you think something happened, but a person operating the doors? It doesn't make sense. Gaia's suggestion that it's evil? Come on, Annie."

"It doesn't make sense to me either, Sam. But it happened.

He's got dark hair, hazel eyes and he's a bit shorter than you are and not as muscular."

Sam sat on the couch and put his head in his hands. "That library has been in my life for over a century. It's saved me more times than I can count." He looked up. "Why would this happen now?"

"How can I answer that? But you were denied the right to work the doors and then I was allowed to do it. Maybe it wants that power for itself. A man as the library makes sense. I can't stand it that you don't believe me."

"I'm sorry, but some of the things you've said seem pretty far-fetched."

"And you turning into a bird isn't?"

"That's different, it's part of me, a part I haven't known about until now."

"The library is all-powerful. You know that. I am not imagining things." She narrowed her eyes. "Jack believes me."

"Fuck Jack. He'd take you away from me if he could."

Annie shook her head and let out a heavy sigh. "He's not interested in me, Sam. But he knows I don't make things up."

"I'm not saying you made this up. I'm saying that you aren't in your right mind. You've been through a lot in the past few days. The energy is strange here. I've felt it. That wind for instance. It wasn't normal."

Annie looked down. "We can't be bickering about this, Sam. I have no way to prove it unless we call up a door. And Gaia told me it was dangerous to do so."

"How do I know you even saw her?"

Annie felt the anger swell. "Ohmygods. You think I made that up too?" She stood up and began to pace. "Maybe it's *you* who's having a break-down. You have never doubted me like this—not ever."

When Jack walked in, he stared at the two of them. "What happened now?"

Sam shook his head and left the room.

"Good luck," Jack called after him. "I used up all the hot water."

Sam didn't answer.

"He doesn't believe me," Annie told him, settling on the couch. She felt sick, upset with Sam and worried about how they would get home.

"Yeah, he's being kind of a dick."

Annie glanced at Jack who was leaning on the counter. "Sam's probably the most susceptible to whatever this is. It's in his mind—he thinks you're after me."

Jack shook his head. "I would love it, Annie, but I'm smart enough to leave that alone. You know how I am, any port in a storm, but you and Sam are together. You have a baby. There's no way that..."

At that moment the candles all went out at once. Annie lurched up from the couch. A second later she ran into Jack and they fell to the floor.

They were lying there, trying to disentangle themselves, when the candles suddenly re-lighted. And a second after that, Sam entered the room.

CHAPTER 26

S am let out a bellow of rage and stormed across the room. In the next second he had Jack on his feet with his hands around his neck. "You lying bastard!" he shouted.

Annie was on her feet a moment later. "Stop it, Sam! It isn't what you think! It's the library, it…"

When Sam squeezed Jack's neck, Annie grabbed his arm. "Stop it! You'll kill him!"

Sam finally let go and Jack dropped like an empty sack. Sam glared at Annie. "As soon as my back is turned, you two…"

"The candles all went out at once! What you saw was us running into each other in the dark. Come on, Sam. Have I ever been unfaithful? What is *wrong* with you?"

"The candles are all fine," he said, glancing around the room.

Annie let out a heavy sigh, her gaze going to Jack who had pushed up from the floor and was trying to catch his breath. His neck was ringed with red. "It's sorcery, just like the wind and the cave. It's doing this to cause problems between us!"

Sam frowned. "Why would the library want to cause problems?"

"I don't know. But I'm calling on Gaia to help us. You need to come to your senses."

"My senses are just fine," he muttered.

"No, they aren't," Jack said, his voice hoarse. "You nearly choked me to death."

Annie turned away, her mind on Gaia. *Please,* she whispered. *Sam's gone crazy. And bring Ares.*

A couple of minutes later Annie heard voices. She ran to the door expecting Gaia, but instead it was Apollo and Constance. "Thank the gods," she muttered, reaching to hug Apollo.

"What is wrong?" he asked once she released him.

Annie glanced at Sam standing like a statue behind her. His face was like marble, a frown etched into his forehead. "I'll let Sam tell you," she murmured, turning to give Constance a hug.

Jack coughed and went to the jug for water. He poured a cup and drank it down, watching warily as Apollo approached Sam.

"What is happening here, Sam?" Apollo asked.

Sam shrugged and turned away.

"Sam!" Annie shouted. "Tell him!"

"You tell him," he said heading toward the door. A second later he was gone.

IT TOOK AN HOUR TO RELAY THE EVENTS OF THE PAST COUPLE OF days, Annie and Jack interrupting each other to fill in details as Apollo and Constance listened.

"Sam is bewitched," Annie finally said, her eyes filling with tears. "I don't know how it happened, but he's lost his mind."

"It does sound as though he's not thinking straight," Constance agreed. She glanced at Apollo. "You were too hard on him," she said, "and finding out that he's a shifter must have put him over the edge."

Apollo nodded slowly his gaze going to Annie. "We couldn't wait for him—we had to get to Seris. It was important to find out what happened there. In the meantime it seems that the library has been wreaking havoc. It is hard to imagine, but I certainly believe what you've told us."

"Thank you," Annie said, her tight shoulders relaxing. "Where are the children?"

"We left them with Cari, our cook and housekeeper." Apollo paced with his hands clasped behind his back. He reminded Annie of a monk. When he stopped and looked up, both Jack and Annie focused on him.

"There is something you should know," Apollo said quietly. "As I've mentioned, the library on Atenua is the original one. There is a chance that Sam's moods and negativity have allowed dark energies into the library he knows. Either that or it is teaching him a lesson. But you have also told me that Gaia is aware of these energies. In that case I would say my first assessment is correct. A goddess can see past the veil to what is hidden."

"And you can't?"

"I am a conduit only. My abilities extend mostly to my senses. Without seeing or experiencing what you have, I am in the dark as much as you are."

"It's like it wants it Sam to be angry and think I'm cheating. Makes no sense."

"Unless this is truly the library's way to bring Sam to his senses. You told me he hasn't been the same since his time in the 1300's. Perhaps something happened that impacted him in ways that none of us can see."

Annie nodded. "We had a honeymoon period when we reconnected that lasted about nine months. He was thinking about killing himself before that."

Apollo frowned and stared into the distance. "Something has infested him, some demonic force. If he was at the point of committing suicide it makes sense that in his weakened state he would be susceptible. And the 1300's experience was enough to begin the process." Apollo gazed at Annie. "These forces are always there, Annie, like the viruses that we carry in our bodies. It is our immune system that prevents them from taking over. This is the same process, but it is the strength of the mind and the will that has to be there to stop it. He almost died several times, correct?"

Annie nodded. "He was in hell when the three Furies had him."

"So he did die. This is what weakened him. He is immortal—did you know?"

"I suspected it, but he won't discuss it with me."

Apollo nodded. "He might not be aware of it, at least not on a conscious level. I will have to approach him carefully." He glanced toward the door. "I assume he has shifted into the hawk. He feels safer in that state."

A sense of relief went through her. "I am so happy you're here."

Apollo's mouth lifted in a half smile. "I am very glad that you are here too, Annie. Sam would be lost if you hadn't come when you did." He glanced at Constance who was sitting on the couch. "I must go my love, and help our son."

Constance waved him away. "Take care of yourself, Apollo. He may be in a fighting mood."

Apollo nodded and was gone. When Annie glanced out the open door she heard only the whoosh of wings.

"He is an eagle," Constance told Annie. "It is how he travels. And somehow he can take me with him. It's how we arrived here so quickly."

"You knew about Sam?"

"Gaia reached out to us. We have worried and discussed our grown son many times in the past months. Apollo feels responsible for sending Sam down this path of destruction. He should have been kinder."

"He didn't know the extent of what was going on."

"True, but it does not excuse him. He knew clearly that Sam had inherited the ability to shift, and yet he refused to explain it to him. I think it was his fondness for you that turned his heart against his son."

Annie felt a pang. "I shouldn't have confided as much as I did."

"Your relationship with Apollo was one of the reasons we sent you away, Annie. I needed him, and I hate to admit it, but I was jealous."

"Which meant I couldn't be close to you. And that hurt."

Constance smiled sadly. "It is in the past now." She glanced at Jack who had been silent. "What is your role in all of this?"

He shrugged. "The doors brought me here—perhaps I am a reminder of the past?"

"Or the joker in the deck," Annie said with a laugh.

Constance glanced from one to the other. "You two are close."

Annie glanced at Jack. "We were once together. But it was a long time ago now. We've been through a lot, some of it good and a lot of it bad."

"But despite that you still love me," Jack said, chuckling.

"I wouldn't go that far."

Constance rose. "Old friends," she murmured, heading to the kitchen. "Would anyone like tea?"

Old friends. Annie glanced at Jack. He had helped her recently and he seemed a different person since he'd been on Atenua. But it was folly to trust him. She headed to the kitchen to help Constance with the tea.

CHAPTER 27

SAM

The hawk landed in a tree and scanned the landscape, looking for prey. Something was bothering the bird, but what it was wouldn't come fully into the hawk mind. Snow had stopped falling, a cold wind ruffling his feathers. Was it close to time to mate? He had a mate—he was sure of that. She would show up and they would fly together and find a place to build a nest.

He saw the eagle soaring in the sky above him, a bad omen. The other bird would catch his prey—it was bigger and faster than he was.

When it flew toward where he perched, he hunkered down, hoping it would merely fly past, but instead it landed on the branch above him.

He refused to look in its direction, pretending that it wasn't there. There was something disturbing about it and all he wanted to do was fly away. Instead he felt attached to the branch where he perched, unable to move. He was struggling to shift his feet when the larger bird descended, landing next to him. Words came from the eagle's mouth. Human words. He knew their meaning.

"Sam, we have to talk," the eagle said, opening its beak wide. "Shift so that we can work this through."

Sam, that was his name. He was Sam. But he didn't like Sam —didn't like who he'd become. And there was something else that he didn't want to see.

"Come down to the ground—we need to work this through."

Sam watched the eagle fly down and shift into a man—he was Apollo, Sam's father. Something in his heart region seemed to contract.

Apollo looked up at him, gesturing. "I was wrong. I treated you badly. I understand that now. Please shift."

Sam felt a softening around his heart, the need to shift coming over him. He dropped to the ground and became what he was—a man.

Apollo came close and pulled him into an embrace. "I am so sorry, my son. I have hurt you. I did not mean to do so. Please forgive me."

But Sam couldn't answer as tears poured out his eyes. He clung to his father and sobbed.

It was some time before Sam got hold of himself. Apollo had somehow managed to bring clothing along and after his initial breakdown he put them on. He felt shattered, like a pane of glass that had cracked into a million tiny pieces. He'd cried like a little baby.

Apollo smiled at him. "I am glad you were able to let go, Sam. That is the first step toward healing."

"I feel like a fool," Sam muttered, wiping his eyes with the back of his hand.

"Better a fool than pig-headed, my boy. I should have explained the bird thing right away. And I should never have ignored you as I did. I am the one who is ashamed."

"What has changed your mind?"

"Talking to Annie and learning what you've been through, for one thing. I believe now that you have been taken over, that your psyche has inadvertently allowed demonic forces to enter. You are seeing things around you through their eyes, not your own."

Sam shook his head and looked at his feet. Was his father telling him he was over-reacting to Annie and Jack? "I don't feel as though..."

"Sam, you died in the 1300's, and you are immortal. That in itself is a clue to what has happened."

"I didn't die, I..."

"Do you remember the three Furies and being in hell?"

Sam frowned. "No."

"Annie came to you there. After talking with the Furies they allowed her to give you another chance to change the things that had happened between you—but you refused."

Sam felt confused, wondering why he didn't remember any of this. "I...I have a vague memory of Annie telling me she was four months pregnant, but it made no sense. She couldn't have been."

"I want you to close your eyes and remember that moment in the past."

Sam did as Apollo said, feeling the heat of the man's fingers on his forehead. It came to him suddenly, so clear that it was as though he was there. Annie stood in front of him, grabbing his hand to place it on her belly. She told him they could change things if he listened to her. And yet he turned her away. He was crying again. He couldn't help it. "I see it," he managed to mumble, wiping his eyes.

"Keep going. I want you to see it all."

Sam closed his eyes and was suddenly in such pain that he let out a scream. He was on a rack and three women were working the controls. He heard Annie's voice speaking to the women, the moment when the pain stopped. He opened his eyes. "I was dead and Annie tried to save me..."

Apollo nodded. "Annie loves you. Whatever you think is going on between Annie and Jack is all in your mind. The library that exists in Edge is a part of this. I have not yet determined why. Because of what you've been through, it is able to convince you of things that are not true. You must use the library here in Atenua to return home."

Sam nodded, a headache brewing. He felt like a child who had been sick for a long time. "I wanted my magic back—that's why I came here. Now I could care less about it."

"Your magic will return once you are healed and yourself again. It will take time."

"What should I do? I'd like to stay here, but our baby needs Annie."

"I will be happy to have you stay with us for a time. Annie can go home to Gaia and you can join her when you feel ready."

"I would like to get to know you and to explore my life to find out who I am."

"Whatever has infested your psyche is very much like an illness. You need to regain your strength. This will require willpower, Sam. I am not saying it will be easy."

"I would like that. And if I can help you in any way, I would like that too—to feel useful."

Apollo put his arm around Sam's shoulders. "You are a good man. But realizing this could take some time. You have been hiding from yourself and your ego has taken over—but that is the least of it."

"I don't understand how I lost myself."

"You will."

Sam let out a sigh as the two men began to walk back toward the tunnels. The snow was still falling and the wind had come up, bits of ice hitting his face like needles. Sam turned to his father, glancing at the warm jacket and wool trousers he was wearing. "Why am I always naked after I shift and you are not?"

Apollo laughed. "I have mastered shifting and know how to make sure I am dressed when it happens. I can also take items and people with me from one place to another. You are new at it. It takes time and concentration."

Sam nodded. "It's kind of inconvenient," he muttered.

Apollo let out a bark of laughter before he frowned, glancing up at the sky. "The planet has moved slightly, but this weather continues. Something is off."

Sam didn't hear the concern in his voice as his heart settled. His thoughts were on being free of the terrible thoughts that had plagued him. Being away from Annie would be difficult, but if it meant finding his true self, and learning the shifting protocol, it would be worth every second.

CHAPTER 28

When Sam arrived back at the underground apartment, Annie didn't move from the couch. If she was honest with herself, she was angry with him. Apollo came in after him and the sight of the older man put her mind at ease. He looked relaxed and had a slight smile on his face. There was a softer expression on Sam's face too as he headed toward her.

"I'm sorry," he murmured, sitting next to her.

"About what? Not believing me or your jealousy?"

"Both."

Annie nodded, glancing at Jack who was drinking tea with Constance in the kitchen. "I'm glad to hear it."

"I'm planning to stay with Apollo for a while. But you should get back to Gaia."

Anna was surprised to hear this. "You're staying? How long?"

"I don't know. It depends."

Annie glanced at Apollo. "You and I being apart again bothers me. If this problem is related to the library, then..."

"Apollo said you need to use the library here to get home." Sam glanced at his father. "He wants us to go to Seris as soon as possible."

"The weather is still bad," Annie murmured.

"He can move us through the ether," he said, not responding to what she'd said. "Apollo thinks what's going on with me began while I was in the 1300's."

"Makes sense to me." Annie rose from the couch and went to where Apollo stood alone. "Can I talk to you privately?"

Apollo glanced at Constance and Jack, his gaze going to Sam who sat alone on the couch. "Of course."

Apollo led the way into another room and Annie followed, her fingers lighting the way. It seemed to be young Sam's room by the layout of the bed and the books strewn about. Apollo lit a lantern and sat on the bed, gesturing to the chair across from him. "I suppose you want to ask me about Sam."

Annie nodded, feeling silly. "He said you want him to stay here for a while. I only wanted to hear what you think now that you've spoken to him."

"He's broken, Annie. His psyche has been destroyed. I do not understand the motives, but demonic forces are in charge of him at the moment. Until we clear them and he heals, he must remain here with me."

"Why did this happen?"

Apollo shook his head. "I have my suspicions that the 1300's are a part of it. Sam is immortal. And to die while you are immortal is unheard of—and yet he did. This weakened who he is and set in motion what is happening to him now." He glanced at her. "He cannot be held responsible for his behavior."

"I'm not truly angry with him, Apollo. I know him on a deep level and I understand who he really is. I've been with that version of him—it's who I fell in love with."

Apollo smiled and reached a hand out to touch her knee. "I figured as much. You are a wise and intuitive woman with your own newly realized magic. Do you understand what I have said about his healing process?"

"Yes."

"We will travel to Seris and I will take you to the library. You need to get home."

Annie felt a shot of adrenaline. "Is something wrong?"

"There will be if you do not go soon."

"And what about Jack?"

"Jack is an enigma to me, but I do not see him as dangerous. If you agree he can travel back to Edge with you."

"It's okay with me, but Sam might think otherwise."

"He understands that he overreacted, Annie."

Annie rose from the chair. "Okay, if you say so," she murmured. "Thank you for explaining things." She was about to leave the room when something occurred to her. "Will Sam be all right—can he come back from this?"

Apollo had risen and was about to shut the lantern down. He turned. "I hope so."

Annie's mouth dropped open in shock. There was a possibility that Sam would never come back to himself. "So, how long do you think it will take?"

"I have no way of knowing. It could be weeks or months."

No words came as she took this in. She hurried down the dark corridor, fear sending her thoughts scattering in every direction.When she reached the lit space, Sam wasn't there. "Where's Sam?"

Constance looked up from her mug of tea. "He did not say where he was going."

Jack glanced at her, a questioning frown on his face. Annie shook her head and headed for the door, but before she reached it Apollo called out to her. "Take these," he said, handing her a pile of clothing.

By the time she was outside the tunnels, she picked up the pace. She was out of breath and had the feeling of floating untethered in a world that made no sense.

Sam was her rock, and now he was not there for himself or for her. He could be away from her and Gaia for months, and maybe never come back to who he really was. The tears came fast and furious, keeping her from noticing the shadowy presence hovering in the distance. When she moved toward it, it dissipated, tendrils of darkness moving in several directions like snakes let loose from a cage.

Annie hurried on, her focus on the trees and the sky. When she noticed the hawk flying in circles above her she stopped and yelled his name as loud as she could.

The hawk did one more circle and swooped down to land not far from her. "Shift!" she shouted.

The hawk stared at her out of one orange-yellow eye for several moments before it transformed. Once Sam was standing there she rushed toward him. When she flung herself into his arms it took him a moment to react, a bewildered expression on his face as his arms finally came around her.

"Sam," she murmured, her tears returning. "Apollo told me. I have to leave you here. I can't stand to be apart like this. Please try and get well for Gaia and me."

"And for myself," Sam muttered hoarsely.

Annie pulled back to look up at him as she handed him the clothing Apollo had given her. "Of course for yourself—that goes without saying. We've been apart so much—too much. I could be pregnant again."

Sam dressed, his gaze on her face. "Are you trying to make me feel worse than I already do?"

Annie smiled a sad smile. "No. I'm sorry. But if I'm having another baby I want you there to experience it with me."

"And you don't think I want that too? Apollo told me that I can't rush things. I have no idea how long this will take, but I can't see it going on for more than a few months."

Annie pressed into his arms again. "A few months?" she repeated, looking up at him. There were tears in his eyes—he was as unhappy as she was.

"I want to be with you, but not like this," he whispered.

A desperate feeling came over her—they'd been separated before and it had not been good for either of them. If she was pregnant it would be a repeat of her earlier pregnancy with Gaia. She couldn't stand the idea of that happening all over again. She gazed at him through a haze of tears. "I have to go home right away. Apollo said things could get dicey if I don't go soon."

Sam stepped back, a frown on his face. "What did he mean by that?"

"I don't know. But Gaia needs me—I can feel it. I told you what Cecily said. If she's dropped our baby off at social services I will never forgive her."

"You won't have to because I'll kill her," Sam growled.

"You won't be there to kill her," she muttered. "And I'm sure she hasn't," Annie added, trying to get control of her emotions. "How are we getting to Seris? Hiking does not appeal right now."

"Apollo has a plan."

When Sam put his arm around her she leaned into him, her body shaking with nerves and the cold. They headed back to the tunnels.

BEDTIME TOOK THEM TO THEIR ROOMS; HOW ANYONE KNEW WHEN IT was time, was a mystery, but like clockwork Apollo and Constance rose and headed off together. Jack passed Sam and Annie on his way to the far bedroom, his impish smile and lifted eyebrows saying it all. Annie ignored him, pretty certain that there would be none of that going on. She was overwrought and worried and everything was too up in the air to even consider having sex.

"We're leaving for Seris tomorrow morning," Sam muttered as he undressed. "Apollo mentioned it earlier—not sure you heard him."

"I didn't hear him say anything." Annie thought what that would mean—she would be leaving for Edge either tomorrow or the next day. She pulled off her sweater and jeans and headed for the bed, her stomach roiling with nerves. But before she reached it Sam's arms came around her from behind. He nuzzled her neck sending shivers down her spine.

"Sam," she murmured. "We can't."

He pulled her around to face him. "Are you kidding me? This is probably our last night together for who knows how long."

"I know, but..."

"But what, Annie? I'm not some sicko who you have to treat with kid gloves. I'm still a man. Can you really leave me like this?"

Annie felt the heat from his fingers that traveled along her arm, her body responding as it always did. When he pulled her close and his hardness pressed against her she couldn't ignore the ache in her lower belly. When she reached up to kiss him he stepped her backward until her legs were against the side of the bed. With a small shove she was on her back. He hovered over her staring down with a look on his face that spoke of love and lust and a million other emotions.

There was no more talking as he proceeded to kiss her, first softly and then hungrily.

Annie moaned and put a hand up to cover her mouth. "Constance and Apollo are in the next room," she whispered.

Sam smiled lazily and ignored her, moving on to other areas with his lips. By now Annie was breathing hard, trying to stay focused. But when he reached her lower belly, she let out a gasp.

"Relax," he muttered.

"How can I relax, I....oh...oh..."

"That's better," he whispered. When Annie let out a little cry he put his finger on her lips. "Quiet, my love."

Annie's laugh was stopped by his mouth and a second later she forgot everything. There was no more thinking as they came together, moving in a languid rhythm as she fought to stop the cries that wanted to erupt from her mouth. When they reached the point of no return he didn't bother asking her if it was all right.

Sam held her against him until their breathing slowed. "If you weren't, you could be now," he whispered in her ear.

"You didn't ask this time," she whispered back.

Sam let out a low laugh. "You didn't stop me, did you?"

Annie stifled the giggles, her body shaking with suppressed laughter. "Do you think...?" she asked, her eyes welling with the enormity.

"I knew it the night Gaia was conceived."

"No, you couldn't have. That was when you decided to remain in the 1300's, even after I pointed it out."

"Annie," he murmured pulling her to him. "I love you—if you're pregnant I will make sure to return early. Apollo and whatever crap is going on with me will not keep me away from you. You have to believe that."

WHEN SHE WOKE UP MANY HOURS LATER SHE THOUGHT ABOUT WHAT they'd done together, wondering why it was that Sam was his normal self when they made love. Any insecurities were gone, and he had no trouble performing. When she turned to him he was watching her with liquid eyes. "No," she murmured, recognizing the look. "I heard people stirring. It's time to get up." And then she asked her question.

"What we do together isn't part of my normal life," he answered. "It's only the outer world that sets me off."

"So why don't we just go home? You don't have to interact much with the world and you'll be there to see our baby growing inside me."

"Are you so sure we made one?"

"I thought it was you who said we did."

Sam let out a sigh. "I said my piece last night. If you are, I will be there." He stared at her, one hand cupping her cheek. "But Annie, please understand that I can't be the man you need until I deal with these demons."

"I'm trying to understand, but we've been apart so much. Who knows what could happen?"

Sam smiled, and pulled her against him. "One more for the road," he murmured in her ear.

"You just hope that…"

"And what do you have against that exactly? I told you I would come home. Don't you believe me?"

Annie met his ardent gaze, her body turning liquid. Maybe she was fertile and that's why she couldn't seem to deny him. She wanted another baby, but not like this. But before she could pull away he was placing kisses along her collarbones, her breasts, his mouth warming her wherever it went. As he continued, she couldn't do much of anything but moan.

"Quiet…" he whispered.

"Gods damn it, Sam," she hissed.

Sam let out a low chuckle. A second later she was gone again, inside the world they made together—the one where it was just the two of them, their hearts beating in rhythm as their bodies connected. When it was over she was crying and holding onto him, shaking with the aftermath and the knowledge that she would be leaving him here on Atenua.

"Don't cry," he murmured in her ear.

But she couldn't help it. "I…"

"I know," he whispered. "Me too."

A knock on the door made them both jump. "Time to get a move on, lovebirds," Jack called out. "Apollo and Constance are ready to go."

CHAPTER 29

The trip to Seris was done through the ether, with Apollo presiding. It was strange to be in one place and then another a minute later, and stranger still that he could take all of them at once. The minute or so that they traveled had been in a white mist—a place of nothingness. She'd been afraid for a second. This nothingness was familiar to her, and not in a good way. But before panic set in they arrived inside the compound.

Annie thought about the library and how Apollo had told her that he didn't need the doors to travel. But she'd heard through various sources that it was quite the trip for them to get to the tunnels every year. Was that a type of pilgrimage that required sacrifice on his part?

They were there before she could puzzle anything out—it was a question for another time. Right now she had the sinking feeling that she would soon need to say her goodbyes. Apollo and Constance disappeared inside to greet their children, while Annie, Sam and Jack waited in the gardens. Snow still fell, making her wonder about the ongoing terrible weather.

Sam moved next to her on the bench and took her hand in his. "Apollo wants you and Jack to leave as soon as possible."

She felt a shock as she gazed at him. "I don't want to leave yet."

"The time will pass quickly," he said hopefully.

She glanced at Jack who was walking the snow-laden garden paths with his head down. "I hope that's true."

"Having time with Apollo is what I've been hoping for. We got off to a bad start."

"Finding out that you're shifter must have been shocking."

"You could say that," he said, smiling wryly. "If you're pregnant will you send me a message? Or if not me, then Apollo."

"I'll do what I can. I hope I'm not."

He put his hand on her cheek. "I hope you are."

"Why? We'll be light years apart."

Sam didn't get the chance to answer as Apollo appeared from the house and headed quickly toward them.

He gestured to Jack and turned to Annie. "Time to go," he said quietly. "If you want to come along to see them off you're welcome," he told Sam.

Jack walked over. "This is a beautiful spot you have," he said, gesturing to the gardens that were covered in a layer of snow.

Apollo smiled. "We are very lucky."

Constance came out the door with Thea and Sam, her eyes glazed with tears. "Just thought we'd say goodbye," she said, looking at Annie.

Annie hugged her and greeted the children as she fought back tears. A minute later Apollo had the door to the compound open and ushered the three of them through.

Conversation lagged as they walked, everyone lost in their own thoughts. By the time they reached the library Annie was in a state of panic. Leaving Sam behind took every bit of her courage, every sense telling it was the wrong thing to do. She was so afraid they would never see each other again.

Apollo took everyone inside the ancient building and closed the outer door. "This weather is not right," he muttered, shaking the snow off his hair. "It should be tapering off by now." He lit a lantern and turned to Annie and Jack. "I will wait while you say your goodbyes, and then I will call on a door to take you to Edge."

"Wow," Sam muttered, glancing at the shelves that disappeared into the shadowy recesses. The woodwork alone was amazing. Annie saw it all again through his eyes. "Beautiful, isn't it?" she whispered.

"This is the original, the first one," he murmured, his eyes wide with wonder.

"We can take a look later, Sam," Apollo said.

Sam turned back to Annie, his eyes welling. "I love you," he whispered in her ear.

"I love you too."

When she reached to kiss him his arms went tight around her, pulling her close. The kiss lasted a while, both of them with tears in their eyes when they pulled apart. They stood very close together, staring at one another until Apollo coughed.

"Ok, ok," Sam said, stepping back.

A moment later a door appeared, smooth metal with a heavy brass handle. Jack went first while Annie said her goodbyes to Apollo. She was inside, blowing a kiss to Sam when the door snapped shut.

"Did he tell it where to go?" she asked.

Jack shrugged. "Are we moving?"

"I don't feel anything." When Annie tried the door it wouldn't open. "I guess we're on our way."

A second later there was a heavy lurch and Annie lost her balance and fell against Jack. He put his arms around her to keep her from slipping. They were rocking wildly and then everything went dark.

Annie was lost in a dream. Everything was white—it was the nothingness again. She was dressed in a gossamer gown and Jack was with her. His clothing was white too, loose white shirt and pants. When Annie looked down, her belly was enormous. She frowned and put her hands there, unsure what was happening.

"Our baby will come soon," Jack murmured from beside her.

"Our baby? This is Sam's baby."

Jack laughed and pulled her close. She could hear the angry screech of the hawk that flew in the air above them. She tried to look up, to call to the bird, but no sound came from her mouth. The first contraction tore through her and she doubled over in pain. "Sam," she muttered, her voice barely a whisper. "Please help me."

ANNIE WOKE IN A POOL OF SWEAT, HER BODY TREMBLING. WHEN SHE looked around there was no door and no Jack, and she didn't recognize where she was. The landscape was empty, the sky devoid of color. It was hot. There were a few buildings in the distance, a haze of heat shimmering around them. She rose to her feet and began to walk. By the time she reached them she was covered in sweat, the unrelenting heat making her feel faint. She'd shed all the clothing she could without embarrassing herself. What she removed was tied into a lump that she'd secured onto her back, using the sleeves of her sweater. She wiped the sweat from her eyes and trudged on. When she saw a figure coming toward her she shaded her eyes to see who it was. It looked like Jack.

CHAPTER 30

ANOTHER TIME AND PLACE

When Annie met Jack on the path he stared at her worriedly. "Where have you been?"

"That landing was weird—I guess I was concussed or something. Where are we?"

Jack frowned. "Annie, are you all right? You went to the market and you didn't come back." He glanced at her belly which she abruptly realized was protruding, just like in her dream.

She placed her hands there. She had to be at least eight months pregnant. "What is going on?"

"You aren't okay—that's obvious," Jack said moving close to take hold of her arm. "Let's get you home so you can rest."

Annie was too confused to pull away, her thoughts tangling as she tried to take in the reality. This had to be a dream, but it certainly felt very real. Once they reached a small wooden house on the outskirts of the town she sort of woke up. "I'm not supposed to be here," she murmured as he led her inside.

Jack shook his head and led her into one of two rooms where a bed took up most of the space. He helped her lie down and pulled a blanket up over her. "I'll fix dinner with what we have since it seems you didn't get any food. Sleep, and I'll wake you when it's ready. Don't want anything jeopardizing the upcoming birth." He leaned down and kissed her lightly on the lips before he left her alone.

Annie tried to get up but felt so lethargic she could barely keep her eyes open. She finally closed them and fell asleep.

ANNIE WOKE SOMETIME LATER, HER BODY CRAMPING WHEN SHE SAT up. She knew the signs. She was in labor. "Sam!" she cried out before remembering where she was.

Jack ran into the room. "Who is Sam?"

Annie shook her head as a contraction rolled through her. This couldn't be happening, and yet it was. Jack was all efficiency, ready for the birth with towels and a basin of water, his brow creased in concentration. "The baby's early," he muttered, helping her off with her clothes.

"Jack," she muttered between clenched teeth. "How long have we been together?"

He gazed at her, a smile lighting up his eyes. "Don't you remember? We wanted to wait on another baby but, well… things happen."

"Where are we?"

"Edge, where we've lived forever. We grew up here. What is wrong with you?"

But Annie couldn't answer as another contraction had her crying out in pain. *Please have me wake up,* she whispered. *This is the worst dream I've ever had.*

The pains continued, Annie crying and sweating as Jack tried to soothe her. "I promise you this one won't be like the first one," he whispered. "Try and breathe, Annie."

"Like the first one?" she managed to mutter.

"Stillborn."

Stillborn. The word went through her mind sending chills down her back and into her legs. She let out another cry and doubled over. Black spots appeared in front of her eyes and she felt dizzy and disoriented. Jack looked really worried. "There's too much blood," he whispered.

Annie glanced down at the bed, seeing the red spreading under her. A severe pain sent a shiver of fear though her and then the dizziness grew much worse. She was about to black out. "Help," she whispered. Jack was there, the look on his face saying it all as he helped her lie back.

"Hang on, Annie," he murmured.

A second later everything closed in on her.

ANNIE FLOATED IN A NEBULOUS PLACE THAT HAD NO EDGES. SHE wasn't corporeal, or maybe she just couldn't feel her body. She certainly couldn't see it.

"Did you like that?" a voice asked.

Annie looked around but couldn't see anyone. "Like what?"

"Your other life."

"Is that you, Steve? Is this another trick of yours?"

A laugh told her that she was right. "No, I didn't like it at all. Where am I and where is Jack?"

"Jack got back safely, but you…I thought maybe you needed to learn a lesson, Annie. You are so sure of yourself, so sure you know what's best for everyone."

"That is not true. Why are you doing this? I want to see Gaia."

"Your baby is safe—don't worry."

"Please take me home."

"You do realize that you and Jack were together, right? That was real, what I showed you. You and Jack have been together in several lifetimes. Unfortunately in that one you died in childbirth."

Annie felt cold all over. "I'm with Sam now."

"Sam is a lost cause. You won't see him again."

"What are you talking about?"

There was a chuckle before he said, "With me in control of the doors, he can't get back to Edge. And you will not be able to reach Atenua. Sorry, but this is your fate."

Annie struggled to see him, but there was only a white fog around her. "Please, Steve, at least let me go home to Gaia."

"We'll see," he muttered. "First you have to atone. Are you willing to do that?"

"Atone for what?"

"For taking over the library when it was not yours. *I* am the library and it is *my* choice how it works. Do you understand that now?"

"I thought the library in Atenua was free of you," she mumbled.

"No library is free of me. How can it be?"

"Please let me go. I didn't mean to step on your toes. I thought the library was in tune with me. What do I need to do?"

"I'm still considering my next move. For now you can rest."

Annie's eyelids were suddenly heavy and her eyes burned. She closed them and fell into a strange torpor. She heard Steve laughing as she drifted off.

ANNIE WOKE LATER IN A BED. BESIDE HER SITTING IN A CHAIR WAS the dark-haired man from the doors. Her stretched-out legs came into view—she at least had a body now. "What's happening?"

He smiled, looking at her with his head cocked to the side. "I'm considering an alternative plan. You will stay with me—we can be a couple."

Annie reached out to touch him, surprised to realize he was corporeal. "That would be nice," she answered carefully, "but I'm afraid that doesn't work for me."

He frowned. "Why not? I have the right to experience what it is to be human."

"You may have that right, Steve, but I'm in love with Sam."

"So what? Humans are humans, aren't they? You and I can have sex."

Annie let out a small gasp, realizing what it was he wanted. "I don't do things like that—I'm loyal to the man I love." *Or at least I try to be,* she thought to herself.

"Can I at least kiss you?"

Annie shook her head as she sat up. "Please send me back. If you do that for me I'll find you someone."

"A woman to mate with?"

"Yes," she lied.

He glanced at the ceiling and then back to her. "How do I know if you're telling the truth?"

"I thought you were all-powerful."

He looked confused for a moment. "I...I cannot read your mind."

"And you can read other's minds?"

"Jack's is easy to read."

"You will have to trust me, Steve. I will find a woman and bring her to the library, just as I promised."

"If you are lying I will punish you," he muttered. "Maybe that punishment will be taking you away forever. We could have a baby together."

"What? You can't possibly...I mean...can you?"

"I am fully corporeal. I have all the necessary parts. I've watched the act and I know how to perform it now."

"How did this happen?"

He laughed before grabbing her and pulling her against him. When Annie tried to twist out of his grip he only laughed more. And then he kissed her. Annie felt his tongue inside her mouth, her efforts to escape him doing nothing but making things worse. She finally decided to give him what he wanted. Maybe it would appease him. Despite the voice screaming inside her head to get way, she relaxed into his arms.

When he finally let her go she felt strange, as though she'd been inside a waking dream. He was real, a man who wanted her. And despite her efforts to deny it, she wanted him too. She stared at him, a frown forming on her face. "How did you do that?"

"Do what?" he asked innocently.

"You meddled with my mind."

He smiled. "Well, yes—I did have to convince you, didn't I?"

Annie fought with herself, trying to come back to who she really was, but something inside her had shifted. "I won't," she hissed.

Steve grinned. "We'll see about that."

He was handsome, Annie had to give him that. But he was a devil, a monster who was way too powerful. And as he gazed at her, her desire for him grew. She finally decided it was his eyes that were doing it and looked away. She glanced around the room they were in. It was furnished like any other room, except it seemed sterile and lacking some essential ingredient. It was like a robot had put it together, a creature who only knew the outer, not the inner. "Where are we?"

"This is my domain."

"Take me home and I will do what I promised. I have to see my baby."

There was an intake of breath before he said, "If I return you to Edge and you do not do what you promised, I will take you again. And this time you will not be able to resist me."

Annie kept staring at the floor. "Fine. I agree to your terms."

CHAPTER 31

EDGE 2325

J ack found himself inside the library—the one in Edge. When he looked around for Annie, she wasn't there. "Shit," he muttered, frowning. The ride had been crazy. When he heard the cry of a baby he hurried through the door that led out of the stacks. Maybe Annie had gone ahead of him. But when he entered the living room there was no one there but Cecily and a distraught baby screaming her head off.

"Where is Annie?" Cecily shouted over the crying.

Jack shook his head. "I hoped she was here."

"What are you saying? You got separated?"

"I don't know—we left Atenua together and then..."

Cecily's eyes widened. "She said three days—it's been ten! I cannot take care of this baby a moment longer." She handed a crying Gaia to Jack and stormed away. "Tell her I quit!" she flung over her shoulder as she left the building.

Jack ran after her. "Wait!" he yelled. "Annie's missing! Something happened to her on route!"

"I don't care!" she shouted without turning.

The baby had quieted by now and was playing with a lock of Jack's hair. He went back inside, noticing the black dog who looked up at him out of amber eyes. "Wolf," he said, remem-

THE LIBRARY OF TIME

bering his name. Wolf wagged his tail. Jack sat heavily on the couch and placed the baby on the floor. A second later there was a rabbit there and Wolf was chasing it. "Jesus Christ!" he yelled, rising quickly from the couch. "No wonder the woman quit!"

Wolf let out a short bark and picked the rabbit up in his mouth. Jack was waiting for him to shake it to death, but instead he carried it over and placed it at Jack's feet. Jack stared at the rabbit and back at Wolf. "What have I gotten myself into," he muttered.

~

SAM FELT A JOLT IN HIS SOLAR PLEXUS. "SOMETHING'S WRONG."

"What did you say?" Apollo asked. They were on their way back to the compound after seeing Annie and Jack off.

Sam looked over at his father. "Annie's in trouble."

"Trouble? What kind of trouble? I told the library exactly where to take her."

"She didn't make it back. That man she mentioned, Steve—he's taken control."

"Of the library here on Atenua?"

Sam nodded. "We have to do something. He's got her sequestered somewhere."

"Did she reach out to you?"

"I'm not sure if she reached out or if I feel her. Or maybe it's the baby."

"The baby? Gaia's in Edge, isn't she?"

Sam let out a sigh. "I think she's pregnant and that's why I know what's going on with her. The fetus is the link."

"A few cells? I doubt that. You and Annie love each other—that's the best explanation. You have uncovered some truths about yourself which has freed up the connection between you two. I'm going to head back to the library to get some answers. In the meantime, share what you know with Constance. She may have some insight."

Constance had nothing to contribute, her widened eyes scaring Sam more than he already was. "Apollo will fix it," she murmured like a lost child.

Sam was frantic by now, wild and frightening thoughts running through his mind. Was the loss of his control over the library the cause of this strange anomaly? It was one thing to have a sentient building with awareness of what Sam wanted, but to have it be a man...and a man that he was fairly certain wanted Annie. In his vision he'd seen them together—kissing. He didn't know if this was his usual paranoia or whether it could be true. And what happened to Jack? And, Gaia. He had to get back there.

SAM WAS PACING THE GARDENS WHEN APOLLO RETURNED. His footprints had tamped down the snow, making a narrow path that meandered in and out of the flower beds like he was drunk. "Did you find out anything?" he called out as his father came into view.

Apollo headed to a bench where he scraped off the snow and sat and put his head in his hands. "I have no say over anything now," he muttered. "The library's door system is gone."

Sam stared hard at him. "I don't understand this—how can this be?"

He let out a heavy sigh. "As you know I don't use the doors, but if I needed to, they were there for me. This may call for extreme measures." He glanced at Sam.

"But since you don't use the doors can't you go to Earth and see what's happening?"

Apollo's mouth thinned. "I worry about leaving Constance and the children. I have not traveled to Earth since I brought your mother here. I am needed. I have many duties."

Sam didn't know what duties Apollo had, but he was aware

of the heavy burden he carried on his shoulders. "Can you teach me how to do it?"

Apollo looked up. He didn't say anything as he stared into space. Finally, after several minutes he said, "Possibly." He glanced at Sam. "But you are barely aware of who you are yet. That was the reason you stayed here under my tutelage."

"I know, but extreme situations call for extreme measures. If this entity takes Annie I may never get her back."

"Why are you so worried about Annie?"

"I saw him kissing her."

Apollo's eyes widened. "Are you sure?"

Sam ran a hand through his hair. "I don't think this is paranoia," he muttered.

"Annie would never be in agreement with this—you know that."

Sam nodded. "The entity wants to experience being human, Apollo. I feel like I know him. It's exactly what I would do."

"You are not in any position to help her," Apollo said decisively. "As you have realized, the doors are now run by this entity. The best thing we can do is to wait it out. Annie is very resourceful and I do not see her in danger. She is tackling this on her own."

Sam sighed. "I feel so powerless. It's infuriating."

"It may be infuriating, but it is what it is. You must allow yourself time to heal, Sam. Rushing off like a hero will not solve your problems."

Sam wanted to scream, to run to Annie—to save her from this Steve character, but Apollo knew best. And Apollo told him that Annie was managing the situation. He realized that he wanted Annie to be vulnerable-he wanted her to need him. He *wanted* to be the hero. But he couldn't—not in the current shape he was in. And he had to acknowledge Annie's strength.

When he let out a bellow of rage, Apollo turned to him. "This is the most difficult lesson there is—to realize that you are in no position to intervene, and also that the one you love is more than capable of saving herself. This is one of your biggest problems. It is what caused you to remain in the 1300's. You must let that hero image of yourself go."

Sam sighed. "I don't know how to be anything else."

"That is why you're here—to learn who you are beneath the archetypes you've used to cover over your vulnerabilities."

"There's nothing there," Sam muttered.

Apollo ignored him. "There is also the magician to get through—another ideal you've used. The magician represents power, Sam. Without your magic you feel like nothing. But the magic is not you."

"Are you saying that I won't find my magic again?"

Apollo stared into his eyes, holding his gaze. "I did not say that. What I am trying to convey is that you must be fully who you are first. Until that happens, you and Annie will continue to go through these periods of separation in which you need to 'find yourself'."

Sam felt utterly defeated. He wanted to cry, but held the tears back. How long would this take?

Apollo put a hand on his shoulder. "Right now we are on a quest to speak with the minister. Can you be here in the present moment?"

Sam nodded.

CHAPTER 32

Annie was in Edge, deposited inside the stacks. There was no door to pass through except the one leading out to the living room. She felt oddly free after being with Steve, as though whatever he'd done to her was now gone. Thank the gods. When she heard Gaia she flung open the small door and rushed through.

"Annie!" Jack stood from the couch and met her halfway, his arms coming around her in a tight hug. "My gods, I didn't know if I'd ever see you again," he muttered.

Annie pulled free and hurried to where Gaia played on the floor. She picked her up, tears flowing as she pressed her against her chest. "My sweet one," she murmured.

But Gaia had other ideas and wriggled free, looking up at her with a frown.

"She's been changing into a rabbit," Jack murmured. "I can't get her to stop." He grabbed Annie's arm. "Where have you been?"

Annie let out a heavy sigh, trying to settle her nerves. "Steve had me. He...he..." the entire scenario rolled through her mind like a nightmare. More tears came and she couldn't stop them.

Jack put his arm around her and helped her to the couch. "It's okay, Annie. Everything is fine now that you're back."

She looked up at him and wiped her eyes. "No, it's not okay. Steve wants me to find him a woman, and if I don't, he..." By now she was sobbing, all her pent-up emotions pouring out as she covered her face with her hands.

Jack sat beside her. "What are you talking about?"

Annie told him what had happened on her trip back, the nightmare scenario that Steve had put her through, including being with Jack and the birth that had killed her.

"He said we've been together in past lives and you died in childbirth? That is horrible, Annie. My gods, who is this creep? Did you believe him?"

"It certainly felt real, from the pain and the blood and..."

Jack reached and out and grabbed her arm. "Stop. Stop thinking about it."

Annie took in a deep breath. When she glanced at the baby, Gaia immediately turned into a rabbit and hid under the couch. "Steve wants to be with me—he wants to be fully human."

"I can only imagine what that means." Jack shook his head. "We have enough problems without this," he muttered. "Cecily is gone—your Tarot reading business is done. The baby—she's impossible. I can't control her at all. If she gets out of this building, she..." He shook his head, unable to finish the sentence.

"We have bigger problems than Gaia being a shifter. I'm not kidding about Steve. If I don't find him a woman he will take me. He's a sorcerer, a monster—he can control my emotions."

Jack frowned. "What do you mean by that?"

"He can make me want him, Jack! It's his eyes. I'm terrified."

Jack sat up straight, staring at her with a shocked expression. "He...got you to...?"

"Not yet, but he will if I don't find someone to take my place."

"What about Elizabeth? She's alone and lonely."

"My sister? My gods, no."

"She looks like you, and she's adventurous," Jack continued. "As I remember, Steve is a good-looking man. We can save her before anything bad happens. Just don't explain things."

Annie glanced at him before her gaze went to Gaia who was now standing in front of her. She smiled and picked her up. "Are you happy to see me now?" she whispered, kissing the top of her head. Gaia gurgled and pulled on a few strands of her hair. She turned to Jack. "He's...he's dangerous. I would never forgive myself if something happened to her."

Jack breathed in and out slowly. "He wants to know what it is to be human. I thought she might like the challenge."

Annie shook her head. "Do you hear what you're saying? I can't do that to her."

"Even to save yourself?"

"She's my twin."

"Steve can go back in time. He can court her. That way she makes up her own mind about him."

"She likes men with manners," Annie answered hesitantly, "but I'll have to explain who he is."

"Talk to Steve—tell him about her. If you don't feel good about it once you get there, don't do it."

"And how exactly do I get away from him? You don't understand what he can do. His eyes...they're weapons."

"Don't look at him and tell your sister not to look at him either. If he can't use his eyes then he can't hurt her, right?"

Annie let out a heavy sigh. "He may have other tricks up his sleeve. Anyone who can create what he put me through is more powerful than anyone I've ever met, including Sam. And what about Gaia?"

"I'll take care of her."

A minute went by while Annie contemplated. "It's too risky ," she muttered.

"I get it. You can't throw her to the wolves to save yourself. But if she knows what he can do, she can defend herself. Don't leave them alone until she understands."

"I don't know Jack. You've been with her. Will she really be interested in him? I mean what happened between you two?"

"You know what happened. I decided to look out for number one. I left her before the marriage could take place. We slept together, if that's what you're asking."

"Was it easy to convince her?"

"Yeah, after we set a wedding date. But it took a fair bit of convincing on my part."

"Why did you leave her?"

"You know me—I'm not one to stick around for long. I was already involved with Izzy and it was easier than dealing with your sister. She can be demanding."

Annie laughed before she remembered the situation. Her thoughts went to the Golden Dawn and what Elizabeth had told her about their connections with Sirius, which extended to Atenua. The Sphinx pointed toward the Sirius star system, so the ancient Egyptians were definitely involved with Sirius. And that meant the goddess Isis. Maybe with Isis, Gaia and Ares they might have enough power over whatever Steve was. To find out more she needed to go back in time and talk to the people at the Golden Dawn. They had to have dealt with this kind of situation at one time or another.

She gazed at Jack. "I can talk to the people at the Golden Dawn. They might be able to help me."

"Steve controls the doors. How will you manage that?"

"I'll tell him that the woman I want him to meet is there. I'll have him wait while I talk to them, and then..." she paused and stared into the distance.

"And then what?"

"I don't know!" she yelled. "I don't know," she said again softly as tears filled her eyes.

Jack put his arms around her. "I'll help you in whatever way I can, Annie."

She looked up at him. "Didn't you say you could move through time without the doors?"

He shook his head. "Something has prevented me from moving through the ether. Maybe it's all this crazy crap that's going on—it's deleting my wizard energy." He chuckled humorlessly. "I haven't done it in a long time."

"Can you at least try?"

"Have Steve take you—it's better that way. He'll assume you're finding him a woman."

Annie let out a long sigh. "If I fail to meet his demands he'll take me."

"Don't look into his eyes."

She made a face at him before she hurried into the stacks, grabbed a book on Victorian London mores, and called out to Steve. "I need to talk to you!"

When he appeared from the shadows she looked down at the book in her hands. "You must dress as they did in Victorian London," she told him, handing him the book. "There's a society there where I can find you the perfect woman. But read up on the mores. Things are formal in the past and there are certain ways you must dress and speak."

He cocked his head. "You're unwilling to sell your sister?"

Sell her sister. What a horrible way of putting it. "How did you know I was thinking about her?"

"I read Jack's mind. Your sister looks just like you."

Annie nodded, keeping her eyes on her feet. "She does look somewhat like me, but she isn't what you need. She's too much of a spinster."

"Spinster—what does that mean?"

"It means a woman who is beyond child-bearing years and who doesn't enjoy what you're proposing."

"She is older than you?"

"Oh yes, quite a bit older—too old to bear a child. I decided that a better choice would be from this society I spoke about. But you will have to give me some time to find the right person. Can you do that?" She saw him nod out of the corner of her eye.

"I'll wait, but if you do not produce what you promised, you

know what will happen. And do not think you can avoid me."
He leafed through the book. "When can we go?"

"Now is as good a time as any, as long as you bring me back
here. Do you agree?"

When he nodded Annie ran into the other room to tell Jack
she was leaving. "If I'm not back in a couple of hours you need
to find a way to come and get me," she hissed.

Jack stared at her. "Jesus, Annie. How can I?"

"Leave Gaia with Wolf and call up a door. Steve should be
otherwise occupied, right?" She grabbed his arm and whispered
into his ear. "He can read your mind."

"What? Are you serious?"

Annie nodded.

Jack glanced at Gaia and let out a heavy sigh. "This better
fucking work."

ANNIE AND STEVE STOOD IN THE COURTYARD THAT BELONGED TO
the Golden Dawn. Trimmed hedges made a square around a
sedate garden filled with marble benches and topiary. It was a
serene and restful spot but Annie was agitated, her nerves like
frayed wires.

"You will not get a door until this deal is settled," Steve
muttered. "If this woman refuses me, I will come for you,
Annie."

"If you are kind and charming, she will accept you. But you
need to court her. Read about it in the book I gave you. You can't
just drag her back to your lair and have your way with her."

"Lair? Not sure what that means but it sounds derogatory."

Annie didn't answer as she walked quickly away, heading
toward the open door that led into the Golden Dawn. Thank
goodness she'd thought to change into her sister's dress.

Inside she hurried to Eva, who happened to be crossing the

wide lobby when she arrived. "Eva, I need to speak with you," she said in a stage whisper.

The woman turned, surprise registering in her eyes. "I thought you had already left for the future."

"I have a slight dilemma that I hoped you might help me with."

"What is it?"

I have a friend who has traveled here from the future. He is looking for a wife. But he is unfamiliar with the mores of this time. He's very handsome."

Eva paused, her gaze going into the distance. "I'm not married."

Annie was surprised to hear this, suddenly worried about what she was about to do. "I can introduce you, if you like," she murmured, her pulse beginning to race.

Eva smiled. "I would love that. If he does not appeal to me, I will not engage."

Eva retrieved her cloak and followed Annie out the door and to the spot where she'd left Steve. He wasn't there. When she called out to him there was no answer and no indication of the residue of a recent door being activated. "I'm not sure where he could have gone off to," she muttered, turning in a circle.

Eva looked around before heading toward the building. "Let me know if you find him!" she called out.

Annie was completely perplexed, but also greatly relieved. The thought of putting Eva in that position did not sit well. Actually, she couldn't imagine putting her worst enemy into Steve's hands. Where was he? After waiting around for what seemed forever she decided to risk calling up a door. She headed between two buildings, hoping not to be noticed before she did so. A few seconds later it hung in the air in front of her. When she stepped inside there was no Steve to greet her. "Please take me to Edge and my baby," she murmured.

~

DAYS WENT BY WITH NO WORD FROM STEVE. ANNIE WANDERED about, cleaning and straightening and trying to keep her mind on Gaia and the present. The baby cried every time Annie was out of sight, even if it was for a minute. Wolf held up his end, playing with the rabbit whenever Gaia decided to shift. It was scary to watch him chasing it, but Annie had learned that he would never harm her.

It was the morning of the fourth day when Jack appeared at the door. "Well?" he asked pointedly.

She shook her head. "Nothing yet."

Jack's eyes narrowed. "You need to go back there and see what the hell is going on."

"How do you propose I do that?"

Jack pressed his lips together. "Summon a door. If he's inside, you can find out what happened."

Annie glanced out at the early dawn frost that had left a glaze over the tree stump and the chairs, as well as the giant woodpile Sam had left. Soon she would need that wood to not only cook, but also to keep warm. She did not relish a winter without Sam.

"And just to play devils advocate, if you're thinking of fetching Sam home, he's probably not ready."

"You just read my mind."

Jack grinned and shrugged. "I can often do that with you."

"Will you watch Gaia?"

"Yes, but I suggest that you change into that dress you wore the last time."

"And that damn corset," she muttered.

Jack laughed.

Annie ran up the steps to the bedroom to find the dress, her mind whirling. She changed quickly, feeling the strain as soon as she tightened the corset. Was she fatter than the last time? She let out a gasp as she pulled the laces tight. When she slipped the dress over her head it barely fit her. Oh gods, was she pregnant again? No point in worrying about it until she knew for sure, she thought, pulling her hair up and twisting it into a chignon.

Jack whistled when she came down the steps. "You look... amazing."

"You just like the pinched in waist and the pushed up..."

"Yup," he muttered, looking her over appraisingly. "Why do you think I enjoy that time period so much?"

"Because of how easy it is to cheat people out of their money?"

Jack laughed. "Yeah, that too." His forehead creased. "Don't stay long. I'm not equipped to take care of your shape-shifting baby for more than a few hours."

"I don't plan to be back there longer than that—all I need to do is find out if Steve's there." Annie glanced at him. "Remember that he can read your mind, Jack."

"You already told me. How did you figure that out?"

"He saw my sister in your mind. I told him she was older than I am and past child-bearing age."

"He wants a baby?"

"I don't know for sure, but I'm not taking any chances."

"He's probably found some woman of the night."

Annie gazed at him. "That's an interesting idea. I'll check with Eva at the Golden Dawn, and if there's no sign of him I'll go and say hello to Elizabeth."

"Hope the door works," Jack muttered.

"Me too."

"Good luck," Jack called out as she picked up her long skirts and stepped into the stacks.

CHAPTER 33

S am followed Apollo into town, his heart in his throat. All
he knew about this minister was that he was like a mayor
and ran things in Seris. It seemed that lately he'd been on
some kind of a spree to scare the shit out of everyone. The snow
was coming down even harder, an icy wind moving through the
small trees and bushes as though seeking them out.

"How did you get him to agree to meet with us?" Sam asked,
pulling his coat tight.

Apollo turned. "We will surprise him."

"And you trust me? I don't feel like the best choice to help
you."

"You have a certain presence, Sam. You're muscular and you
carry yourself in a way that can be intimidating. I don't expect
any problems, but if we have them, I can count on you to fight."

Sam thought about that. Apparently he was the brawn. So far
they'd barely scratched the surface of Sam's past, most of the
time spent on chores and mundane things. They'd flown
together a couple of times, which was invigorating and made
Sam felt better about himself afterwards, but mostly he'd been
following his father around like a lost puppy.

By now they'd entered another area of the city. There were

many people living on the streets. And the ones he saw huddled into their coats would be dead by morning. "What about them?" he asked his father.

Apollo gazed toward where he pointed. "I have tried to get them to shelter, Sam. They refuse. I cannot force them."

"They'll die."

Apollo grimaced. "I know that. This is the worst winter we have ever had."

Once they reached the tower where the minister lived, Sam hung back, watching as Apollo move forward to knock on the heavy wooden door. The drifts were high around the building, covering the lower windows.

When the door opened, a small woman with gray hair was standing there, her eyes furtive as she scanned the streets behind them. "What is it?" she asked.

"I would like to speak with the minister," Apollo said, gesturing to Sam to come forward. "My son and I have some business to take up with him."

"The minister is not at home. Who shall I tell him called?"

"I'm Apollo and this is my son, Sam. When will he be back?"

The woman seemed afraid for a second, blinking and stepping back. "He...I don't rightly know. He has been away for some time..."

Apollo frowned. "Away—where did he go?"

She shook her head and made to close the door, but Apollo put his foot in the opening. "Are you alone here?"

She hesitated before giving a slight nod. "The Minister...he left here some time ago. He...has changed."

"In what way?"

"He was not kind to me and left without giving me my pay."

"And this is not normal for him?"

"Of course not. He looks out for me. I know he has a very bad reputation in Seris, but he is not who you think he is. Or at least he wasn't until recently."

"He is the reason the factions here have not come together."

"That is not his doing, sir. It is the ones who work for him. I have heard him arguing with them. I even heard him mention reaching out to you."

"When did this change come about?"

She thought for a minute or two, her hand on her chin. "It seems to have coincided with the explosion that happened, but I am not altogether sure."

Apollo frowned, turning to Sam. "That's interesting," he muttered. "Thank you for your time," he told her, reaching into his pocket for some bills. He handed them over. "Hope this helps."

She smiled. "Thank you, kind sir. I do appreciate it." A second later the door closed and they heard the lock click into place.

Apollo frowned and shook his head. "This is odd." He glanced at Sam. "Did you intuit anything?"

Sam was surprised to be asked. He closed his eyes and let his mind clear. He saw something shadowy rush by, followed by a strange laugh and the sound of a door slamming shut. He was reluctant to repeat it for fear of being ridiculed, but he had to chance it. "Is it possible that this minister is the same entity that has taken over the library?"

Apollo lifted his brows in surprise. Finally he nodded, his narrowed eyes staring into the distance. "You may be onto something. I have never seen him, nor have I spoken with anyone who has. I have wondered from time to time if he is supernatural. There have been several happenings in Seris that could not have been performed by an actual man. But what his housekeeper just told us is even more unsettling. He was talking about reaching out to me? Why he would suddenly decide to take over the library makes no sense. We must uncover the truth of the matter."

"And that will be impossible."

Apollo sighed. "Not impossible, but difficult. We may have to call on the big guns."

"The big guns?"

Apollo smiled. "The gods."

"What does this minister do that is so bad?" Sam asked.

"He, or as she said his cronies, seem hell bent on dividing people, as though if he creates a population consisting of the very rich and the very poor, he will gain by it." Apollo stopped and glanced at Sam. "I suggest we talk to those who fear him. Perhaps we can come up with a purpose to his madness, or at least some understanding of who he is."

"Has he always been here?"

"As far as I know, yes. I assumed he was a recluse. It was a long time before I discovered what he was doing to the townspeople."

"Aside from division?"

"There are many races here on Seris. Barriers have been erected between the factions, barriers that lead to more poverty and more racism. The minister is the acting head of the town. From what I have discerned he allows the ones with money to do as they please, which causes trouble, especially down at the docks. What she said about the meteor is interesting. What could that have to do with this change in attitude?" He cocked his head to one side, thinking.

"*Telchines*," Sam mumbled, remembering a book he'd read in the library. "They're wizards."

"What?"

"*Telchines* are mythological creatures who can shape-shift. One could have arrived on the meteor and taken over the minister's body. They are envious of others. If this one is on his own, he must be very lonely."

"So they are corporeal. What do they look like?"

"From what I've read they originally came from the Island of Rhodes. One description mentioned them looking like fish. They can bring on bad weather and choose any form. He could have been a townsperson, for all you know. They're sorcerers."

Apollo nodded. "This envy you mentioned might explain his

branching out into what is mine—the library. I'm the only other powerful person here in Seris."

"Makes sense."

"There are people missing, Sam. I have heard this from several families. He might be using the library to remove people from Seris. What would a *telchine* want from them?"

"Perhaps companionship, or…" Sam paused thinking. "He might want to mate."

Apollo put his hand on Sam's arm. "Let's go home."

CHAPTER 34

When Annie called for a door one arrived almost instantaneously. She hesitated at first, gun-shy after her encounters with Steve, but when the image began to waver she decided to chance it. "I want to go to London, October 2nd, 1893, by the building housing the Golden Dawn," she murmured. Last time she was there was in early September. By this date she should know what Steve was up to.

When she walked out she was met with a cold rain. She had forgotten her umbrella and her cape. She let out a huff and hurried toward the Golden Dawn building, rushing through the door before she got drenched. When she reached the desk, a man was there instead of Eva. "Excuse me," she murmured. "I am looking for Eva Moore?"

The man glanced up from his work and removed his round spectacles. "Hello, Elizabeth. Eva is at a lecture. Can I give her a message once she returns?"

Annie smiled. "I'm not Elizabeth, I'm her twin, Annie. This might seem a strange question, but has Eva recently been courted by a dark-haired man with hazel eyes?"

He frowned. "Not that I am aware. She has been here for all

her shifts and lectures, and I have not seen her stepping out with anyone."

Annie let out her held breath. "Thank you. Please let her know that Annie Morgan stopped by."

Annie hurried outside and across the cobbled boulevard, lifting her dress before stepping around puddles and piles of manure. She waited until there was a break in the chaos before she rushed to the other side of the street and headed to her sister's townhouse. She was looking forward to a cup of tea and a short chat before she headed home.

At the door she picked up the knocker and let it fall.

It took a few moments before the door opened. Instead of her sister, Steve stood there, eyeing her suspiciously. He was dressed casually with no frock coat and no cravat, his vest open over a white linen shirt that had pulled out of his gray trousers. "What are you doing here?"

Annie was tongue-tied for a moment, unable to speak. After a long moment she said, "I could ask you the same question. I did not tell you to come here."

Steve let out a bitter laugh. "Do you think you can order me around? You lied to me, Annie. Your sister is definitely not older than you are. She looks identical and has told me that she is of child-bearing age."

Annie felt a twinge of fear. "Last I knew you were supposed to wait for me outside the Golden Dawn."

"I got bored, and since I had your sister's address I decided to call on her. I thought with her advanced age and wisdom, she might be able to steer me in the right direction." He laughed.

A shiver moved down her spine. "How did you get her address?"

"I read Jack's mind."

Annie couldn't help staring at him. "You...and you've been here ever since?"

"Of course. Your sister is lovely."

"I...was worried about her, Steve. That's why I wanted to hook you up with someone more appropriate."

"I go by Steven now," he hissed, glancing over his shoulder. "Your sister is in the kitchen. Shall I fetch her?"

"Can I come in?"

"I would rather you didn't," he muttered. "We are still in the courting stages."

Annie scoffed. "You look pretty relaxed to still be courting. How far along are you two?" she asked, fearing the answer.

He frowned. "That is none of your business."

"I want to see my sister."

Steve frowned at her before closing the door in her face. She waited there for what seemed an interminable time before the door opened again. Elizabeth stood there, her eyes wide when she saw who it was. "Annie! I did not expect you." Her robe hung off one shoulder and her hair was down and untidy. Despite it being nearly noon, she had not dressed for the day.

"Elizabeth, are you all right?"

Elizabeth glanced over her shoulder before she smiled. "Yes, of course. Why do you ask?"

"Steve, I mean Steven. Is he your beau?"

Steve came up behind her before she answered, his hand on the small of her back. Elizabeth's eyes glazed over.

"I live with her now," he answered.

Annie glanced at her sister who had turned to face Steve. Shock went through her when he bent and kissed her. Her sister would never display such intimacy in front of anyone. She was a private person, any displays of affection done in the bedroom. When he released her, Steve stared at Annie, his cold gaze making her feel slightly ill. "We are busy," he told her. "Elizabeth and I have things we must do."

"Elizabeth?" Annie said, reaching a hand out to her sister. "Are you happy with this situation?"

Elizabeth turned to Annie, her gaze remote. "Tell her," Steve muttered from behind her. "Tell her how happy you are."

"I am happy," Elizabeth said in a monotone.

A second later Steve moved forward and kicked the door closed.

Annie stood there for a full minute, trying to decide what to do. Her sister was bewitched. Could he make her pregnant? Annie was suddenly in terror mode. Steve was...what? Supernatural for sure, but he had to be alien. Her breath hitched in her throat and she felt dizzy for a second.

She moved to the window, standing on tiptoes to see through the lace curtains. The two of them were there, Steve's arm around her sister's waist and Elizabeth smiling up at him. Annie watched him lead her toward the couch where he helped her off with the robe, leaving her standing there in her light shift. His eyes met Annie's. *Thank you,* he mouthed as he removed his vest and unbuttoned his shirt. Her sister stood as still as a statue, a vacant look on her face as he undressed. But as soon as he tilted her chin up and met her eyes she smiled. He pushed her gently back onto the couch. Elizabeth seemed happy to comply, her eyes on his as she reached for him.

Annie moved away from the window, not wanting to witness what came next. A second later she retched into the bushes. She took off without thought or plan, dodging cars and horse-drawn carriages and slipping on the rain-slick cobbles as she raced toward the Golden Dawn. She burst though the door and ran toward the desk where Eva was now sorting through papers. "Eva," Annie gasped. "Do you remember me?"

Eva looked up. "Of course. You are Annie, Elizabeth's twin. Franklin mentioned that you had come by. Where is she? We haven't seen her in weeks!"

"Elizabeth is in trouble. I need your help."

The next moments were fraught as Annie attempted to describe what was going on.

"But you said she mentioned she was happy..."

"Only when she looks into his eyes, Eva. He's...I don't know what he is," she said, planning the current wording for the rest of her sentence, " but he could *get her with child* and then leave her unwed with a baby to take care of. She would be shunned."

Eva shook her head, loosening a couple of strands of pale hair from her complicated up-do. "Elizabeth has always been a sensible woman. She is quite aware of how to prevent a baby. All the women who are members of the Golden Dawn are aware of such things."

"But he isn't...this is what I'm telling you. Steve...he's not human—not really."

Eva seemed surprised, but she answered as though not being human was perfectly normal. "If that is the case how could there be a baby between them?"

Annie let out a heavy sigh. "I don't know if there *will* be a baby, it's my fear that there *might* be. I don't know what he's capable of. My sister is not equipped for this man's sorcery."

"So, now you call him a man, and yet...I have never encountered such a being as you describe. Perhaps we need to consult with other members here."

"Yes. Speak with Curtis and others—we need an intervention."

Eva pulled out a pin and reattached the wayward strands. "What exactly is an intervention?"

Annie realized too late that this term was not in use in the late 1800's. "We need to get her away from him."

Eva finally nodded. "I will fetch Curtis. Perhaps he will have a better understanding of what you are trying to tell me."

Curtis wasn't much better, his frown of confusion making Annie even more frantic. "Has anyone here had a relationship with my sister?"she finally asked. "Romantic, that is."

"There was that one fellow," Curtis muttered, glancing at Eva.

"Oh yes, Randolph. He left the order a month later." Eva turned to Annie. "How does this help?"

"I don't know—I thought that if she had been with a

member, that member could talk sense into her. But if he's gone..."

"We can reach him," Curtis said, "if you think it might help." He glanced at Eva. "If Elizabeth misses any more classes she will not be allowed to continue with the order."

"Can you contact this Randolph? Perhaps he could help bring her out of her bewitchment."

"As I remember they parted on bad terms," Eva answered.

"And he's now married to that woman, what is her name? The one he met here who was only a member for a month or so."

Eva nodded. "Ah yes, Sarah."

"That's it," Curtis said.

By now Annie was in panic mode. "Would you two be willing to accompany me to her house? Whenever you can manage it, but the sooner the better. You need to tell her that she might lose her place here. Maybe it will bring her back to her senses."

"Once our next class finishes, I would go with you," Curtis said, glancing at Eva. "Eva?"

She looked up at him and nodded. "If you are willing to take this seriously, I will as well."

Annie's shoulders dropped back to where they belonged. "I'll wait for you here," she murmured, looking around for a place to sit. She watched Curtis and Eva head away before she settled onto the ornate loveseat upholstered in deep burgundy velvet.

Elizabeth, a woman steeped in the Victorian era, was like a lamb to the slaughter for someone like Steve. Nausea rose up again, the idea that she was responsible clawing at her belly. She placed her hands there and took in a deep breath. With their help everything would be fine, she told herself over and over.

By the time Eva and Curtis returned, Annie was pacing back and forth across the marble tiles. She took one look at them and headed for the door, signaling them to follow her. Outside she pointed, "The house is over there, the pinkish one between…" She stopped in the middle of her sentence. The house was gone, leaving an empty spot like a missing tooth. "That's impossible," she muttered. "The house…it isn't there," she whispered.

Curtis frowned, squinting in the direction she pointed. "That would demand the highest sorcery there is." He glanced at Annie. "I am sorry to say that this is far beyond anything I have ever encountered. Sorcery of this nature is…well it is unheard of."

Annie felt like she might explode, the dress tightening around her as she attempted to draw in breath. Dark spots appeared in front of her eyes before she felt herself falling. By the time she hit the floor she was unconscious.

CHAPTER 35

SERIS

S am stopped in mid-stride. "Annie..." he muttered.

"What is it, Sam?"

Sam turned to his father. "I'm not sure. It felt like a light went out."

"A light—the link between you?"

"Maybe. I can't feel her."

Apollo closed his eyes, going utterly still. Two minutes went by before he opened them again and gazed at Sam. "She's in the past. Something has happened to her sister."

Sam began to pace up and down. "I have to go to her."

"As I said earlier, Annie is able to take care of herself. This is the hero again, the part of you that wants to gallop off on your white charger with sword in hand to save her. You cannot do anything about this. If the minster is really this creature you mentioned, we have yet come up with a plan of attack. And from what you felt, it seems that this is the crux of the matter."

"You said call in the big guns."

Apollo sighed. "I am still in the pondering mode. I am gathering my thoughts regarding these *Telchines*. I have more reading to do."

Sam looked ahead to where the wall began, his impatience

making him blurt out all he knew. "They were the children of the primordial gods. Maybe this one became separated and went slightly mad. Perhaps he was living on this meteor that crashed, or perhaps he's been here for longer than that. Will we call on the gods once we get back to your house?"

Apollo smiled. "You must learn to calm yourself. We will arrive home, I will greet my wife and then we will have tea. After that we can talk again."

Sam wanted to grab his father by the lapels and shake him. "But what if…"

Apollo held up his hand. "Annie is all right for now. The bigger problem is who this Steve is and how we combat him. Settle your thoughts. We will talk again in an hour or so."

An hour? "Steve is a *telchine*, I know it," Sam muttered. He tried to calm his thoughts, but he kept seeing Annie's face—or was that Elizabeth? He was suddenly confused. The woman was wearing a Victorian dress and was lying on the floor with her eyes closed. He was suddenly up in the air, flying above the trees and above the compound. He no longer worried, all thoughts drifting away as the cold air ruffled his feathers.

"WHERE IS SAM?"

Apollo gazed at his wife. "He is a bird right now. It is probably for the best."

"Apollo—what is going on?" she asked, staring at him.

He pulled her to him. "My dearest Constance, you always know."

"I know you and I can tell when something disturbing has happened."

"The minister was not at home, and apparently has been gone for some time. Sam suggested that this entity who has taken over the library could be one and the same. I may agree."

Constance raised a hand to her mouth. "The minister has

taken over the library? That means he...he is impossibly powerful."

"Yes, he is."

∽

By the time Sam returned, Apollo had uncovered more information in his extensive library regarding the *Telchines*. There was confusion about whether they were the children of Titans, or born from the blood of Uranus. They were skilled in metallurgy and were said to have built Poseidon's trident, the same trident that Poseidon used to kill them. Had one escaped and lived on the meteor which crashed? It seemed impossible, but if they were as strong as the text intimated, it could be true.

Sam placed his mug on the table. "I saw Annie or Elizabeth lying on the floor of a large room with her eyes closed. Is this enough incentive to do something?"

Apollo placed his mug down and turned. "I thought you might have calmed yourself by flying, but it seems I was wrong."

Sam's eyes narrowed. "It isn't your wife down there, is it?"

Apollo's eyes darkened. "Do not speak to me in that tone. I am your elder and I demand respect, no matter what is happening. I do understand your worry, but I can see that no one is in danger at the present moment. We will proceed with caution, not rush to judgement. From what you just told me, this woman could merely be asleep."

"She isn't asleep, she's hurt!" he shouted. "I am also capable of *seeing*," he ground out angrily.

Apollo stood from the table and left the room.

"Sam, you must respect him," Constance whispered. "He knows things that you do not. Believe me when I say he will not allow Annie to come to harm."

"We need to contact Gaia and Ares. Something has to be done to stop this creature, whatever it is."

"All in good time. Apollo has his methods. You must trust him."

Despite his mother's words, Sam was unable to settle his mind. He kept seeing vague images of a house floating in the ether, and a familiar woman, either Annie or Elizabeth, inside it. He roamed the grounds and breathed deeply, taking the cold air into his lungs as he thought about everything they'd talked about. Apollo had mentioned that the weather was not normal. Sam knew from his reading that the weather was one thing that the *Telchines* controlled.

He'd read stories about them whipping up storms that came out of nowhere, winds so high that they could topple houses, and snow deep enough to bury entire towns. He thought about the wind that had taken Annie, a sudden epiphany arriving in his mind. Annie had been right all along. This entity was doing all of it.

He hardly felt the snow falling on his uncovered head as he walked. He finally sat on a bench and closed his eyes, letting the scurrying thoughts drift away. And that's when he saw Annie standing in an alleyway, her lips moving as she summoned a door.

"Annie, no!" he shouted, as if she could hear him. She was wearing a loose shift that looked like it was made of silk. Was she pregnant? It certainly was loose enough to hide it if she was. But then he remembered she'd only been gone a few days. Nothing would show this early.

It seemed that she heard him as she turned and looked up, but a second later a door was there and she stepped inside. He jumped up and ran for the house, rushing inside to find Apollo, and babbling his news.

"Annie was using the door system?"

"It was either Annie or her twin, but I don't think Elizabeth knows how to summon a door."

Apollo frowned. "She must know something we do not. Perhaps this *telchine*, or whatever it is, is otherwise occupied." He turned to Sam. "I do not see her in any danger, Sam."

Sam let out his held breath, trying to calm his racing heart. "Maybe not in this moment, but…"

When Apollo fixed him with a cold stare, he stopped talking. Sam was aware that it was only when he was calm and centered that he could see her. And right now all he saw when he closed his eyes was a wasteland of white fog. "What can we do?" he muttered.

"There is not one thing we can do about this, Sam. As I said and continue to say, Annie is powerful in her own right. She is doing what she feels is the best course of action. We must allow her to find her way through this."

Sam shook his head and wished he could summon a door. He didn't think that Apollo was seeing clearly—but then, he probably wasn't either.

CHAPTER 36

When Annie's eyes opened there were several men and women standing around the couch where she lay half dressed.

"Ah, glad to see you amongst the living," Curtis said, smiling. "Why women are forced to wear such abominable clothing is beyond my understanding."

Annie sat up and glanced down at the loosened corset. Her dress lay in a heap on the floor. "I fainted."

"Yes. You could not breathe," Eva said. "You should wear what we wear," she continued, pointing to her loose caftan.

"It wasn't just the dress," Annie muttered. "My sister's house is missing."

"Yes, a shock makes matters worse," Curtis agreed. "Now, as far as the missing house, for that to happen, some very strong alchemy was used. I have never heard of such power. Who could do this?"

Annie looked into his intense stare which told her that he lusted after power. "I told you. It is the entity who now has my sister. How will I ever find her?"

His eyes lit up. "And this person hails from where?"

"From the Library of Time," Annie answered as she rose from the couch.

When she swayed, Curtis grabbed her arm to steady her. "What is this library?"

Annie shook her head. "We are wasting time. I have to find Elizabeth before he does something even worse."

"Worse than kidnapping her and using her as his dollymop?" Eva asked, her eyes widening.

Annie reached for her dress and pulled it on, but when she tried to button the front, the two sides did not come together. "He could kill her," she muttered, reaching around to try and tighten the corset. She finally gave up and shook her head. "Eva, do you have an extra robe I could wear?"

Eva nodded and hurried away.

By the time Annie was dressed in Eva's extra caftan, night was coming on. Should she try for a door or was Steve now back controlling them? And where should she go? Could the door take her to her sister's house? She wondered how the doors were controlled now that Steve was gone. Maybe he wasn't the library after all—maybe he was using sorcery to control it. Which meant that the library might possibly be hers again. "I have to go," she told Curtis and Eva who were obviously waiting for her to leave so that they could go home for the night.

"Where will you go?" Curtis asked, a hint of worry in his voice.

Annie let out a sigh. "I don't know. But I must find my sister. It is my fault she's in this predicament."

ANNIE WAS STANDING IN THE VACANT LOT WHERE ELIZABETH'S house had been. A few bricks had fallen, but other than that it was just a muddy lot and looked as though the house had never been there. She had to get home to Gaia. From there she would decide what to do next. Maybe Jack might have some ideas—

THE LIBRARY OF TIME

he'd been more than helpful recently. Good thing Sam wasn't around to see him taking care of their baby.

When she asked for a door it seemed to take a while, as though the library was thinking—either that or there was no one to run the doors at all. But as that thought went through her mind, a door appeared, hanging in the air like a misty mirage. She stepped inside and immediately felt herself moving. She had not yet thought about a destination, waiting to find out if Steve was there or not. "I want to go home to Gaia," she whispered.

It wasn't long before she felt the thunk that indicated she'd arrived. But when she opened the door she was met with a fog so thick she couldn't see through it. And on the edge of this fog, rising up like a pinkish apparition, was her sister's house. She ran toward it, hoping that she wasn't on a cloud or something nebulous from which she could drop through. It felt solid under her feet, spongy, but it held her weight across the short distance to the house. She opened the door and went inside. "Elizabeth?" she called out.

It was only a minute before her sister appeared. "Annie! Where did you come from?"

Annie didn't answer as she rushed to her sister and pulled her into a hug. "Are you all right?"

Elizabeth pulled back frowning. "I am fine, but you are behaving in an odd manner."

Annie glanced around. "Where's Steven?"

"Who is Steven?"

Annie stared at her. "Elizabeth, don't you remember me visiting the last time? You were with him—he was controlling you!"

Elizabeth looked confused. "I had a strange dream about a man with dark hair and a hypnotic stare who...oh my goodness," she whispered, turning red.

Annie let out a heavy sigh. "Have you ventured outside lately?"

She shook her head. "Way too much fog today."

"We are not on Earth. Steve is controlling you and your house. I'm not sure why you can't remember anything."

At that moment a fish-like creature appeared in the opening to the kitchen. Elizabeth let out a shriek and fell against Annie in a dead faint. As Annie eased her to the floor, the creature shifted into the entity she recognized. "How did *you* get here?" he asked.

"Better question is how did you bring this house here. Where are we?"

Steve smiled. "This is my invention. Since I will have to ease her into this new reality, I took her memories."

Annie was still wondering about the fish she'd seen. "What *are* you? You're certainly not the library."

He cocked his head and grinned. "But I am in control of it."

She glanced around the familiar room. "Everything about this house is the same."

"Of course it is. I didn't want to scare your sister by taking her to my realm without her things around her. She will love it once she gets used to it. I have learned how to be what she needs."

Annie glanced toward the fog swirling outside the window. "Is there anything out there?"

"No. I can also take her to my home on Atenua—without the house, I'm afraid. But that is for later once she accepts me."

"Home...on Atenua? I don't understand."

He laughed and a second later Elizabeth stirred, her hand going to her head. "Did I faint?"

Annie bent down to help her up. "You did faint," she murmured, glancing at Steve.

"Will you introduce me?" he asked in a posh accent. "I would love to meet this gorgeous creature. Annie has brought me here to court you, my dear. I am an old friend of hers and she believes that we are well suited."

Elizabeth rose to her feet, unsteady for a moment before her gaze went to his. She smiled before glancing at Annie. "Well, will you introduce us?"

"This is Steve. He is not a friend of mine and he will hurt you."

Steve lunged at Annie and knocked her down. In the ensuing scuffle a door appeared. Annie struggled to her knees to open it, kicking at the creature that had now turned into a fish. Grabbing her sister's hand she dragged her inside. "Home!" she shouted as the door closed behind them.

CHAPTER 37

EDGE 2325

Once she felt the familiar settling, Annie opened the door, peering out to see the familiar bookshelves. She was home in Edge. "Come on," she said, grabbing her sister's hand. When she opened the door into the living room, Jack jumped up from the couch. "Annie!" he called out. "And Elizabeth…"

Elizabeth was behind Annie and gave him a cold stare. "What are you doing here, you…you…skilamalink!"

Jack laughed. "That's a new one. I am here at your sister's behest. She left her child in my care. Is that any way to treat a person trustworthy enough to take care of a shape-shifting toddler?"

Annie had already rushed by, calling to Gaia as she went. A rabbit bounded under the couch before she could grab it. "Is she afraid of me, now?" she asked.

Jack shrugged. "She does that occasionally. I think she feels safer under there."

"What is happening here?" Elizabeth asked, looking from one to the other.

"I thought I mentioned that Gaia is a shape-shifter."

Elizabeth's eyes widened. "If you did so, I do not remember it. My goodness, what an interesting life you lead!"

The rabbit peeked out from under the couch before curiosity got the better of her. A second later Gaia was standing there, trying to decide which sister to go to. It didn't take more than a second before she chose her mother, making her way to Annie and holding her arms out to be picked up. Annie lifted her up and snuggled her against her chest. "My sweet one—how I have missed you!"

Jack stood alone by the door, watching them. Finally he asked, "What is the latest news regarding the library and Steve?"

Annie glanced at her sister, who looked confused. "Steve had control of her in London. I tried to get help from the Golden Dawn, but by the time we were on our way, her house was gone."

"What are you talking about?" Elizabeth asked. "My house is perfectly fine."

"Do you remember the man who turned into a fish?"

Elizabeth's eyes widened. "Was that not a dream?" Her hand went to her head. "I have had several very strange dreams of late."

Annie sighed and sat on the couch. "Come sit next to me, Lizzie. I have several things to tell you."

Elizabeth laughed. "I have not been called that since our parents were alive."

When Annie glanced at Jack he was staring at Elizabeth with a forlorn expression. "And you too, Jack—come sit next to us."

Jack moved carefully to the couch and sat as far from Elizabeth as he could get. "I am so sorry for my former behavior," he whispered, looking at her. "I've changed since then."

Elizabeth ignored him as she turned to Annie. "And what is this news?"

"It's for Jack too," Annie began, gazing at the man she now trusted. "It turns out that Steve is not the library after all. He is some kind of shapeshifting demon who is actually a fish-like creature. I have no idea what he really is, but he has the power to move an entire house into the clouds. I only got home with a door because I kicked him before he could take control."

"That's good, I guess," Jack said hesitantly. "But how do we know when he's in the library? He's probably in control again now, especially if you grabbed Elizabeth away from him."

Annie did a one shoulder shrug as she shifted Gaia onto the floor. All she wanted was to bask in her home and be with her sister and her baby. When Wolf appeared, Elizabeth let out a shriek. "A wolf!" she cried out, picking up her feet and tucking them under her dress.

"His name is Wolf, but he's a dog, Lizzie, and as gentle as a lamb."

Wolf wagged his tail and glanced from one sister to the other. He finally moved to Annie and licked her outstretched hand. She rubbed his ears and bent down to kiss the top of his wide head. "There's more I have to tell you," she muttered, gazing at her sister. "He...Steve, had you under his spell. He may have..." she couldn't go on as she watched her sister's eyes go wide.

"The dreams," she murmured, her cheeks turning pink. Her eyes filled with tears. "What did he do to me?"

"He bewitched you. I don't know how far he got—your dreams will probably tell you. Do you remember me coming to see you? Probably not if he wiped your memories. And then he took you and your house into some strange nebulous place."

Elizabeth frowned, her expression confused. "Are you saying that you knew about this? How could you?"

"I was attempting to fix him up with someone from the Golden Dawn, but he knew your address."

"How?"

Annie glanced at Jack. "He plucked it out of Jack's thoughts."

Jack frowned and shook his head. "Are you saying this is my fault?"

"No, Jack. But he did say it was easy to read your mind. You should probably hide your thoughts a bit better," Annie told him. "I guess you were thinking about Lizzie's house and he saw the numbers."

Jack put his hand up to his head, a startled expression on his face. "What the hell," he muttered.

Elizabeth stared into space before she gasped. "Oh no," she moaned, tears welling. She put her head in her hands and wept.

At that moment the door to the stacks flew open and Steve was standing there, anger wafting off him in waves. "You utter bitches," he growled. "You will pay!"

Gaia immediately shifted and disappeared under the couch. Wolf began barking, his lips curled back in a snarl. With one flick of Steve's hand, Wolf was thrown across the room. Annie ran to him, but luckily the dog was unharmed.

By now Jack was facing Steve, his expression not just angry but furious. "Get the fuck out of here," he growled.

Steve laughed. "And exactly who is going to make me?"

"I will," Jack said.

Annie watched him, surprised by his bravado. He couldn't stand up to this entity, and yet he was.

When Jack stepped forward, waving his hands, Steve seemed confused, his eyes darting from one hand to the other as he decided what to do. In the next second Jack had run full force into Steve's stomach, sending him sprawling. Annie watched in shock as Jack muttered a string of words, throwing something that looked like a small lightning bolt at Steve. Steve fell back but righted himself quickly. A second later Jack had disappeared. "Who wants to be next?" Steve asked. "No one? Well, then I think it's time for the three of us to go."

Annie felt herself lifting into the air, her gaze going to her sister who was in the same position. A moment later they were inside Elizabeth's house.

"Two are better than one," Steve muttered with an ugly laugh. He grabbed Annie's face and stared into her eyes. She managed to close them before his spell had done its worst, but she still felt weak and shaky. He let her go and ran to Elizabeth who was not as fast to stop his sorcery. Annie watched in horror as he lifted her and carried her quickly up the stairs. A second later she heard the door slam. When she pounded up the steps, she heard her sister moaning and then a terrified scream.

She grabbed the handle, expecting it to be locked but it opened easily. Elizabeth was on the bed, a glazed look on her face, her dress hiked up to her waist. Steve was staring down at her, his eye contact steady as he pulled off his belt. Annie rushed toward him, her nails raking across his exposed back as she tried to drag him away. When he turned on her, he was the fish, his ugly scaled face revealing a wide open mouth full of tiny teeth. "Get out of here, Lizzie!" she shrieked, trying to keep the fish-man in check. But her sister didn't move, her eyes wide as she watched him.

It was a second later that Jack appeared out of nowhere, lifted her sister into his arms and vanished. A second after that everything around her went dark.

CHAPTER 38

S am was done taking orders from Apollo. After sucking in several deep breaths and trying to calm himself, the visions returned. And this time he let them come. He knew that something was wrong and he intended to do something about it. He ran the entire way and flung himself into Atenua's library of time. "Send me to Annie!" he shouted. When nothing happened he let out a bellow. "Please forgive me for being an arrogant asshole. I promise not to do that again—but *please*—Annie's in trouble."

Before a door appeared, Apollo burst into the library. "Sam, what in hell are you doing?"

"Trying to get to my woman—she's in trouble!" he shouted.

Apollo grabbed him by the arm. "We've discussed this need of yours to be the hero, have we not? Annie is discovering who she is. If you interfere you will keep her from knowing what she's capable of. Believe me when I tell you that she's not in trouble."

"I saw her, Apollo. That creature has her."

"No, he does not have her. She has her own magical ways. She is a witch in her own right. I saw it when she was here and I see it now. Jack is there to help."

"Jack? That bastard!"

Apollo tugged Sam out of the library. He held his shoulders and stared into his eyes. "Jack is not a problem—*you* are the problem. It is why you're here."

Sam's eyes welled and he fought back tears. "I'm not the problem—Jack, he…"

"Listen to me. Jack is only there to help. He is not trying to steal Annie away from you. This situation is playing itself out the way it's supposed to. If you interfere now you could ruin everything. You will stay here and face your fears."

"That's what I'm trying to do," Sam muttered, his eyes narrowing in frustration as he wiped at them with his sleeve.

"Rushing off when you do not understand the dynamics is not facing anything. These visions are only showing what you choose to see. You are too worked up to see the truth. Facing yourself square on and realizing your destructive tendencies is what you must do. Is that not what we discussed when you made the decision to stay here?"

Sam let out a heavy sigh. "What do you suggest we do about this *telchine*?"

"We will decide that in a timely manner without losing our minds over it. Now come home and have a glass of mead."

"Mead? You have mead?"

"Yes, Sam." Apollo laughed and shook his head.

SAM WAS DRUNK BY THE TIME HE WENT TO BED. YOUNG SAM AND Thea had gone to bed early, leaving the adults to talk. There was no talk of Sam's issues, or *telchines*, or gods and goddesses. The alcohol had helped him loosen up and he and Apollo and Constance had laughed a lot about subjects he couldn't recall. He pulled off his clothes and fell face down on the bed. A second later he was snoring.

Annie's large belly swayed as she walked beside him along the trail.

Sam smiled, glancing at her. Gaia was on his shoulders and he felt like the world was his plaything.

A second later it was like someone turned off the light. He was in a place of utter darkness, fear rising into his throat. "Annie?"

He struggled against the walls that seemed to be closing in around him. "No!" he shouted, beating against the hard stones until his knuckles were bloody. "Is anyone there?"

There wasn't a sound, and in the stillness he realized that he was alone and would be for the rest of his life. And it was all his fault.

Sam woke with a scream on his lips. It was dark in his room as it always was. He felt the same sickening claustrophobia as he had in the dream. He had to get out of here. He needed light, the sun, his child, and his woman. He needed Annie with a fierceness he'd never felt before. Without her he was like an empty shell. And yet Apollo had told him over and over that he had to find himself before he could go home. What did that even mean? It might mean something for Apollo, but to him it meant nothing. Sam was literally as old as the hills. If he hadn't found himself by now, he never would. It was Annie who had discovered him, Annie who had reached deep inside him so that he could see himself through her eyes. He turned his face into the pillow and sobbed.

Some of what Apollo told him was true—he was arrogant and he went off half-cocked, so to speak. But he was also many other things—the parts of him that Annie loved could be riddled with faults. Would she love him the same way if he came home like a replica of his father?

He'd discovered the bird—wasn't that enough? Now if he needed to get away all he had to do was fly. It was better than engaging in a long ago war that took place in the 1300's. But how could he convince Apollo that he was ready to go home? He wondered what Annie's opinion would be if he explained his visions and what they made him want to do. Would she chastise him or praise him for caring? Could it be true that rushing to her was actually keeping her from her destiny? If that were true what was the meaning of love? Was he supposed to allow her the same freedoms of a woman he didn't care about? Was Apollo the only one who knew when she needed him and when she didn't? He frowned and shook his head. That was bullshit for sure.

He sucked in a breath and tried to stop the cascading thoughts—but they continued, all his suppressed feelings rising up at once. When it came to Annie, Apollo was wrong. Energy filled him, all thought gone. Annie was his responsibility, not Apollo's. Loving her came with taking care of her. He had to go to her. Now. He only hoped he wasn't too late.

CHAPTER 39

A nnie woke in a place of no light. She heard the shuffle of feet, a strike of a match and then saw a small flicker of light. When she tried to move she found that she was paralyzed, her body not responding to what her brain was telling it.

"Awake already?"

When Annie tried to speak her throat closed up and no words emerged.

"Sorry about that. I shouldn't have asked a question while you're in this compromised state. Shall I tell you about myself? I know you're curious."

Annie lay like a dead thing, unable to utter a noise or a word or move any part of herself. She didn't know if she was naked or wearing clothes since she couldn't feel fabric and couldn't see any part of her body. She was glad her heart was beating—she could feel it pulsing against her chest in a rhythm that was way too fast.

"I'm the last one of my kind—maybe that will pluck at your heartstrings, or maybe not. In any case you can't speak so it is of no consequence."

He was still in human form and sat down next to her and placed a candle between them.

"I like this body I inhabit," he said, staring down at her. "They call him the minister. He's not a good man, but he suited my purposes perfectly. I know he's handsome from the looks I've been getting from those shaped like you."

Annie was unable to move her eyes, so when he gazed at her she couldn't stop him from working his magic. She felt his power over her, but since she was paralyzed it didn't affect her in the way it had earlier.

He laughed, watching her. "I have poison glands in my mouth. I can kill with it. But I decided that keeping you still and quiet would be better—at least for now. We'll see how things go." He turned and looked into the distance. "Your friend is interesting. He seems to have some hidden talents that went undetected." He leaned over her. "What's that? Oh you can't speak." He laughed. "Yes, Jack is a mystery. I didn't see what he could do until it was over."

Annie couldn't move or speak, but she could feel, and the claustrophobia was terrifying, the panic worsening with every second that went by. Sweat poured from her, the adrenaline fueling a flight or fight response, neither of which could be activated.

He was now rolling a cigarette, his fingers holding a small pouch that he removed from his vest pocket. He poured tobacco into the rolling paper, deftly filling it before using his tongue to seal it. "I recently learned how to do this," he told her with a short laugh. "It is soothing in a way I've never experienced." He used another match to light it, pulling in a long breath of smoke before blowing it into her face. She felt a cough inside her but she couldn't cough, her body rigid as she fought against the paralysis. Her eyes watered and tears rolled down her face.

A smile appeared on his face. "Not being able to move or speak is difficult, but I wanted you to know what happened to me after my kind were all killed off. I was one of a very select group in my real life, thousands of years ago." He took another tug on the cigarette and blew it into her face again. "We were supernatural beings and unstoppable until Poseidon did away with us."

When he glanced at her again her unblinking eyes could not turn away. More tears rolled down her cheeks, itching as they slid onto her neck. He reached over and wiped them away with his sleeve.

"We made that trident for him and then he killed us with it," he continued. "We were skilled metal workers, revered for it. And then one day we were no more. I suppose we were too powerful to be allowed to live," he muttered. "Obviously I escaped. I've been on that rock for more years than I can count. "I am not sure how I found my way there...there are moments of blankness in my memories after the massacre." He smiled down at her. "Do you feel sorry for me yet?"

Annie wanted to shake her head, to scream, but she couldn't move a muscle. Where this was headed was what scared her the most. He could anything to her and she would have no power to stop him.

"We were known as wizards, as gods," he continued. "We were the original inhabitants, the children of the Titans. Can you imagine what it is like to lose every single one of your kind?" He frowned. "I've been alone for a very long time, Annie. I want to know what it is to be human—to love and bring another into the world. I'm hoping you can help me. I watched that friend of yours—I saw how he accomplished things with the female he called Izzy. It looked to be very satisfying for both of them."

Annie felt sick with a loathing she couldn't express. It was becoming obvious what he was planning. And she could do nothing to stop it.

"I could perform the act with you as you are now. It wouldn't be as much fun, but it would still achieve my purpose. I am not absolutely sure if you as a human can carry my offspring, but I hope it will not kill you. I know that you are opposed to this coupling—that is the reason I worry about waiting. Once you have your faculties and your strength you will use it against me. I will have to fight you." He stared at her. "I figure love comes with the act. If we can couple then you will love me."

Annie wanted to scream at him, to tell him that was not how love worked, but all she could do was lie there. Her insides roiled with revulsion, visions of what he was planning like a horror movie that kept replaying.

He turned and lit another cigarette, one that he'd been fiddling with while he talked. He blew out smoke and watched her face. "That bothers you, doesn't it? I can see it in your eyes. I'm sorry for making you uncomfortable. All I need is for you to allow me this one small act, and then you will know me and love me. I would be good to you. I want you to understand what I am —for you to know the anguish and pain I've been through. What I put inside you will reveal my history. It is not so much to ask, is it? You should be interested to learn about an alien species. After all, you are intelligent and curious."

The adrenaline running through her veins was making her feel as though she might explode. She knew if she wasn't paralyzed she'd be shaking like a leaf. Her sweat permeated the air and her eyes burned from the smoke from his cigarette. Terror lit up every cell in her body. How long did this paralytic last?

"It will wear off soon," he said, answering her question. "That is why we must decide. Shall I accomplish this with your permission or without it?" Steve rose to his feet and picked up the candle. "I will let you think about things. Perhaps when I return you can answer my question, at least with a nod of your head," he said, leaving her in darkness.

ANNIE MUST HAVE FALLEN ASLEEP BECAUSE THE NEXT THING SHE WAS aware of was being able to wiggle her toes. But when she tried to move her fingers, nothing happened. Her throat was raw and trying to swallow was still impossible. How long would he keep her like this? *Sam,* she thought, *please, if you can hear me. I'm in trouble.* The thought of Steve's return filled her with a terror she'd never experienced. If she could nod it would be to say no to his question, but that wouldn't stop him. He thought that if they had sex she would automatically be in love with him. And without being able to speak she couldn't tell him that love didn't work like that.

CHAPTER 40

S am ran the entire way to the library. It was very early in the morning and he hoped that Apollo was not yet up. She'd called out to him, waking him from a deep sleep. There was no question about it—Annie was in serious trouble. He looked behind him before hurrying inside the library. He took one longing look into the shadows where the shelves housed every book known to man. He didn't have the time to inspect the secrets that were hidden there. "Send me to Annie," he ordered, his hands turning into fists.

The library responded, a door hanging in the air less than a second later. He opened it and entered, closing his eyes as he pictured her in his mind. It moved suddenly, throwing him violently from one side to the other. It was only a minute or two before the movement settled and came to a halt.

When Sam rushed out he was caught inside a fog so thick it was like a white wall. When he swiveled, he saw a house that belonged in the 1800's, with coarse pinkish brick and the ornate style synonymous with Victorian row houses. He didn't stop to question where in hell he was as he headed toward it.

Inside it was dark and silent. But he felt her. Annie was here.

He decided to stay as quiet as he could, letting his intuition take him where he needed to go.

ANNIE THOUGHT SHE HEARD THE SOUND OF A STAIR CREAKING.

"You can nod now. What is your answer?"

"I can't move," she muttered weakly.

"That is not the question, Annie. I want you to love me and the only way to accomplish that is..."

"That isn't how love works," she interrupted.

"What do you mean? The act itself is love."

"No, it isn't. Love is what brings people together to perform the act."

"That cannot be. My kind..."

"I am human. Humans do not like to be forced."

"Who said anything about force?"

"You did when you made the decision to rape me."

"Rape. This is not a word I understand."

"It means to take me by force, Steve. I don't want to do this. I love another. And it will have the opposite affect of what you want. I will hate you."

"Haven't I impressed upon you what it feels like to be the last of my kind?"

"It makes me sad for you, but it does not make we want to do what you propose."

"What I deposit inside you will grow quickly. All it needs is darkness and the womb you carry." He gazed at her, his head cocked to one side. "I have studied your species in the books on those shelves. Your anatomy is quite different, but I am hopeful that with your help I can bring one of my species into existence. You will feel differently once it's done."

Annie tried to move but she was still mostly paralyzed. Her body tingled all over, as though it was close to wearing off. "I won't feel differently. And it is quite possible that our two species are not compatible. Do you want to kill me?"

He came close and kneeled next to where she lay on the bed, his fingers running along her neck and cheek and across her chest. "You are a fine specimen. Your proportions are pleasing. I think the combination will be interesting."

"No!" Annie tried to shout, her voice hoarse and weak. She didn't want him touching her or looking at her like that.

"Why do you resist me?" he asked with a puzzled look on his face. He moved closer and pulled up her dress. "This is the place where we connect?" he asked, looking down. He pulled off her underwear and explored. "I watched the act but was not close enough to see how it was accomplished."

"Stop," she muttered, watching his body begin to change into the creature he really was. Part human and part fish was the only description she could think of. She lay frozen as he got into position, his mouth moving like a fish underwater as he assessed what to do next. She saw the part of him that would enter her, a long protuberance that waved in the air. Bile rose in her throat, sickness taking over as she attempted to twist away. "Please don't."

He glanced at her, his weird fish eyes staring at her as he lowered his body. She felt it against her, desperation making her cry out as she attempted to twist away. He was going to do it and there was nothing she could do to stop him. She would die from this. It was at that moment that she heard the crash of the door and saw Sam storm into the room.

He let out a bellow and threw himself against the creature. They fell off the bed together as he grappled with the scales, his hands unable to keep hold of the slippery monster. Sam let out a cry when it bit him in the neck, blood pouring from the wound. He tried to get his hands free, but the creature pinned his arms. Annie watched in horror, trying to move.

A sudden storm erupted in the room, winds swirling, and freezing rain making the floors slick. The wind howled like a wild animal, the sound eerie inside the closed space. Annie covered her face as the rain pelted down, freezing as it hit her cheeks and her exposed legs and lower body. She began to shake.

She struggled to move, her entire focus on ridding her body of the paralytic. She had to help Sam before it was too late. When she got control of her fingers, fire flashed across the scales, an unearthly shriek coming from the creature. Annie's body was boneless as she slid off the bed and landed on the floor. Her eyes met Sam's as he grappled with the fish man. By the time Sam pulled off his leather belt and looped it around the creature's upper body, she had gotten control of her legs and arms. But her movements were still jerky and un-coordinated.

"Call up a door," she muttered hoarsely, taking hold of her shift and ripping a strip off the bottom. She crawled to where Sam held the creature and tied the piece tightly around his head, covering the creature's eyes and his mouth. "His sorcery comes from his eyes," she explained.

The fish tail thrashed wildly as he tried to escape, but Sam held onto him, the muscles in his arms bulging. "Where do we send him?"

"Back to where he came from."

Sam stared at her. "Ancient Rhodes?"

Annie didn't register what Sam had said, only wanting the creature gone. "Do it before he uses sorcery again."

When Sam called up a door it appeared immediately, hanging in the air like the miracle it was. He opened it, and with Annie's help they pushed him inside. "Take him to Rhodes where he originated!" Sam shouted.

When the door closed and disappeared, Annie fell back on the floor, her eyes closing. Sam knelt beside her. "Annie?" he whispered.

"Sam," she whispered, reaching for him. He pulled her into his arms, rocking her like a baby as tears fell from his eyes.

. . .

IT WAS A WHILE BEFORE ANNIE REGAINED ENOUGH STRENGTH TO move. Her body felt strange and loose-jointed. Sam helped her stand and held her against him to keep her steady. She leaned into him, tears welling and trickling down her ashen face.

It was several minutes before she let out a long sigh and pulled away to look at him. "He…"

"Don't think about it, Annie. You're safe now."

"I called to you."

"I know—I heard you."

" Did Apollo send you through the doors?"

"NO!"

Annie's eyes widened at his vehemence. "What happened?"

Sam's mouth thinned and he shook his head. "He…he under-mined the last shred of confidence I had left. He told me that you needed to deal with your life without me, that your destiny was only achievable if you were on your own."

Annie stared at him. "What?"

Sam frowned, looking away. "He said that I always have to be the hero, riding to your rescue. According to him you don't need a hero because you have magic of your own."

Annie frowned. "If you hadn't come when you did I might be dead. That thing wanted me to have its offspring—some kind of horrible creature that would probably kill me while it was in the womb." She glanced up at him. "It poisoned me—I was para-lyzed for… I don't know how long. It just wore off."

Sam's expression clouded. "Gods, Annie, I'm so sorry. I wish I'd come sooner. "

Annie was truly crying now, hiccuping sobs releasing the fear and horror she'd experienced. "He told me it would grow quick-ly…" She let out scream at the thought of it being inside her, and how close he'd been to accomplishing what he wanted.

"I need you," she muttered through her tears. "I need you to be the hero—I love that part of you." She shuddered. Sam pulled her close again, tucking her head under his chin. "You're safe now. That thing is gone."

Annie felt the blood on his neck. "He bit you. I'm surprised you aren't paralyzed or dead."

Sam reached up and felt the spot that still burned, his fingers coming away covered in blood. "Maybe I'm immune," he muttered.

"We need to clean and disinfect it."

Sam didn't answer, his head buried in her hair as he let out a ragged sigh.

ANNIE WAS IN NO SHAPE TO GO ANYWHERE, AND SO THEY LAY together on the bed, going over things as she slowly recovered her equilibrium.

"Apollo insisted that the magician isn't me either," Sam muttered. "He said I need to find out what's underneath all that." His brow furrowed. "I tried, but all I came up with was emptiness. The hero and the magician are who I am. Can you love me even with my faults?"

Annie managed to smile. "What you call your faults are what I love about you the most."

Sam let out a heavy sigh. "Now that I know I'm a hawk, I can use that instead of heading into timelines where I don't belong."

Annie shivered in his arms. She kept reliving what had happened, the terror replaying inside her mind. "That thing was about to impregnant me, Sam. I saw its anatomy and it is not like ours. I told him that it might kill me, but it didn't matter."

Sam shook his head, an expression of fury on his face. "You shouldn't have been in this situation. The first time I tried to leave, Apollo stopped me. He was adamant you were fine. You weren't fine, and if I'd come earlier you wouldn't have had to go through this horror."

Annie grabbed his hand and twined her fingers through his.

"The creature seemed to think that having sex would result in me loving it. I told him that wasn't true, but he refused to believe me." Annie let go of his hand and pulled the pillow case off the pillow and reached up to staunch the blood on Sam's neck. "And how would Apollo know? From what you describe it seems that he's the arrogant one. He's not who I thought he was."

Sam gazed at her. "He was trying to do what he thought was right, but his behavior surprised me too."

She felt along his neck where the fangs had sunk into the skin. "And what is that *thing*?" she asked. "He said he was a god, but when he shifted he looked half fish."

"He's a *telchine*, an ancient fish-like creature that was part of a group of sea-god magicians and smiths who built Poseidon's trident. I remembered reading about them. Poseidon killed them, but apparently one survived."

"He told me his story but I was so terrified I can hardly remember what he said. I knew what was coming, and that's all I could think about." Annie shuddered and crawled into his arms and put her head on his chest. "Please don't go back to Atenua."

Sam pulled back and met her eyes. "Are you kidding? I would never leave you after what just happened." He wrapped his arms securely around her body. "The doors worked for me," he whispered.

Annie glanced up at him, her eyes misty. "I hope it means what you think it means." She glanced at the room where they lay together on the bed. "This house is Elizabeth's and belongs in London. How will we get it back there?"

Sam's eyes widened. "Even if my magic is restored, I'm not sure I can perform a feat of that caliber."

"Maybe with the two of us?"

"That's an interesting idea. Where's Elizabeth?"

"Jack rescued her—he probably took her to Edge. He saved her, Sam." Her eyes filled again and she dabbed at them with her sleeve. "I haven't told you about how many times he's taken care of our daughter."

Sam stroked her hair. "Let's go home. From there we can discuss what to do about the house. Jack might have some ideas."

"That's a new one—Jack on our side?"

Sam laughed and then tipped her chin up so he could kiss her. He felt his love as though it had been buried beneath a thousand pounds of heavy stones. Something good had happened from his time with Apollo, but it wasn't what either he or Apollo had expected.

CHAPTER 41

Apollo searched the compound for Sam but didn't find him.

When he entered their bedroom Constance woke up. "What is wrong?" she asked, watching him pace back and forth.

"Sam's gone."

"Gone, where?"

"I do not know. But he is not in his room and not on the grounds."

When Thea let out a cry, Constance rose and hurried out of the room. When she returned with the baby she sat on the bed to feed her. "Where would Sam go, Apollo? He can't use the doors. Maybe he's in bird form?"

He shook his head and let out a heavy sigh. "I might have gone too far, Constance. I might have pushed him past his limit."

"Limit? Of what?"

"My reminders that he should not give in to his hero side. I told him Annie needed to find her way through whatever is going on."

Constance stared at him. "I read about the archetypes in the library. Sam has always been the hero. Think of our young Sam.

He's the same. He lives for saving whatever needs to be saved, even me when I'm unhappy."

Apollo looked away. "I told him he needed to find himself underneath all that. And his magic too. I think he needs to face who he is without those props."

Constance let out a huff of annoyance. "Props? They don't prop him up—they *are* him. How can you have steered him so wrong?"

Apollo turned, his face a mask of anger and frustration. "I have tried my best. I thought he agreed with me—he seemed to realize his mistakes. He understands that rushing in to save Annie is not needed. She has magic of her own."

"He obviously had a vision, Apollo—you can't expect him to ignore that. What is the point of being together if he can't help her when she needs it?"

Apollo ran frustrated fingers though his hair. "She doesn't need it! Annie is a self-sufficient woman with her own magic who doesn't need anyone!"

Constance stood so quickly that the baby became dislodged from the nipple and began to cry. "I cannot believe you actually think that! Annie needs our son. And he needs her!" She left him standing there as she hurried out of the room, the baby in her arms.

Apollo sat on the bed and put his head in his hands. Was Constance correct? Had he steered their son toward an impossible future? He'd been so sure of his guidance, his knowledge of what Sam needed from him. But now—now he wondered if he was wrong. He closed his eyes and thought of Sam, trying to discern where he might be. What he got back was an image of Annie and Sam together. He'd somehow found his way back to her. How had he done it?

Apollo was angry and upset with himself and with Sam. And if he was honest, he was angry with Constance too. How arrogant Sam was to ignore his superior wisdom and leave like that. And why was Constance taking Sam's side? But then he had the same thought about himself. His arrogance had put Sam over the edge. And if Sam had a message from Annie there was no way he wouldn't follow up on it. He let out a sigh and shook his head. Constance had spoken the truth as she always did.

"Godsdamn it!" he yelled, picking up a vase and hurling it at the wall. When it broke into a million pieces he saw the irony of what he'd done. His arrogance had taken over. The same arrogance he accused Sam of having.

APOLLO WAS IN THE LIBRARY, SEARCHING FOR ANY TRACE THAT A door had been used. A whiff of something he couldn't define and a misty residue lifted into the air. Sure enough, a door had been used—it must have taken Sam...somewhere. But where that might be was not revealing itself. The only way to find out where he'd gone was to ask the doors to take him to Sam. But first he had to talk with Constance.

On his way back to the compound he thought about the situation, wondering why the door was listening to Sam again. It must mean that the creature was occupied elsewhere. But it had to be more than that—was Sam's magic back? Maybe the *telchine* was doing something to Annie. That could explain the doors allowing him in since the library responded to Annie now. But that wasn't what his visions had shown him. Earlier he'd seen her with her sister and Jack. Something must have happened after that.

When he reached the compound garden he was met with a stony-faced Constance. "I am very angry with you," she whispered, her eyes narrowing.

When he reached for her she backed away. "Do not touch me. Why did you not mention what you and Sam had discussed? I could have helped."

"Constance," he began, trying to find the right words, "I... thought I knew what he needed. I know now that I was wrong."

"Why not discuss this with me?"

Apollo looked at the ground. "I was afraid you would dissuade me from what I knew to be the right course of action."

"So, you knew that I would disagree." She stared hard at him, her eyes darkening.

"I suppose I feared that you might. You are softer than I am."

"Softer or more discerning? Honestly, at this moment I feel the need to be away from you. I have to work through my anger. You will sleep in the guest bedroom," she said, turning too leave.

"Constance, you can't mean that!" he called after her.

She turned. "I do mean it. I want you to take a good hard look at what you have done. Our grown son will more than likely never visit us again. When will I ever see him?"

"Where do you think he is?"

"He's exactly where he should be—with Annie."

Apollo wondered how she knew. She had no magic whatsoever. He let out a sigh, his heart heavy as he watched her disappear into the house. The only way forward was to ask the library to take him to his son.

He left the compound and hurried back to the library, hoping that the doors would send him where he asked to go. He had little affinity with the doors, but maybe in an emergency they would listen to him. This one was the original and would belong to young Sam once he came of age. The library had never belonged to Apollo.

Once he was inside, he thought of how to word his request. He glanced at the shelves disappearing into the shadows, the books mocking him as he stood there—an intruder. "Please help me. I need to reach my grown son," he begged. He was suddenly stripped bare, the knowledge of what he'd done making him bow his head in shame. What a fool he'd been.

It didn't take long before a door hung in the darkness, dust motes floating around it. He pulled down the handle and stepped inside.

CHAPTER 42

E ven though she wriggled to get away, Annie pressed Gaia against her chest and kissed the top of her head. When Sam held out his arms she handed the baby to him. Gaia seemed much more interested in her father who she hadn't seen for quite some time. She babbled a few nearly recognizable words as she played with his hair.

Annie watched and laughed. "Your hair is so long, Sam!"

Sam shrugged and put Gaia down, watching in wonder as she toddled across the living room and stopped in front of Jack and Elizabeth. When she crawled into Jack's lap, Sam glanced at Annie, his expression saying it all.

"You've been away," she whispered. "With Cecily gone just be glad that Jack was here."

He smiled and reached for her hand. "I can hardly believe I'm home."

Annie smiled. They had not yet had a minute to themselves. There were many things to discuss, not the least of which was her sister's house still lurking in some nebulous cloud system. She moved to the couch and sat down next to her sister. "Are you staying in Edge for a while?"

Elizabeth glanced at her before looking at Jack. "I might stay for a day or two."

Annie noticed the look exchanged between them. Was it possible that they were now friends? "If you go back to London we have to figure out how to get your house back."

Elizabeth glanced at Jack again before she said, "That settles it, I suppose. There is no place for me in London at the moment. I hope the people will not suspect witchcraft when it suddenly appears again."

Annie widened her eyes, trying to imagine the scenario. "First we have to decide if it's even doable. Sam does not have the power of the *telchine*."

"Do not mention that creature," she hissed, her face blanching. A second later Jack placed the baby on the floor and took her hand in his. He leaned close and whispered something in her ear that Annie couldn't hear.

Gaia came over to Annie and held up her chubby arms. "Mama?"

Annie laughed. "Did you hear that, Sam?" she called.

Sam was across the room, his arms folded as he leaned against the wall watching everything. "Does she know Papa too?" He left his spot and kneeled in front of where Gaia sat in Annie's lap. "Want to come to Papa?" he asked her.

"Papa," she repeated, her gaze going to Jack.

"I'm Papa," Sam said, an expression of frustration appearing.

"Give her time," Jack muttered. "Once I'm out of here things will get back to normal."

"Where are you going?" Elizabeth asked, creases appearing in her forehead.

"There's no room for us here," he told her.

"Us?"

"Yes, you and me. I thought maybe we'd...get a room in town."

"A room," she repeated.

"Or two rooms," he added quickly.

Annie glanced at her sister. "Have you and Jack reconciled?"

"Jack saved my life," she murmured. "That thing would have...well, you know. We had a long talk."

Annie didn't say it, but it seemed to her it might have been more than a talk. "You and Jack are okay then."

Elizabeth glanced at Jack who answered for her, "Lizzie and I got our misunderstandings straightened out. We realized that a lot of our animosity was caused by our mutual attraction."

Elizabeth nodded. "Jack apologized. I do not know whether to trust him, but I must admit that he no longer resembles the man who jilted me."

"Did Atenua do it, or was it taking care of Gaia?" Annie asked Jack.

Jack smiled, his eyes going soft as he glanced at Elizabeth. "It was mostly Lizzie. I'm utterly smitten."

Annie examined his expression, looking for a hint of his calculated deviousness. Jack had always been a woman's man, but he never stuck around for long. She wondered if he was serious about this. The idea of him leading her sister on again was not a happy thought. "I suggest we do a tarot reading," she said.

Instead of refusing, Jack nodded eagerly. "Happy to."

Elizabeth clapped her hands and laughed. "What fun!"

When Annie glanced at Sam she was struck with the expression on his face. He sat with Gaia on his lap, a contented smile hovering around his lips as she looked up at him and tugged at his long hair. Had she ever seen that look on his face?

Annie rose and grabbed the worn Rider-Waite Tarot deck from her desk against the wall and handed it to Jack. "Shuffle and cut it three times from left to right. Ask any questions while you're doing it—the tarot will answer."

Jack did as she asked, watching her as she stacked the three parts back into one on the coffee table in front of the couch. She pulled a card from the top and turned it over. *The Fool.*

Jack chuckled, looking up at Elizabeth who had risen and stood next to the couch watching. "Yup—that's me, about to walk off a cliff into the abyss."

"This card represents someone who is starting out, Jack. New beginnings, and not knowing what to expect. It is a positive card, and if I'm right, it seems in line with what's going on with you at the moment."

Jack raised his eyebrows at Elizabeth who smiled. "I'm willing to walk off a cliff," he murmured.

Annie turned over the next card, revealing the three of swords. Before telling Jack the meaning, she turned over the next card which was the three of cups.

She looked down at the two cards—an interesting combo. "Emotional turmoil," she said, glancing at Jack. "These two cards together usually represent what is happening right now, not in the past or the future. And two threes represent growth and a creative solution to a problem. The three of cups usually has to do with a sense of belonging. An abundance of emotion," she added. "With the three of cups there could be some tears involved."

Elizabeth's mouth opened, her eyes on Jack. "This is what we were speaking about last night," she murmured.

Jack looked confused. "Was it?"

Elizabeth blushed and looked down. "How to manage a relationship," she whispered, "after everything that has happened between us."

Jack nodded slowly. "We did talk about that. I'd forgotten since we covered so much. As I remember, a few tears were shed."

Elizabeth nodded, her cheeks going pink.

Annie turned over the next card in the layout. *Judgement*. "A period of awakening," Annie told him. "Self-reflection."

Elizabeth smiled. "Exactly right," she murmured.

Annie glanced up at her when she turned over *The Queen of Cups*. "This card is you, Lizzie."

"What does it mean?" she asked, peering at the woman wearing a crown and sitting on a throne. She wore a beautiful gown and held a golden chalice.

"I suspect that in this reading it is telling Jack that there is a woman in his life who represents compassion, caring and emotional stability. I would say it's telling him to go for it."

Jack reached for Elizabeth's hand. "See? I told you, didn't I?" He pulled her down on the couch next to him, both of them studying the layout.

Annie watched her sister's expression go from dubious to elated, her eyes sparkling as she looked up at Jack. *What a change*, she thought to herself. But the Tarot had spoken loud and clear. This was meant to be. She smiled to herself.

~

LIZZIE AND JACK HAD GONE TO FIND A ROOM IN TOWN AND ANNIE and Sam were in bed when they heard the slam of a door and some incoherent mumbling from downstairs. Wolf was next to the bed and let out a loud bark before rushing for the door and racing down the steps. And then Gaia began to cry, woken out of her slumber.

Sam was already up and pulling on his trousers. He glanced at Annie. "Stay here."

She nodded and reached for Gaia, pulling her close as she watched Sam head away. She finally rose and headed to the door to listen in on the mumbled conversation going on downstairs. It was Apollo.

"Why did you leave like that?"

"I had to. Annie needed me."

"I told you that rushing off…"

"I know what you told me and I disagree. And Annie disagrees too. What she loves most about me is exactly what you wanted me to get rid of."

There was a long moment of silence before Apollo said, "Constance is angry with me. We are not speaking because of this."

"Because of…what exactly?"

There was heavy sigh and the sound of shuffling feet before the creak of the couch springs. "I…I have to admit that I might have been hasty," Apollo muttered. "To me it seemed that you were hiding under a heavy mantle of what Constance referred to as 'archetypes'. I wanted you to discover who you are beneath all that, but when Constance told me that you've always been the hero, I realized I might have been wrong."

When Sam didn't speak, Annie took the moment to pick up the very awake Gaia. She carried her downstairs, gazing at the two men, so alike, who sat next to one another on the couch. "I have something to say."

Both men looked up.

"I need what Sam is," she began, her gaze focused on Apollo. "I need all of him, not just the parts that Sam or you deem to be his best parts. It's his faults that bring us closer together. We've literally been to hell and back. And what I've learned is that we are meant to be. If he goes off like he has in the past, then so be it. I can deal with it as long as I'm not worried that he'll end up dead somewhere in a 1300's ditch."

Sam laughed at that. "I have my bird part now. The hawk knows how to rid me of my restlessness. But I appreciate your faith in me, Annie."

"It isn't faith, Sam, it's love."

Apollo watched her, nodding. "I've just learned something."

Annie gave him a quizzical look, waiting as he rubbed a hand across his stubbly face. "I've just figured out that my beautiful Constance is my tether to reality. She keeps me grounded. Without her I would be an arrogant asshole."

At that Sam let out a roar of laughter, glancing at Annie before staring at his father. "I guess we're more alike than either of us knew."

Apollo laughed too, the atmosphere lightening.

Annie left them to it, picking up Gaia and heading up the stairs to bed. She was still exhausted from her ordeal and she had a feeling that Apollo and Sam would be up talking for the rest of the night.

CHAPTER 43

"You did *what?*"

Annie laughed at Apollo's surprised tone and the look of shock on his face. "Sam sent the *telchine* to...well, I don't know exactly where...he told the library to take him back where he came from."

Despite her interrupted sleep, Annie had risen when she usually did and headed downstairs with the baby to make tea. The two men had never been to bed. It seemed that things had been settled between them by the softness in Sam's tired eyes and the feeling of calm they both exuded.

Sam turned to Apollo. "The *telchine* was in fish form at the time. I wonder if that means the minister is back in Seris?"

Apollo glanced at Annie. "What did he do to you?" he asked, his expression worried.

"He...he tried to impregnate me. Sam arrived in the nick of time."

Apollo stared at her. "You must have been terrified, Annie. And I would wager to say that if he managed what he intended you would die in the process of it. From my reading, the *telchines* have a completely different anatomical system. Your womb and reproductive system is not compatible for either carrying their offspring or giving birth to it."

Annie shuddered, remembering how she'd felt in that moment. "I told him as much, but he wasn't planning to stop. Thank the gods for the hero in Sam."

Sam glanced at his father before rising to stand next to Annie. "I would have come sooner if I had known," he murmured, putting his arm protectively around her shoulders.

Apollo shook his head and looked down. "It was because of me that Sam wasn't there for you. I am so terribly sorry that you had to go through that. I am grateful to my son that the *telchine* was stopped before he managed to complete the act."

Annie leaned into Sam before she placed her mug on the table and sat. "So, the body I called Steve is actually the minister? Apollo, are you sure? Have you met him?"

Apollo leaned forward to pour himself tea from the earthenware teapot Annie had placed on the kitchen table. "I have only heard rumors, but have never seen the man. It seems from talking with his housekeeper he might not be as bad as I once thought."

Sam poured himself a cup and took a sip. "If the *telchine* came in on the meteor, as he told Annie, he was not in Seris for more than a a few weeks."

"The housekeeper said he'd been gone for some time."

Sam stood and began to pace. "How much time? You need to check—see if he's there. And if he is there, does he have a memory of being the *telchine*?"

Apollo nodded and rose from the table. "All interesting questions, but I should get back. Constance will be worried."

"Perhaps she has forgiven you by now," Annie murmured, watching him.

"I hope so. Constance angry is like having a hive of hornets after you."

Sam laughed, glancing at Annie. "I know the feeling well."

"Do you think we can really be rid of the *telchine*?" Annie asked worriedly.

"From what you two told me, it could be the last of him—his home is ancient history—he's way back in time now. Using the doors should give you the answers."

"But you don't use the doors."

"I did this time, but normally I don't need them."

Annie glanced at Sam. "Are we brave enough to make sure he's really gone?"

Sam let out a sigh. "I think we have to be, Annie. If we are to get on with our lives we have to know that the library is ours again."

Annie glanced at Apollo as her thoughts cascaded down a terrible road. "Can you see into the future?"

Apollo shook his head. "You are on your own with this one. But I think Sam is right. If you don't test it, you will worry."

"Can you test it?"

Apollo smiled and shook his head. "I have no affinity with the library. The only reason it provided a door is because I begged it to take me to Sam. We have the original library in Seris, but it has always been my son's project, not mine."

Project. Annie thought about that. The library was hardly a project. It was alive. Would they be able to trust it after what they'd been through? Steve and the thing he turned into haunted her.

APOLLO LEFT SHORTLY AFTER THIS CONVERSATION. ANNIE WAS STILL tired, her arms and legs fatigued as though she'd run a marathon. The paralysis and the terror of her experience must have done more than she thought. When she glanced at Sam she noticed the dark shadows under his eyes. He'd had no sleep at all.

As soon as Gaia was ready for her nap, Annie picked her up

and headed for the stairs. "I'm going to take a nap," she told Sam who was reading a book on the couch.

He looked up. "I'll join you once I've finished this chapter."

"What's the book?" she asked.

He turned it so she could read the title. *Ancient Creatures from Ancient Times.*

"*Telchines.*"

He nodded.

Annie turned and headed up the stairs, too tired to even ask what he'd learned.

ANNIE WOKE WHEN SAM CURLED AROUND HER BODY AND PULLED her against him. She was sleeping on her side and relished the warmth and closeness, letting out a sigh of contentment. But a moment later she felt him. He was not in a sleeping mood. "Sam? Did you sleep at all?" she whispered.

"A little. But being with you is not conducive to rest right now. We haven't celebrated our reunion."

Annie turned her head. "What about Gaia?"

"She's sound asleep. She lost sleep last night too."

"That's true," Annie whispered. By then Sam had turned her to face him, his mouth finding hers. She sank against him, her body relaxing, but a second later she had a vision of the *telchine* and had to pull away.

"What's wrong?"

"It's…what happened to me…I…"

Sam held her and ran his fingers through her hair, his mouth against her ear. ""We can go as slowly as you need."

Annie was on the verge of tears, her body shaking. "I don't think I can right now…"

But Sam had other ideas, his fingers working along her skin as he kissed her neck. Annie fought against herself, trying to let go of the claustrophobia, the feeling of being trapped, but she couldn't relax. "Sam...I..."

He pulled back to look at her. "If you don't want to I can wait."

"I want to, it's just that..."

He let out a heavy sigh and moved away. It was a good thing because a second later Gaia woke up.

CHAPTER 44

Annie was plagued with nightmares, her screaming waking both Sam and the baby. Sam was always there for her, trying to calm her racing heart and taking care of Gaia until Annie was settled again.

In the daytime Annie tried to get hold of herself. She did the Tarot, focusing on her fears and how to let go of them. She got the *Tower* and the *Hanged Man* more than once. The tower card was obvious, sudden unexplained change and destruction. The hanged man card had to do with having patience, surrendering and gaining new perspectives. They both made sense but they didn't help pull her out of what was going on. Both her body and mind had been injured during the encounter. She tried several times to explain to Sam what was going on, but his answer was always the same. "You need to let me in. I can heal you."

"But I can't right now—that's what I'm trying to tell you!"

Weeks went by in which Sam tried to make love to her. But every time she came close to allowing it, a vision would pop up and she would be paralyzed with fear again.

"What can I do?" Sam asked her one morning, his expression verging on desperation.

Annie could see the frustration in his expression. "I wish I knew," she murmured. "The visions are always of that thing hovering over me. The feel of him examining me, and then..." she shivered and began to cry.

Sam pulled back, frowning. "You didn't tell me about that. Gods, Annie. No wonder you're feeling this way. Did he actually touch you there?"

Annie nodded, shivering again. "He wanted to figure out..."

"I get it," he interrupted. "But my gods--what you went through. If I had known..." He shook his head. "You need to talk to someone about this. I promise I won't bother you again until you feel ready. But please try, for us."

Annie pressed her face against him and sobbed.

Two months went by, two full months of horrible visions. Sam was holding himself together by a thread, his frustration simmering. He'd given up on trying anything, their bedtime ritual now sleeping far apart and turned away from each other. Annie wondered if the *telchine* had cast some horrible spell on her. It wasn't normal to have these nightmares go on and on. When she mentioned it to Sam, he just stared at her.

"How could the *telchine* accomplish that? You didn't complete the act and he's long gone. Please reach out to friend—talk with someone other than me. Please, Annie."

"Maybe he did something to me when I was paralyzed."

"I think it's trauma. And the only way to get past it is to work through it."

Annie gazed at him, tears forming. "You mean I have to allow you to..."

"No. What I'm saying is talk to someone—how about Cecily, or one of your friends in town? Once you do that you and I can work through it—but not until you're ready."

"I know you're frustrated. I am too. But every time I think

about it, terror goes through my body— I'm like a rape victim even though I wasn't raped."

"How do rape victims get over it?"

Annie shrugged and turned away to deal with Gaia. She picked her up and walked toward the door. "I'm going for a walk," she muttered, heading out. Winter was in its last throes and the sun was a welcome sight.

"Can I come?"

Annie turned. "Not now, Sam. I need to be alone."

The expression on his face nearly broke her heart. She was hurting him every day and didn't know how to stop. His patience would not last forever—she knew him too well.

WHEN CECILY APPEARED ON THE PATH, ANNIE WAS SO SURPRISED she stopped in her tracks and stared. She hadn't seen her in months and with what Sam had suggested it seemed more than coincidental. Annie expected her to turn around and hurry away, but instead the pixie-like woman asked her how she was.

Annie put Gaia on the ground, watching her toddler run toward the ocean in the distance. "Not great," she admitted.

Cecily walked closer, a frown appearing her face. "You don't look well, Annie. You've lost weight."

"Have I?"

Cecily nodded, taking the lead toward the baby in the distance. Gaia had stopped and was watching a flock of seagulls. "What's happening now? Is Sam off on another ill-advised trip?"

Annie shook her head, tears welling. "It's way worse than that," she muttered.

"Okay, spill," Cecily said, moving to a log and sitting down.

Annie watched Gaia who was now collecting shells. She began her story haltingly, but as Cecily asked questions she found it was easy to let it all out. When she came to a stopping place Cecily let out a heavy sigh. "This is serious. How long did you say this has been going on?"

"It's over two months since it happened."

"Poor Sam," she muttered.

"What about me?"

Cecily looked up. "You are a victim, Annie. I understand how hard this must be. I only said that because I know how he is. Sex is important to him."

"It's important to me too."

Cecily gazed at her. "You and Sam have always connected in this way. Without it, you must feel estranged."

Annie nodded. "It's horrible. Every time he comes close I cringe. I hate to be like this. I've been wondering if that creature put a spell on me—he was a powerful sorcerer."

Cecily shook her head. "This is major trauma. You were paralyzed without any control over anything. He touched your private parts and you saw his anatomy and pictured what he was going to do to you. You were vulnerable in a way you've never been before. You thought he would impregnate you with an alien who you would have to carry inside you and then birth. That is beyond terrifying, Annie."

"So, how do I get over it?"

"I think Sam is right. The only way out is through. You and Sam have to find a way together." She glanced at Annie. "You love each other and you are very attracted to one another. Try and focus on that. You'll figure it out." She chuckled. "But don't wait until he's so frustrated that he leaves."

Annie smiled. "He's very frustrated."

Cecily laughed. "I can only imagine."

"Want to come back and say hello?"

Cecily shook her head. "I think I'll wait until you two have worked this through."

Annie gave her a hug, tears welling. "I've missed you."

"I've missed you too. Now go home and find your man and take the steps to deal with this."

Annie rose and collected Gaia and headed up the path toward the library.

~

Two days went by before she told Sam what Cecily had suggested.

"That's what I've been saying for over a month now," he said, shaking his head. "I promised I wouldn't push you and I haven't, but it's been torture for me."

"I'm willing to try now," she muttered, feeling a shiver of apprehension. "Talking about it to a friend really helped."

"Tonight then?" he said.

Annie looked away, her arms going tight around her body.

"Annie," he said, taking hold of her arm, "It's only me...do you think I would force you?"

She shook her head and tried to smile.

The rest of the day went by in a blur as Annie kept envisioning what might happen. Her thoughts went from rising from the bed and rushing away, to bursting into tears, to a feeling of terror that took over her stomach.

When it was finally time for bed they waited until Gaia was settled and sound asleep before they embarked on their plan. They'd placed her crib on the far side of the room where it was the darkest.

They undressed together, something they hadn't done since Annie's experience with the *telchine*.

"You've lost a lot of weight," Sam murmured, looking her over worriedly.

Annie glanced at him. "Nerves," she muttered.

"My gods, if I had known I would have suggested this sooner."

"I wouldn't have done this sooner, Sam. I don't even know if I can do it now."

"Annie," he murmured, taking her in his arms. "I love you."

She tried hard not to pull away, but it went against everything she was feeling. "I might not be ready for this."

Sam let her go and gazed at her. "You're ready. You have to be. We can't go on like this."

She glanced up at him, her eyes welling. "I know. I'm sorry."

"Don't be sorry, just try. That's all I ask."

Sam moved to the bed and pulled back the comforter. He lay down on his side, waiting until she did the same. Annie climbed in and faced him.

"Did Cecily say how to go about this?" Sam asked.

Annie shook her head. "She only said to let our mutual attraction guide us."

"Fine for her to say—mine is there, but is yours?"

Annie gazed at him, her eyes roaming across his bare chest, his wide shoulders, and the tawny hair tangled around the familiar face she loved. His eyes were dark with longing. She felt a pang of guilt. "I'm sorry."

"Guilt doesn't cut it right now. Can I touch you?"

"Where?"

"Where do you want me to touch you?"

Annie wanted him to touch her all over in all her secret places, but she knew she would balk if he did. She felt torn in two, one part that wanted him and the other terrified. She reached a hand out and caught his. She placed his hand on her breast, hoping she wouldn't suddenly have to pull away.

He left his hand there and moved closer, his leg leg sliding along her thigh. She fought with herself, every instinct wanting to pull away. She let out a heavy sigh and tried to focus on his face. He was watching her with a look in his eyes that normally set her on fire.

"Progress," he muttered. "Your turn."

Annie moved closer until her breasts touched his chest. She took in a deep breath.

"Okay so far?" he whispered.

She nodded.

"My turn," he said, moving so that his lower body was pressed against hers.

When Annie felt him she pulled away.

"Shit, Annie. What's wrong?"

"I...I got scared for a second."

"Scared of what? It's only me and you here."

"I know—I'm..."

"Don't say you're sorry again. Can I kiss you?"

"Yes," she murmured.

His hands went to each side of her face as his lips slid along hers. Instead of deepening the kiss he pulled back.

She opened her eyes. "What are you doing?"

"Teasing you."

She laughed and pressed her mouth to his before she realized what she was doing. This time he deepened the kiss and pulled her tight against him. When it was over they stayed that way.

"Are you okay?" he asked.

She felt his warmth, and the part of him that was pressed solidly against her lower belly. If they stayed like this she could manage it. She nodded.

"Can I touch you in the places you used to like?"

Annie took in a deep breath. She was free to move around, free to get out of bed if she wanted to. She was not paralyzed and there was no monster standing over her. Sam would never force her. She gazed at him, their eyes meeting. "I forgot what you look like and how it feels to touch like this."

"Without clothes you mean?"

She nodded and smiled. "I love your body."

Sam grinned. "And I love yours. I would like to worship it right about now."

When Annie laughed it released some of the tension she felt.

"Are you going to answer my question?"

She hesitated until she realized that there was a deep ache inside her, a feeling of tension that indicated that she was ready.

Mentally she wasn't so sure, but she nodded. "I have the physical part down, but..."

"And mentally?"

"I'm not sure..." When his fingers moved along her thigh, inching upward she let out a gasp.

He stopped. "Annie?"

She breathed in and out, aware that a lot of what was happening was desire. She was very turned on. "It's good, Sam," she managed to murmur.

He continued with his explorations until he felt her shivering. "Are you all right?"

"I...I think so. Keep going."

"Your turn," he said, folding his arms across his chest.

Annie stared at him. She wasn't used to taking the lead. But this was different. She had to participate. When she slid her hand along his thigh he let out a moan.

"It's been a long time. I'm...on the brink," he explained.

"Oh," she said in surprise. "Should we, I mean, will you...?"

"Will I what?"

"Can you keep going with this, or should we...?"

He was pressed hard against her now, his hands on her hips. He let out a ragged sigh. "Are you trying to torture me?"

She gave a little laugh and realized that she was more than ready. "Oh...gods," she whispered, her eyes closing.

"Sweeter words have never been spoken," he murmured.

In the next moments Annie was lost to herself, clinging to him as he kissed her. He was careful with her, going slowly and waiting for her to indicate that all was well. When they finally connected she felt all the pent-up emotions he'd been keeping at bay. *My gods, the poor man*, went through her mind for the one second she had coherent thought. As she opened to him, it was like the first time, her eyes on his as they connected. She leaned in to kiss him, the sweetness of what they were doing enveloping her in a feeling of rightness. "I love you," she whispered.

"I love you too," he whispered back. From then on it felt like the world had righted itself, all her fears and worries lost within the intense sensations and the fullness of their mutual love.

When a cry came from her that surely would have awakened the baby, Sam placed his hand over her mouth. But his bellow of release was even worse. When it was over they were silently laughing, rocking back and forth as they came down from where they'd been.

"She didn't wake up," Sam said, glancing at the crib.

"No thanks to either of us," Annie whispered.

They stared at one another in silence until Sam said, "Thank the gods we made it thorough this. I wasn't sure I could last another day."

"And what would you have done?"

Sam shook his head. "I don't know—exploded, maybe?"

Annie laughed. " I feel like a different person. Like the world shifted and righted itself."

He leaned in and placed his lips gently on hers before he said, "I feel closer to you now than I ever have. Going through this has opened up something inside me—something deep that I buried."

"Love?"

He smiled. "And a connection I've never felt with anyone else."

Annie decided not to ask who the 'anyone else' referred to. He was older than the hills and surely had had many relationships with other women. "Can we go again?" she whispered.

Sam raised his eyebrows in surprise before he glanced down. "Looks like the answer is yes," he murmured.

CHAPTER 45

A loud knock had Annie running for the door. She had hoped for Cecily, but it was Jack who stood there. She stepped back to let him inside.

Over two months had gone by since she and Sam had bridged the gap between them. They'd moved Gaia out of the bedroom, afraid they would either wake her or traumatize her forever with their night time antics. Annie's nightmares had not returned.

"Hey," Jack said, looking at her flushed face. "You look... better."

"What's happening?" she asked, peering out the door. "Where's Lizzie?"

"She's taking a walk. We have some news."

"Hey, Jack. How's things?" Sam asked, joining them from upstairs.

"Couldn't be better," Jack answered, moving to sit on the couch.

"He has news," Annie told Sam.

"And what is this news?"

Jack smiled widely. "Lizzie and I...she's..."

"Pregnant?" Annie asked, her eyes going wide.

"Yes," he answered proudly. "I can hardly believe it."

"Will you get married? The 1800's frowns on unmarried couples having children."

Jack's smile faded. "We've been discussing the house. We don't know what to do about it. She wants to live in London."

"And you?"

"You know how I feel—living in that timeline is good for business. I hate to admit it, but I can make a killing." He glanced at Sam. "Can you help me get the house back to where it belongs?"

Sam lifted his brows. "I can try, but I'm not promising anything."

Annie thought about the *telchine* commenting on Jack's abilities. She hadn't had a chance to talk to him about it. "Jack," she began haltingly, "when you rescued Lizzie—how did you do it?"

He frowned and stared into the distance. "I'm not sure. It seemed like I was taken over by something."

"You said you're a wizard. Is what you did so odd?"

"Not odd, exactly, it's just that I barely remember any of it. I don't think I could repeat it."

Annie smiled. "Love can do that to you," she said softly.

Jack's eyes widened. "You think it was because I love her?"

"Yes, Jack. I do. It's why you can't remember and think you couldn't repeat it. She was in dire straits and you saved her."

"But how did I know to...?"

"Good gods, man," Sam said. "Have you never been in love?"

Jack looked confused for a moment. "Maybe not," he mumbled before looking up. "Maybe I never have."

"Until now," Annie added. "That creature was impressed by you—and seemed confused by your magic. He said he hadn't seen it coming."

Jack laughed. "I didn't see it coming either! Lizzie, she's... she's everything to me. I would give up my life for her."

Annie laughed. "I have never heard those words come out of

your mouth, and I never thought I would. Selfish is your middle name."

Jack looked down at the floor. "Used to be, yes. When I'm with her I want to protect her, to keep her from anything that might be uncomfortable or dangerous."

"Does she want to go back to work at the Golden Dawn?"

Jack nodded. "After the baby's born."

"And a wedding?"

"I don't know—we haven't decided yet."

Annie laughed. "If you're worried, maybe you should have the wedding there. Otherwise what will you tell them—that you got married in the future?"

Jack nodded. "Good point. However she's pretty far along—already four months, and it shows."

"Why don't you just buy her a ring and say you're married? No need to do it if it isn't something you both want. Sam and I aren't married." She glanced at Sam.

"We could be," Sam said, looking at her.

Annie shook her head, surprised. "Are you serious? Why would we?"

He smiled. "Why not? An excuse for a party."

"There's not really a reason…"

Sam made a face. "There are all kinds of reasons, Annie. For one, Gaia needs a last name."

"We don't have to be married for that."

Sam frowned. "Are you saying you don't want to?"

Annie opened her mouth and closed it. "If we are giving the baby a last name I want mine included."

"Morgan-McDougall or McDougall-Morgan?" he asked as Gaia ran by. A second later she shifted into a rabbit and slipped under the couch.

Annie laughed. "We can leave that for another day," she said, turning back to Jack. "I want to see my sister before you two disappear into the past."

"Don't worry, you will. Lizzie would never leave without

saying goodbye. But first we have to deal with the house. What do you think, Sam?"

Sam made a face. "I think I have no idea how to manage it. I'm not even sure what I can do anymore. Magic has been the last thing on my mind," he continued, glancing at Annie.

Annie smiled at him, knowing exactly what he was talking about. Sam had not spoken about magic since they'd reconnected, and he didn't seem at all concerned about it. He went about his days whistling, his happiness infectious.

"The *telchine* put the house where it is. I got there once, but not sure I could do it again. What do you think?" Sam asked, turning to Annie.

"How am I supposed to know? You and Jack are the ones who appeared out of nowhere. The doors worked for you then, why not now?"

Sam frowned. "I have the sense that it's what you said before —love brought me there."

"Yeah, it was love for me too," Jack muttered. "Maybe since Lizzie wants the house so much something will come over me again?"

"You two are ridiculous," Annie said, shaking her head. "Neither of you knows what magic you have? And you're talking nonsense."

When the door opened and Lizzie arrived Annie hurried to greet her. "Jack told us the news," she whispered in her ear.

Lizzie smiled. "I need to get home so that I have the proper clothes. These blue pants everyone wears are too tight and uncomfortable."

Annie looked her over, noticing the bump and the zipper that was half way down, her sweater pulled over it. Instead of her prim hairstyle, her hair hung loose around her face, softening her expression. "What happened to your beautiful caftan?"

Her eyes darkened. "Left behind when that creature had me."

Annie put a hand on her arm. "Let's not revisit any of that," she murmured.

"What about my house? Is there a way to return it to London?"

"We were just discussing that," Jack told her as he slung his arm around her shoulders.

Annie watched her reaction to this gesture. Instead of being embarrassed by the public show of affection, she smiled up at him and leaned into him.

Her staid sister was loosening up. And this time it was real love that did it.

AFTER MUCH DISCUSSION REGARDING LIZZIE'S HOUSE, JACK AND Sam made the decision to try the doors. They hadn't done so since Apollo's visit, and it was high time to find out if the creature was really gone. Annie and Lizzie sat together on the couch as the two men disappeared into the stacks.

Annie was nervous, her hands twisting together as she thought of the shapeshifter. Was he really gone? What if he wasn't, and Jack and Sam were caught?

Lizzie broke the spell when she said, "I'm sorry we have not visited sooner."

Annie let go of the dark thoughts and turned to her sister. "I suppose you and Jack have been busy?"

Lizzie smiled. "With the baby coming I have not felt myself. And we needed the time to get to know one another again. I guess you might say it has been a honeymoon for us." She laughed. "Strange to say such a word when I'm embarrassingly enormous. Women in this condition are in confinement and do not see or sleep in the same bed as their husbands. But Jack has convinced me that this is all normal for this time period. I have to say I would be lonely without him." She blushed after this statement.

Annie smiled. " I can hardly believe it, Lizzie. Someone finally tamed the irrepressible Jack."

"He told me that you two were together for a while. When I asked if he loved you, he told me he thought he did at the time, but being with me had proven him wrong." She glanced worriedly at Annie as if this might upset her.

"I was sixteen at the time—who knows what love is at sixteen?"

"Yes, that is exactly what I thought." She placed a hand on her lower belly. "This baby will be here in less than six months. I am concerned about how to hide it once we return to London."

"I suggested to Jack that he give you a ring and you two say that you've been married for...well, whatever amount of time you deem prudent. Tell them that you were secretly married because of the earlier scandals."

Lizzie thought about that. "Yes, that is one solution." Worry lines crossed her forehead. "What about Izzy? Jack told me that he'd seen her recently."

"And how does he feel about her?"

"He said she was good for a fling, which he explained means a 'brush', nothing more. What do you think?"

"I think that his telling you about her means he's coming clean. He didn't need to say anything. Do you believe him?"

Lizzie glanced down. "I do, Annie. He's professed his love for me over and over again. The person I remember is no longer who he is. He dotes on me and talks about the baby nonstop. He's already coming up with names!"

"Do you have a midwife?"

"I know one, but we *do* have doctors, you know."

Annie thought about the butchers from the past, her mind slipping easily into bad scenarios as she visualized the eight-pronged cervical dilator and the half vector, which was an early form of forceps and looked like an instrument of torture. The tools used in miscarriage were even worse.

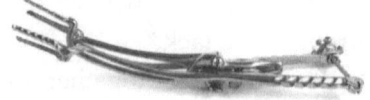

She shuddered. "Please go with a midwife, Lizzie. It will be safer for you. And I could travel there to help."

"Would you? I would be so grateful," Lizzie gushed. "Jack wants to be with me during the birth, but that is simply not done."

Annie smiled. "It's the custom in our times. I wanted Sam with me when Gaia was born, but he was lost in the 1300's."

Lizzie gave a little shiver. "A husband witnessing the delivery? I cannot imagine the embarrassment of it!"

"Times have changed, Lizzie. I wish you could understand how much better it is. Men and women are equals now."

She made a face. "Jack has talked nonstop about the advances in so many areas. He says women wear dresses short enough to show their thighs! Outlandish!" She twisted a lock of her hair in her fingers, staring into space before she said, "I do enjoy the freedom in certain things. Jack will not allow me to pin up my hair, although he helps me braid it at nighttime."

"Honestly, Lizzie, it is so much easier to live in this timeline. I wish you would stay."

Lizzie's mouth turned down in a sort of pout. "But you have had horrible wars and you still have shortages of everything. The shops are quaint but too small and do not have what I need. And the barter system? My goodness, how archaic."

"Sad to say I think money will be coming back soon. I've seen some coins lately in the marketplace. I like the barter system. It keeps the community spirit going."

Lizzie shook her head. "I like my life the way it is. We are experiencing a flood of new inventions. The electric light is all the rage. And automobiles are becoming more and more the norm."

"If you lived here you could wear the type of dresses you wear at the Golden Dawn. Not everyone wears jeans or short skirts."

Lizzie widened her eyes. "You would be shocked by how loose I've become. The utter madness of what Jack has encouraged! He sleeps naked," she whispered, a blush rising into her cheeks. "He wants me to do the same."

Annie laughed, thinking about what she knew of women's nightgowns during Victorian times—high-necked with bows and frills and falling to the ankles—she could see why Jack might not like it. "And do you?"

Lizzie turned beet red and turned away. "Sometimes I do," she whispered.

Annie rose when she heard a clatter coming from the stacks. A second later the door opened and Jack and Sam appeared.

"Well?" she called out.

"We found the house," Jack said, moving toward Lizzie on the couch.

"And?" Annie asked, staring at Sam. "No Steve or creepy creature, I presume?

"No sign of the creature at all. As far as the house, we tried various methods, but none of them worked," he answered.

"It's because it isn't an emergency," Jack added, frowning.

"But it is an emergency," Lizzie said, staring at Jack. "We are having a baby and I need my house!"

Jack shook his head. "Not enough for my wizard powers to emerge," he muttered.

"Or mine," Sam added.

"So what now?" Annie asked, looking from one to the other.

"Call on Ares and Gaia?" Sam asked, grinning.

Annie thought about that for a moment. "You know, Sam, that isn't a bad idea."

∾

ANNIE'S CONNECTIONS WITH THE GODDESS PROVED TO BE invaluable. Gaia managed what neither Sam nor Jack could do. Lizzie was thrilled.

When Sam asked Gaia if there was a way that he and Jack could have done it without her, she said, "You should both explore what lies beneath. You are more than you think you are."

Before Sam could ask what she meant, she was gone.

Once Gaia left, Annie realized that it would soon be time to say goodbye to her sister. And as far as her promise to be there for the birth? She talked with Jack and Lizzie, hoping to persuade them to travel to the future for the birth. Jack seemed happy to comply, but her sister shook her head. "I feel safe in my house, Annie. I will hold you to your promise."

Annie counted forward in her mind. "I will certainly try."

Lizzie reached for her hand and squeezed it.

THE MORNING THAT LIZZIE AND JACK LEFT FOR THE PAST WAS HARD for everyone. A lot of tears were shed and baby Gaia was so upset that she stayed a rabbit nearly all day. In the days after, Annie wandered aimlessly, the loss of her sister weighing heavily on her heart. They hadn't seen much of one another, but just knowing she was close had been enough. Now Lizzie was very far away and about to have a baby.

She smiled thinking about how they'd left in such a flurry. It was her sister who had managed it. Her magic had finally been acknowledged.

CHAPTER 46

T wo months went by in which Annie and Sam moved on with their lives. Gaia was growing like a weed and they spent many hours down by the beach, collecting shells and walking together. When the weather warmed they took Gaia swimming, teaching her to keep herself afloat, laughing and playing in the surf. Wolf went with them, barking at them when they splashed each other. He swam for sticks and shook his long hair out afterward, bright rainbow spray flying in an arc around him.

Gaia was talking non-stop these days, her bright eyes everywhere as she made up games and talked to the rocks, the shells, and Wolf. Sam couldn't get enough of her, pointing out how smart she was nearly every day.

Annie was as contented as she'd ever been, Sam's devotion to his daughter and to her, warming her heart. He had not mentioned magic at all.

IT WAS EARLY INTO THE THIRD MONTH WHEN SHE DECIDED IT WAS

time to share her news. She and Sam were in bed together when she whispered in his ear.

He pulled back and let out a bellow. "Are you sure?"

She nodded and smiled.

"When did it happen?"

"It must have been that night—the one that brought me out of my nightmares."

Sam smiled. "I wondered at the time if we might have made a baby. It was intense and both of us were pent-up—how many times did we do it that night?"

Annie laughed. "At least three."

"That was months ago." His eyes narrowed. "You knew and didn't tell me?"

"I didn't want to say anything until I was sure."

Sam pulled her close. "This time I'll be here for all of it."

Annie hoped those words would prove to be true.

THE DATE FOR HER SISTER'S BIRTH CAME AND WENT. ANNIE WAS very pregnant by then and Sam refused to allow her to travel. She agreed with him that it might be too much or cause premature labor. She worried about her sister until Jack appeared at their door.

When he saw her his eyes went wide. "Another baby!"

Annie laughed. "And how is yours?"

Jack grinned. "He's amazing, Annie. Strong. A genius. He's already talking in sentences."

"How old is he?"

"Nearly a year."

"A year? Good thing I didn't try to be there for the birth. Does he have red hair?"

Jack nodded. "But luckily he has Lizzie's temperament and her eyes. We want to visit, but now that I see how close you are, I think we might wait."

"And how was the birth?"

Jack grimaced."When she went into labor her midwife was out of town. She wanted a doctor but I refused. I've read all about the practices back then. Lizzie was horrified by all of it, from her enormous belly to her overlarge breasts. At seven months she began hiding her body from me. But once the contractions began in earnest, she turned to me for comfort. And you know what's it like—she kind of forgot about me being there once the pains got bad. I delivered him, Annie. It was the most incredible experience of my entire life. And I think it's brought us even closer."

Annie laughed and reached out to hug him. "What did you name him?"

Jack turned red, his gaze going to Sam who. was coming down the stairs. "Samuel," he whispered.

Annie was shocked. "Why Samuel?"

"Sam has been instrumental in my life. Without his influence I'm not sure I would have become who I am. I've said it before, but he is like a brother to me. And Lizzie was fine with it. She said that Samuel is a Hebrew name from the bible that means 'name of God'."

"What did I just hear?" Sam said, coming close.

Jack smiled. "Don't let it go to your head."

Sam clapped him on the back. "Congratulations."

"What about the wedding?" Annie asked.

Jack laughed. "We never bothered. I did get her a ring though, so everyone thinks we are."

Annie looked up at Sam beside her. "Where's my ring?"

Sam raised his brows. "Do you need one?"

Annie made a face. "No, but the gesture is kind of nice."

"I want to marry you, Annie. I want to have a party. But let's wait until after the baby's born."

"I don't care to be married," she muttered, but by now the two men were talking and didn't hear her.

EPILOGUE

T he baby was born on a cold and windy night. The moon was full, peeking in and out of the clouds that rushed by. Annie had been in labor since the night before and Sam was becoming worried. Her water had already broken and when he checked her he was convinced that the baby was turned in the womb.

Annie was skeptical about his knowledge regarding such things, but he was adamant that he had helped others through similar situations.

"Just other women or women you were with?" she muttered between contractions.

Sam let out a laugh as he pressed down gently on her belly, encouraging the baby to shift position. "Are you seriously jealous?" he asked her. "Do you remember how old I am?"

"Don't think you ever told me," she hissed just before she let out a shriek of pain.

"Sorry," he muttered, concentrating. "Almost there."

Annie was gasping and trying not to scream when she felt the baby move. "I think you did it," she whispered. A moment later she felt a sudden need to push. From then on it was nonstop excruciating pain until he arrived.

"He's strong," Sam said, holding him up. That's when he let out a lusty cry, making both of them laugh.

With his dark hair and dark eyes, they named him Apollo, after his grandfather.

THEIR WEDDING TOOK PLACE TWO MONTHS LATER WITH CECILY AND their other friends from town joining them outside in the unusually warm spring weather. Jack and Elizabeth and their baby arrived that morning, setting up the festive air that continued through-out the day. And when Apollo and Constance arrived, the day was complete.

Annie wore a dress of cream lace that her sister had brought for her, one that did not require a corset. It had long sleeves, a low neck and a tight bodice that showed off her figure. Elizabeth did Annie's hair in a complicated up-do, on top of which she wore a garland of fresh flowers.

Sam was dressed in a cream shirt and a brown leather vest with his pale linen pants, retrieved from his trunk where he stored his things from the distant past. His hair had grown long and was pulled back from his face and tied with a leather thong. His eyes were bright with happiness.

Their vows were short, with merely a few words said to convey their love and devotion for one another. Jack acted as officiant, tying the silk ribbon around their hands to bind them to one another.

When Sam produced an ancient and beautiful ring in a Celtic knot design with a moonstone in the center, Annie gasped in surprise. She'd never seen it before and when she looked at him with a question in her expression he raised his eyebrows and smiled. "Is it magic?" she whispered. But he didn't answer her, only grinning enigmatically.

It fit her perfectly and she knew as soon as it was on her finger that Sam had imbued it with a protective spell. When she looked into his deep blue eyes she saw what he hadn't revealed. His magic was surely back, but the form was different. Instead of being the ego-packed heaviness, this magic was delicate and protective, filled with love instead of brawn.

She'd taken the scarab into town and had the silversmith work it into a ring design for Sam. He was utterly surprised and overwhelmed when he saw it, his eyes welling with tears as she slipped it onto his finger.

When they finally kissed everyone hooted and clapped, happiness rising around them like bubbles.

Once the wedding was completed, Apollo produced the mead that he'd made and brought from Atenua. The food was from the bakery in town with lots of bread and cheese and delicacies that Cecily had managed to concoct.

For the first time Annie met Cecily's beau, a man who she decided was a good match for the pixie-like woman with his slight paunch and smiling eyes. He obviously doted on her and she on him. They would be next, she thought to herself, trying to picture Cecily with a baby in her belly. How old was she, anyway? She had known Sam for years and years and yet she looked to be in her early thirties. It was all a mystery that she hoped to unravel one day.

Late in the afternoon Annie and Elizabeth settled inside on the couch while the partying went on outside. "How are things with you?" Annie asked her as she pulled one shoulder of the dress down to feed the new baby.

Elizabeth laughed. "You will not believe it. I am expecting again."

Annie watched Samuel toddle by with Gaia in pursuit, their giggles filling her heart. "That was quick," she said, laughing.

Lizzie made a face and turned red. "He will not leave me alone," she whispered, here eyes going wide. "He wants…" she stopped in mid-sentence, her hand going to her mouth. She glanced at Wolf carrying a rabbit in his mouth and little Samuel trying to keep up with him before she leaned close and whispered, "Every time I turn around Jack is there, ready to take me to bed. It is...well, it is rather unusual, is it not?" She laughed again, her cheeks flaming. "I have to say I love it, Annie. I would never have expected to have a man so devoted. He makes me feel...well...beautiful. It is hard to imagine the man he was when we first met."

Annie smiled and took her sister's hand. "I am very happy for you. And I love that you are here for this special day."

Lizzie smiled. "I would not have missed it. One of these days we will do the same, and you will be there for us."

"You will?"

"Oh yes. Jack wants us to be formally married. There will be a priest and a church. He has made many friends and we will invite them all, as well as the entire Golden Dawn contingent. But if I am to be constantly with child I am not sure how much I will be able to attend classes."

"Are you okay with this?" Annie asked worriedly. "There are ways to prevent it, you know."

Lizzie smiled and patted her belly. "I know what to do to prevent it. I am very happy to have another."

Annie let out a sigh of relief. "Maybe prevent another—at least for a while? You will be very busy, Lizzie."

"We have a housekeeper and someone to help me with the children now. He has made a lot of money, Annie. He is quite the provider."

"I'm not surprised," Annie murmured. Jack had always had a talent for making money. She didn't know what he was up to, but if it was illegal she hoped he wouldn't be caught.

"As far as our marriage," Lizzie continued, "we will say that it is a celebration to renew our vows." She glanced down at the gold band on her finger. "He is designing another ring for me."

"Let us know when the marriage will take place and we will be there."

I~T WAS LATE THAT NIGHT WHEN SHE AND S~AM WERE IN BED THAT SHE turned to him. "Am I correct that you have your magic back?"

He turned to her, his answer a kiss that sent her down a path into another place and time. Wherever they were was filled with golden light, and within that space she knew without a doubt that Sam was not only a hero, but a magical being who could transport her into other realms.

Fin

AFTERWORD

Please leave a review at your site of choice. It really helps! And thank you for reading. I hoped you enjoyed this book.

To find more books and information about Nikki Broadwell, please visit:
www.nikkibroadwellauthor.com

Facebook: https://www.facebook.com/NikkiBroadwellBooks/
Instagram: https://www.instagram.com/earthgoddesswriting/
substack: https://nikkibroadwell.substack.com/
Medium: https://medium.com/@nikkibroadwell

ALSO BY NIKKI BROADWELL

Wolfmoon series:

Moonstone-Book 1

Willow-Book 2

Raven-Book 3

Faery-Book 4

Loki's Bargain: (formerly Gypsy series)

The Tower-Book 1

The Page of Pentacles-Book 2

The Ten of Swords-Book 3

Coyote series:

Just Another Desert Sunset

Coyote Sunrise

Dreamcatcher

Summer McCloud paranormal murder series:

Murder in Plain Sight

Saffron and Seaweed

Black and White and Red all over

Finlay's Folly

The Night of the Jaguar

The Case of Missing Books

Fehin and Airy series:

The Bridge

Time Gap

Salem Witch Series :

A Witch in Time Saves Nine

The Moon in Her Eyes

Raven and Hummingbird series:

Siobhan's Secret—book 1

Dagda's Daughter—book 2

Kat's Conundrum—book 3

Raven's Runes—book 4

Dark Goddess Series:

Echoes--Book 1

Forbidden—Book 2

The Library of Time:

Book 1

Book 2

Single Books:

The Last Keeper of the Light

Rosemary for Remembrance

Burning Night

Finding the Tree